To my Family.

The Dubs, The Tyronians and all in between.

Original Sin

Isabella Coughlan

Published by Rockstar Reading Limited.

Cover Design by Grock AI

Printed in Great Britain.

CHAPTER 1

Jonathan

The moment I saw her lying there, I knew that she was dead.

Is it always so obvious? I don't know exactly but I presume not. Sometimes, I watch those crime dramas on TV and the police detectives really make this show of ascertaining the fact for certain.

On this occasion, there was no question. Lorraine Blackwood was no longer a living person.

She was a corpse.

In death, she was just as elegant as she had been in life. Possessing the decency to die a most down-to-earth death. Well, I suppose that isn't *quite* possible if you get my drift. Especially given that she was murdered. Lorraine though, gave it a fairly good try.

But I'm getting ahead of myself.

Understandably proper etiquette dictates that I must introduce myself first. Here it goes then: my name is Jonathan Crookshank and I like to take people home.

No, not like *that*.

I swear, *honestly*, not like that.

For *I* am an estate agent.

Oh yes, one of those.

I know that at the precise second of reading this piece of information you are experiencing one of two thoughts. Option A is that I am most definitely a highly contemptible individual (this assumption is grossly unfounded, most of the time it's the solicitor's fault and we're left picking up the slack.) Option B is that I am a rockstar.

I assure you; it is the latter.

Quite literally the latter in fact as I have the honour and privilege of working for the finest real estate practice in County Dublin and, if you are of my persuasion, all of Ireland: Rockstar Real Estate.

When Lorraine failed to make an appearance at work on that morning, the initial amount of trepidation aroused in the office was minimal. The policy practised amongst us is generally one that encourages a... self- motivated mindset. That's not to say we all constantly go on the mitch (for anyone reading unfortunate enough to lack knowledge of the Dublinese language, that translates to play truant.) Most definitely not. Due to our position at the forefront of the Irish property market we cannot afford to lose focus. It takes effort to be killing it the way we do.

Actually... potential poor word choice on that one, Jono.

Anyway, as the day progressed, concern did begin to germinate. Early in the afternoon, I was unfortunate enough to answer the office phone only to be rewarded by the effusions of one of her irate sellers. His potential buyers had arrived at a property for a scheduled viewing only to be left locked outside in the pouring rain when she didn't show. He proceeded to inform me that we were "the biggest shower of incompetent eejits" he had ever encountered and would, as a result, be relieving us of his listing.

That is never good.

If we lose a listing or a sale falls through, our boss Frederick Featherington-Smythe (I like to call him Mr. FFS because his general demeanour makes you want to say his initials) puts us in the Sin Bin. That means we are assigned all the less than desired office tasks for the next week. These generally include the rental inspections on tenanted properties. Trust me, you really don't want the details. Suffice it to say that sometimes, the difference between a good and bad renter is one who knows the disparity between the bedroom and the bathroom. I mean it.

It was following this exceedingly pleasant conversation that I began to wonder in earnest as to her whereabouts. You do *not* miss a viewing in this business. You just don't.

Upon her repeated failure to answer her mobile or respond to my texts, I knew that something was wrong.

Seriously wrong.

Attempting to think logically, I decided that a reasonable first step would be to go to her house. I hoped valiantly that I wasn't overreacting. Like, for all I knew, she might have gone out on the lash last night to get banjoed and woken up this morning hangin' like a sign (if you'll pardon the pun to our profession.) However, despite the fact that I pounded persistently on her door for almost half an hour, there was no response. Peering through the windows, I was met with darkness.

With an antithetical embrace, tendrils of fear wound their way around my heart, squeezing insistently in a most nauseating manner. If she wasn't home and she wasn't at work, then where was she?

Calling the Gardai was becoming rather appealing at that point but I restrained myself. A fifty something year old woman not showing up at her office was unlikely to come high on their list of priorities. She lived alone and had no relatives whom I knew of so I was left uncertain of the best course of action.

After plenty of pondering, I began to formulate a plan. The previous evening, she had left work to conduct a viewing on the way home. We deal with plenty of luxurious gaffs but the place in question was extraordinary even by our standards. I suppose you could call it a *deadly* gaff.

I know, I know, I need to work on my word choice a bit.

Anyway, all other apparent options exhausted, I concluded that paying a visit to Maycroft Demesne might offer some answers.

The property was located in Howth, a highly affluent area of north county Dublin. It boasted a panoramic view over Dublin Bay, a square footage fit to make your eyes protrude from their sockets and a price tag that would detach them completely and send them on a spin across the floor.

I made the journey there in my Porsche (what can I say? The commissions are plentiful in Rockstar Real Estate) and as I did, a decidedly unpleasant emotion settled upon me like a shroud. Foreboding.

Some subconscious intuition informed me that all was not well.

I was sent spiralling back to earth by the emerging visage of the gates. An intercom buzzer was attached to the left pillar and with the distinct taste of bile rising in my throat, I parked the Porsche on a grassy verge and pressed the button. My finger trembled as I did.

"H...Hello?" I ventured tentatively.

The silence was deafening.

"It's Jonathan Crookshank... from Rockstar Real Estate," I tried again, unsure to whom I really was addressing this.

The house was uninhabited as the owner lived abroad so the only people who had been permitted within its walls in the last few months were Lorraine and any clients she brought on viewings.

Following the gentle persuasion of my fingers, the gates swung inwards on their hinges with a guttural moan. It was eerily reminiscent of an awakening corpse, confined to reside in the earth beneath the living for time immemorial, eventually seeking the power to satiate his hunger for walking among them again. There was something in the sound that was almost pitiful, that invited sympathy for a household exiled from the perpetual rotation of human life.

The darkness had gathered. It was here, it was there and it was everywhere. In the apple trees lining the drive that wavered, it was not refused admittance but welcomed willingly in whisper, its breath caressing the forbidden fruit. Lethargy gripped me. The unnatural forces meandering in the air bade me to unite myself to them and accept them. When the dawn broke, I would inhabit the reality that lingered in their wake. I would journey on with the mysteries of the night buried to rot alone.

Rain fell. It fell to greet the gravel drive and brush the slumbering flower petals. It fell to mingle with the wind, each droplet, so fragile and insignificant, obliterated to a negligible size by the force of the breeze. It fell to fondle my fingertips. It fell to muffle all sound. It fell to muffle all thought.

Wise up, Jono, I reprimanded myself.

I have to do that sometimes. Reprimand myself *and* wise up, I mean.

Stepping back, I surveyed the stone façade critically. The place was bedecked with window boxes teeming with technicoloured foliage. It wasn't quite as dark as it had originally seemed, the lampposts lining the drive cast a warm glow over the house and overall, I was forced to concede that it appeared an innocent abode.

That was not the case.

Still quite distracted, I tried the door and, foolishly shocked at its refusal to open, remembered the spare set of keys in my pocket. My heart hammering in my chest, I let myself in and shut the door in my wake.

Then though, I was dazzled by the sight that was the entrance hall. In the centre of the chequer board floor, there sat a circular table, adorned by an aromatic arrangement of fuchsia roses. Sweeping off to the left and right were two Italian marble staircases, resembling the train of a royal bride's wedding dress. Along the sides of the room, were gilt edged mirrors and side tables, lending the space an air of symmetry. It oozed money, extravagance and class but in a comfortable ratio that did not overwhelm the onlooker.

Selecting the first mahogany door on the right, I entered the room beyond it. It was well-oiled in contrast to the front gates, I noticed.

Honestly, if it was possible, this room was even more overtly opulent than the entrance hall. There appeared to be some theme of palatial Arabian grandeur at play in the drawing room. Persian rugs of ruby red, deep purple and emerald green were draped over every available surface, including the walls, which also boasted richly woven tapestries that looked as if they had been purchased in some Egyptian souq. In place of typical sofas there were three low day beds and two chaise lounges arranged in a circle on the central rug. Drapes of a floaty gossamer fabric were drawn closed across the windows and yet more artistic floral displays spilled from gold vases embossed by a curlicued ancient Arabic script.

It was then that I saw her.

Lying prone on the mat was the petite figure of Lorraine Blackwood.

Very still and very, very dead.

As I have previously said, she did not die dramatically but with a modest humility; the same that characterised her life.

Lorraine was like a mother to me. Especially given the fact that my own is... well, we'll come to her later. At twenty-five, I'm a fairly recent addition to the real estate world and at times it can be challenging. Should I have found myself overwhelmed by the vicious valuations, censorious clients or my bawdy boss, she was there with a soothing smile and maternal murmur of reassurance.

And she never would again.

An enervated gasp was emitted from my mouth and I fell to my knees beside her body. Customarily dressed in a navy pencil skirt and blazer, her tight blonde bob was pristine. Marred only by the neat circle of congealed blood where the bullet pierced her skull.

It was miniscule in diameter. It was mighty in impact.

The gesture was senseless but still I felt for a pulse. Such a signal of life was elusive.

Unapologetically, I began to bawl.

CHAPTER 2

Jonathan

It meant little to me whether or not the pressed folds of my Armani suit were to be imprinted by the shallow puddles of damp caressing the front steps on which I sat. For a change.

Falling like the unobtrusive precipitation of my tears, darts of hail shot from the sky, reporting off the ground in a vitriolic bombardment. All colour had fled the landscape, rendering it lifeless, a twilit street from which the youth flee at the coming of nightfall. Encased in their cocoon of glass, the amber bulbs of the lampposts lining the driveway metamorphosed into licking tongues of fire ripping through my soul in the anguish customary of when a comrade has fallen.

"Close to her were you?"

I was startled by the voice, coming compassionate and unassuming, from behind me. With great effort, I summoned the energy to twist around in my perch on the top step. Standing within the shadow of the doorway was Detective Joyce.

He was the lead Garda appointed to the case of Lorraine's death. Or, as it was now officially declared; her murder.

Sandy hair gradating rapidly towards grey, I suspected he might once have been as blond as I am. Those days though, were a memory and the silver strands harmonised his lined complexion. His comportment was indicative of kindness but something in his air spoke of a certain... resignation. Almost as if he was used to existing on the sidelines, a quiet observer. Powerless yet somehow controlling the narrative. In the way you'd least suspect.

"I... was," I admitted tentatively, unwilling to say more lest he should drag me off in handcuffs right there and then. I was not blind to the wary glances being shot my way earlier by certain members of the Gardai team who had been dispatched to the crime scene.

What is it that they say? The person who finds the body is always the most likely culprit. Something like that anyway.

But I did not kill her. I genuinely didn't.

An instinct suddenly told me that Detective Joyce did not believe so either. In that, there was at least a glimmer of a positive sentiment.

"Was... was it murder? Definitely?" The words broke from my lungs, uncensored by my brain.

"We're treating the death as suspicious, yes," he confirmed. That was basically Gardai code for "this is definitely a cold -blooded homicide." Not that I blame him for utilising the lingo. I'm guilty of it myself. For example, if I tell you that a property 'is in need of some modernisation', you may as well bring the bulldozers now.

"Just... seeing her like that. It was horrible. Really horrible." Discontentedly, I scuffed my toe along the marble surface, knotting my fingers together.

I risked a glance sideways at the Detective. His steely grey eyes had glazed over as he gazed out into the louring night. For a brief moment, I indulged myself in wondering what he was truly thinking. Was this sort of thing... a common occurrence? Surely not. Yes, he might be a high-ranking Garda but it was unlikely he dealt with murders every day of the week.

When he spoke, it was with an avuncular edge to his words. "I know, Son," he said, clapping me on the shoulder. "Nobody should have to see that. There's been a few unpleasant sights in my time but it doesn't get any easier."

"I... I'd say that."

Taking a deep breath, he asked: "Jonathan, isn't it?"

"Yeah. Johnny, Jono. I don't mind."

He shifted heavily, seemingly uncomfortable. "Look, it's probably the last thing you want to do but...would you mind answering a few questions? Just for formalities' sake."

I would rather have listed a rodent infested one bed but, feeling that in spite of his congenial tone I had no option, I complied.

"Of course."

"Thank you, Jono. Now, did Lorraine have any... enemies?"

Considering my reply carefully, I answered: "Well, we're in real estate so..." I shrugged. My silence said it all.

A sceptre of a smile frolicked on his lips. "I see. Was there... internal competition over the listing? A property such as this," he gestured around him, something akin to envy ruminating in his irises, "is sure to invite contention."

"Well, yes," I said slowly, "none of us could really understand why Lorraine had been given the listing specifically."

It *had* proved something of a contentious issue. As the highest performing salesperson in the office in spite of my rather infantile career, I *had* expected to be entrusted with the property. I managed to restrain myself from boasting of my prowess however, as I suspected it may enhance my motive in the eyes of the Gardai.

"But not enough to kill her," I hastened to add at his crumpled complexion. "Absolutely not. You can count anyone in our office out of this."

He made no reply.

"But then there's Regal Residences," I began, unnerved by the silence. "They're our main competitor and they've done some... weird stuff in the past."

A frown dutifully returned to his lips as he assessed me with blatant wariness. "Weird stuff... how exactly?"

“Well, a while back, a few of our “To Let” signs were vandalised. You know, someone wrote an ‘I’ in between to make them say ‘Toilet.’

At this, he snickered audibly.

“Are they six?”

“They act like it,” I muttered wryly. “Not that... obviously that sort of thing doesn’t equate to murder. There’s just a bit of an... ongoing rivalry really.”

That must be the greatest understatement I have ever verbalised. If we’re champers, then Regal Residences are prosecco. If that doesn’t paint the picture, I don’t know what does.

“How well did you know Lorraine on a personal level?” Detective Joyce questioned with an abrupt change of tack.

“She... kept herself to herself really. Quite a humble person, no airs and graces. Unusual enough in our business.” I ran a hand through my hair distractedly. “I’ve only been in the office two years but she’s always looked after me in a way.”

He nodded thoughtfully.

“I liked her,” I finished simply.

“She lived alone, I believe?”

“Yes.”

“Did she have any family?”

“She... might have mentioned a sister but... she never really talked about herself much. I couldn’t say, to be honest.” A rather disconcerting guilt entrenched itself in my gut. Should I have... asked her more questions about herself? Then though, she was far from an open book and you don’t want to infringe on someone. Do you?

In retrospect, I think that was the point at which I realised how little I truly knew about Lorraine Blackwood.

"And Jonathan," the detective pronounced with a procrastinatory air, "did she seem happy to you?"

My abrupt intake of breath indicated my bewilderment. "Why... why would you ask that? You don't seriously think she..."

Clearing his throat abashedly, he said: "No! Absolutely not. Given the position in which the body was found we came to the conclusion that suicide was impossible."

This sentence was uttered impetuously, in the taciturn manner of law enforcement.

"Right..."

I ran my tongue over my lips.

"That was abrupt, I'm sorry."

When I looked at him, his expression was rueful. "I was merely asking. We're exploring every avenue and, with a murder... there's always the possibility that the victim was...being threatened or blackmailed by someone. It's only a line of enquiry naturally."

"No... I get it," I made to stand up, the weariness falling from my limbs like the brightness from the sky. "I'd better be getting home."

Detective Joyce stood then too and appeared to deeply deliberate on his next words before they left him.

"Jono... you've had a shock, lad. You shouldn't be driving after that."

"Sure, I'm grand, Detective," I reassured him. "Honestly." Suddenly, I desired nothing other than to put as much distance as possible between myself and that bloody property.

Oh, poor word choice *again* there Jono.

"Come on with me for a drink. Back to mine like. It'll do no harm."

He clapped me on the shoulder once again, an encouraging grin subtracting at least half a decade from his features. A shift completed and the stress depleted. To survive in his line of work, I suspected you became rather skilled in depositing the atrocities at the door. Still, his offer was philanthropic if a little peculiar. At the end of the day, I was fairly confident that I was technically a suspect and a Garda shouldn't socialise with a suspect on their case. Lacking the energy to protest though, I found myself oddly acquiescing to his request.

CHAPTER 3

Julia

My secret was safe.

Or at least it was until daddy arrived home from work with Jonathan Crookshank in tow.

Lorraine Blackwood had been murdered. Lorraine Blackwood was dead. I could not say that any emotions I harboured were deeply melancholic. After all, it's what she deserved, isn't it?

Well, you don't know that yet I suppose. But trust me; she did.

You don't know me either: my name is Julia Joyce and I am rather familiar with killing people. Don't take that literally but metaphorically. I'm an author you see, so I do have a bit of a penchant for metaphors. And killing people. Oh, relax, in my books obviously. Could I do it myself? I don't know really. I've never thought about it much. Probably though. If I had to.

Someone was certainly able to do the deed on Lorraine. Did I mention I had a fair idea who it was?

No, I don't believe I did actually. Be patient please, dear reader, I promise you I will get there.

Mathematically speaking, I was about ninety nine percent sure. Audacious to be that certain in a situation devoid of concrete evidence but there we go. I was.

They say you can never be completely certain of anything. That *is* true. I've learnt it the hard way. You can't be certain that you won't be betrayed. You can't be certain that the people you thought you knew best in life won't be altered beyond your recognition by some invisible force. You can't be certain that they, or even you, will not sin.

We are all human and therefore we sin.

You'll understand that a little more when you know my story.

Before I get into it though, the first thing I must do is recount the night that I met Jonathan Crookshank.

It was a highly peculiar occurrence in and off itself that daddy would bring someone home from work. Least of all, a suspect on a case. Strictly prohibited, probably, if you were to concern yourself with the legalities. But there you go.

I warn you now; little about this tale is going to be usual.

Indulging myself in a sabbatical from studying (I'm a medical student, by the way) I was cocooned in my personal hideaway: our library. Should I seek solace, I often search amongst the spines that have been the real backbone of my upbringing. There is a certain placid air that is only understood by books. The way they stand steadfast, soldiers sentry, sympathetically ignorant of the fact your life is about to change for ever.

The slamming of the front door roused me from my reading. It was the geriatric stage of evening, night being imminent, and that meant Daddy was home.

"Hello, Daddy," I trilled cheerfully, bounding out into the hall. "How was wor-"

The person standing in front of me was most certainly not daddy. Most definitely not. A description to which he may have aligned, however, was that of the most pathetically gorgeous man I have ever encountered.

Outside, in the last throes of day, the sun fled like a criminal from his misdemeanour, slashing the sky with seething full stops of red. The setting sun accentuated his golden fair hair, thick waves that ended at the nape of his neck. Rosebud lips that seemed permanently disposed to grin lent a devilish glint to his large sapphire eyes while a dimple anointed each cheek.

If Mr. Bingley were to join a boyband, I suspected the man before me may have made his twin.

"Julia pet," my dad appeared from behind Mr. Handsome. "This is Jonathan. Jonathan Crookshank."

"Hello, Jonathan," I proffered a hand. "Nice to meet you."

His grip on my palm was surprisingly firm, eyes refusing to depart from mine. "Julia," the embryotic grin flourished fully. "You're... you write books don't you?"

"For my sins, yes." I winked coquettishly.

"I... I've read them... I... I love you... or them, I mean..." Clearing his throat, his words petered out, leaving only the self-conscious curve on his lips.

Of all things he could have said, that took me by surprise.

"Oh, thank you, I..."

Mercifully, my dad intervened then and ushered us into the front living room. Crossing to the drinks cabinet, he selected a bottle of Jameson whiskey and poured two measures into crystal tumblers. He handed one to Jonathan and perched on the sofa, taking a satiating gulp from the other.

"Drink up, it'll help with the shock," he advised.

"Shock?" I questioned tentatively. "What... shock?"

"My colleague," Jonathan swallowed hard, "was murdered. I... found the body."

"Goodness, that's awful." My brow furrowed. "What happened?"

"She... went out to do a viewing yesterday ... we're agents from Rockstar Real Estate... and, well, she didn't show up to work this morning." He shrugged helplessly. "I went to the property and..."

Picking up the thread, my dad intoned: "Maycroft Demesne, Julia."

My heart ceased to beat. No, no it couldn't be. Surely not.

"Lorraine was shot," continued Jonathan. "She was just lying there..."

Lorraine. This wasn't happening. I was dreaming. I was going to be roused from slumber's farcical caress. Wasn't I? Oh God, how I wished I could wake up.

"A tragedy." Although daddy's words were sincere, the pointed stare he afforded me was palpable.

When I reminisce upon it, I am never quite capable of recalling how the remainder of the conversation passed. It took concerted effort on my part to present a collected exterior, play the unaffected hostess. Morph myself into an innocent character; a character who had most definitely not encountered Maycroft Demesne or its unfortunate victim before. A character who was perfectly ignorant of the property's history. A character who would not transpire to alter poor little Jonathan's life forever.

I will leave it up to you, dear reader, to decide whether involving himself with me would ultimately be for better or for worse.

An impassive face giving nothing away. That was what I had to be.

He didn't appear suspicious. Not for the time being anyway. Whatever we did, we had to ensure it remained that way.

We did not have a choice.

Vigilance was imperative.

"Julia?" The question that came as I was preparing to show him out surprised me.

"Yes?" I was mindful to keep my tone jovial.

He fumbled in his pocket and retrieved a business card, pristine at its perpendicular edges. Smirking up at me from the lacquered rectangle, was his distractingly dashing visage. The wording read simply: "Mr. Jonathan Crookshank: Sales Negotiator Rockstar Real Estate."

“My number, in case you... need any... property services sometime.” A blush fissured through his cheeks. “Just give me a call.”

“Thank you, Jonathan,” I responded with a tranquil air. “You can be sure that I will.”

CHAPTER 4

Julia

"Daddy, we are *screwed*!"

This outburst was expelled in a fit of something akin to hysteria as I re-entered the living room and flopped down onto the sofa.

"I wouldn't say that, Julia pet. The poor fella's clearly a bit clueless." Scratching his head, he betrayed how truly perturbed he was.

"Well, what are you going to do?" I spread my arms wide in exasperation. "We need a plan here. What if he... knows something and isn't letting on?"

"Trust me, he doesn't know anything. You should have seen him when he found the body. He was green!"

"But if they're selling the place, daddy, they're going to know the score. Even if he doesn't, somebody in that estate agent's probably does. They'll have a bloody thesis of the 'period features' plastered all over their website," I made air quotes to highlight the sales jargon. "You have to shut the investigation down as quickly as possible. The longer it goes on, the bigger the chance we're found out!" For emphasis, I slammed my fist down on the coffee table. Hard.

Standing, he smoothed an imaginary crease from his uniform. "You honestly think they're going to wax lyrical about the fact it used to be a mental institution? They're hardly going to be all 'Come! Make yourself at home, channel your inner skitso!' "

At this, I couldn't prevent a rather reluctantly mirthful snort.

"Anyway, I'm leading the investigation. I control it, Julia. There's nothing to worry about, I promise you." He bent down and kissed my forehead. "I mean it."

"Do we tell mammy?" I murmured half to myself.

At this, a carmine veil enshrouded his features. "Absolutely not," he said through gritted teeth. "Eve doesn't need to know. It'll only stress her out. You know that. And she was 'Doctor on call' tonight. This is the last thing she needs."

"I think she needs to know! We all have to be on guard now."

Lungs producing a laden sigh, he sat down beside me and took my hand in his. "Julia, we don't know anything for certain, pet. It could all be coincidence. There's nothing to say otherwise."

My laugh was mirthless. "A coincidence. So, you think what? Lorraine started a new life as an estate agent and wound-up dead in *that* house?"

"Maybe." He rubbed my cheek with his thumb and forefinger. "It might have been some... rival agent or... spiteful client." Noticing my dubious expression, he added hurriedly. "Seriously! It could have!"

Stilling myself, I conjured the words I knew deep within me were the truth: "He's back, daddy. Your brother is back."

"Jonathan?"

"Oh, hi, Julia. Nice to hear from you. Decided to sell up?" I could almost see the mischievous smirk through the phoneline.

"No...no, nothing like that," I giggled with a mildly flirtatious edge to my words (alright, maybe not *mild* exactly.) "I just thought I'd say hello.... see how you were. It must have been horrific earlier, all that..."

"Well, it wasn't pleasant, no." He gulped audibly.

"I...can imagine."

"Yeah."

Never had noiselessness spoke of such anticipation. He was considering his next words with caution.

"Look, Julia… I…know we've only just met but… you seem absolutely lovely and… I'd like to meet up with you again." There was a short pause. "What do you think?"

Silently, I punched the air in ecstasy. This was unfolding precisely according to my meticulously constructed scheme. The poor boy would be utterly under my spell before he knew he had wandered into the embrace of a lioness.

Do you feel sorry for him already? You should.

"I'll tell you what," I began, slathering the sentence in copious enthusiasm. "I've got two tickets for 'Macbeth' in The Gaiety next Friday night. I was supposed to go with my mum but it turns out she's working late so… if you wanted, you could come with me."

His response was delivered so immediately, he almost cut across my final syllable. "That's perfect! I… I'd love to. Thank you, Julia."

Eager. Almost pathetically so.

I'm sorry Johnny, I really am.

"At least it'll take your mind off things anyway," I said with evident empathy. "Nothing like theatre for a distraction."

"No." His laugh was generous, deeply meant. "There isn't. D'you go often?"

"You'd think I'd shares in The Gaiety." I fondled my bedspread between my thumb and forefinger, its fabric silken and gentle as love. "Do you?"

"Yeah, I know it's nerdy but… Shakespeare's my favourite. So much better than all that commercialised nonsense."

My voice a murmur, I mumbled: "It's not nerdy at all. I absolutely agree."

Handsome, a gentleman and a lover of literature. Was I in heaven?

Not that I had any intentions other to find out what exactly the little nuisance knew and make certain he stayed stumm.

As his light giggle petered out, the silence relapsed.

"I really like you, Julia," he conceded eventually. "I really do."

"Hmm..." I simulated scrutiny of my reply. "I think you might just be tolerable."

"Thanks for the invite. I appreciate it you know," he mused. "'Macbeth' is the best. Tragic but..."

"Meaningful," I finished.

"The way she manipulates him... crazy, really."

Oh, how ironic. If only he could have known.

The one difference? I refused to succumb to my sin.

CHAPTER 5

Jonathan

Julia Joyce.

Throughout the vast majority of that encounter, it seemed a glaringly large possibility that I would metamorphose into one of those emojis with the hearts for eyes.

She was... enchanting.

Captivating. Tantalising. Inherently beautiful.

There was some quality about her that I could not quite place. Yet it lingered in my consciousness. Lingered like the scent of her perfume. Like the impression of her hand in mine.

I'd never really had a proper girlfriend (something my colleagues rather liked to tease me about) but there'd just never been any girl who had interested me enough.

Julia interested me.

She *more* than interested me.

Everything about her was different. From the way she dressed (chic, stylish yet slightly bohemian) to the way she talked about things that actually *mattered*. Big talk, not small.

I knew the moment I laid eyes upon her that I would love her more than I had believed was physically possible.

Hydrating ourselves with a round of pre-theatre drinks in the antiquitarian bar of The Gaiety Theatre, it was a great exertion not to simply gawp gormlessly at her.

Her hair, naturally fair, rippled meanderingly in a hypnotising motion about her shoulders. As I watched the cascading waves, I noticed too her expressive eyes, her endearing features and her dazzling smile. What little makeup she wore was tasteful, scantily applied.

"So," she began, sipping from her champagne flute, "tell me then. What are the secrets of the Dublin property market?"

I smirked at the manner in which she phrased her question, as if anticipating the revelation of some carefully concealed conundrum. "What makes you think there's any secrets?"

"Oh, come on," she pouted beguilingly, "*everyone* has secrets, Johnny."

"Do they?"

"Yes!" Her exclamation was made in exasperation, voice lowered. "Even me."

The bubbles of carbonation in my own drink rose to the surface, sparking insistently against the side of the glass as they burst. I averted my gaze from hers before I replied.

"What's your secret then?" I asked, almost amused.

She smiled to herself. "Time will tell. Patience, Johnny, is a virtue." Her wink was deliberately calculated. I had to gulp.

"You... you're studying medicine?" Rather hurriedly, I seized on the first coherent question that entered my head, hoping it didn't seem mundane.

However, she nodded eagerly in response. "Yes, I am."

"You enjoy it?"
"I do..." Momentarily, she hesitated. "Writing's my real vocation though. *Fraught* with peril."

"Is it? In what way?"

"Because it comes from here," she placed her clasped hands on her chest. "You put pen to paper; you put a lot on the line."

Something in the words stunned me with a beauty they were not trying to possess. In many ways, like Julia.

"I... suppose that makes sense. But I... really admire your work. I do."

Although she rolled her eyes dismissively, she couldn't quite conceal the blush. "You flatter me."

"I hope I do."

When a short silence had elapsed, I resumed: "Must be tough, writing and studying?"

I remarked that she deliberated her response. "Sometimes very but... I wouldn't have it any other way."

"Swot," I teased good humouredly.

Playfully, she swiped at me across the table. "Watch it! Just because you were the class clown."

"No," I admitted. "I was the studious one too."

"Bet you went to private school."

"Why all the assumptions about me?" I questioned jocularly, leaning back further in my chair. "Do I really give that impression?"

"You actually do."

Expelling an overexaggerated sigh, I replied: "Alright then, I did. You win."

"I always do," she winked again.

"Had its downsides though," I continued. "Mainly a maths class where everyone was high on pot and it wasn't news to anyone."

She chortled heartily and fixed me with a thoughtful expression. "That would have been *exceptionally* cringe if it hadn't fallen on a receptive audience. Please tell me you weren't though?"

"God, no," I said hurriedly, "stick to the champers me." Seizing my glass, I took a slug.

"Did you go to Trinity?"

"Yeah, I did a business and finance degree. Went to DTU then to do a Real Estate Masters." I prodded my waterlogged beermat, pirouetting it with my fingers as it began to disintegrate between them. "My dad's a developer. You know, Elysium Estates?"

She nodded slowly. "So have you been with Rockstar Real Estate long then?" When she asked, there was a genuine interest in her words. It was like she cared and I wondered; what *did* she feel about me?

"Only two years. I was lucky to get the job as soon as I qualified because it's... you know... it's a good job." My colouring darkened in embarrassment, not wanting to seem boastful.

She gave a light giggle. "You don't need to be modest, you know. I've seen your Porsche."

"Well," I hesitated. "Yeah, I should probably be saving up but like... I indulged myself a bit on that one."

"That's allowed." She whispered this almost confidentially and it struck me that she was being quite... flirtatious really.

I hoped she was.

"I still live at home so... I don't have to be responsible all the time."

"In Malahide?"

"Yes... my mum, she left when I was two.... so, it's always been just my dad and I. We only really hear from her a few times a year. And that's at most. Dad remarried a while back-" Suddenly, I trailed off, surprised at myself for divulging this information. I rarely revealed that circumstance to anyone unless I absolutely had to. Julia though, she made me feel so... at ease.

"That's... that's awful about your mum. I'm sorry, Jonathan. People can be horrible. They really can." Sincerity coated every syllable. It was clear that she understood.

"Betrayal's tough," she finished firmly.

I saw something then. Something I now know she strives to conceal beneath a perfectly polished façade: Julia Joyce had been *hurt*. Hurt deeply. Back then, I did not know exactly how.

But I knew that, in her own way, she had suffered.

"Yeah well, you can say that again," I muttered wryly. Reaching for my champagne, I found the glass empty.

At that moment, someone entered the bar and hollered around at the assembled tables that it was the fifteen minute call.

"Come on, we'd better go," Julia suggested, standing. "I like to be in my seat early."

I made to stand too but was almost rendered incapable. One of the evening's last straggling sunbeams had slid unobtrusively through the glass pane behind her head, casting her features in shadows of several shades. White, black, grey.

"Yes, you're right, Julia," I agreed.

CHAPTER 6

Julia

He was so painfully attractive.

Why did he have to be so attractive?

It was nothing but a hindrance. One thing was clear though; he didn't know. He didn't know who his colleague really was. He didn't know what she had done.

And, most imperatively, he did not know that I had played a part in it.

Maybe I should clear something up now. Dear reader; I am not an evil person. I'm not. Honestly. Morally grey in the odd area, admittedly but not evil.

Or at least, I don't think I am.

You, however, may have a differing opinion.

Was I simply stringing the poor boy along?, I hear you ask. No. I said it before and I'll say it again; he was highly endearing. He was intelligent, thoughtful, well-read and well-travelled. And gorgeous.

Not that it was of any consequence whatsoever.

He was exactly the sort of interesting individual I relished spending time with and I could see that the feeling was mutual.

When he looked at me, it was with great affection. Maybe with... a trace of something else too.

In spite of the fact we had not known each other long, a bond between us had been forged.

It was unusual for me to warm to someone so rapidly; usually it takes time on my part. That said, I have a tendency to develop a certain feeling towards everyone I encounter rather quickly after meeting. I'm a skilled judge of character.

Well, usually I am. There was just that *one* time when my judgement didn't quite stand me in *such* good stead.

In the case of my uncle.

But more on that later.

The theatre was overlayed by hospitable darkness, considerately guiding all eyes towards the proscenium arch. A pleasant warmth emanated from my companion, close at my side. Strangely, it was a feeling I felt I could feel with pleasure again.

Treading the boards with purpose, was the character of Lady Macbeth. A powerful performance, deeply affecting the audience I was certain.

But then; when you think of a theatre, who really is acting? Is it those upon the stage bedecked in their costumes and guised in greasepaint?

Or is those who sit latently in the stalls, expressions impassive, features utterly exposed?

All too often, it is the act which conceals the act.

Bleating alarm bells, the words of Lady Macbeth's monologue rang out. No compunctions visitings of nature would shake my purpose. There was no access to remorse. Bleeding, like thick blood the words bled into my veins.

They curdled and they glinted.

They glinted like the knife

CHAPTER 7

Julia

"Well, what did you think?" I questioned Jonathan as we negotiated our way through the dispersing throng congregated outside the theatre doors.

"Fabulous, I thought the..." He was interrupted by the shrill ringtone of my mobile phone.

Fumbling in my handbag, I retrieved it and glanced at the screen. My mum.

"Excuse me, I have to take this," I apologised, moving to the side to accept the call. It crossed my mind that it was rather peculiar for my mum to phone me at this time of night. Wasn't she in work?

"Hello, mammy?" I answered hurriedly, drawing my blazer tighter around me against the burgeoning chill of the night. "Is everything alright?"

"Julia!" Relief almost suffocated her exclamation. "Thank God. Oh my God Julia." Without warning, she began to sob hysterically.

My heart flapped like an eagle's wing in my chest.

"Mammy, what's wrong?" I had to restrain myself from outward screaming. "You need to tell me. What is it?"

Somewhere in the distance, a firework exploded into the night. Molten fingers of fire, its terracotta sparkling hues bled through the sky, washed out watercolour.

She was breathless now. "Just...just get home. Please. I can't say it now, I can't. Because it can't be true. It can't be. Oh Julia, tell me that it can't!"

Darts of undiluted panic shot through every cell of my body, harmonising the fireworks. They seemed poised to continue perpetually as the world, the life, I had known prepared to cease its being. Forever.

"You need to tell me what happened! Mammy, you're scaring the crap out of me. What's wrong?" I *was* screaming now and attracting a few dubious glances from the crowd. Jonathan was staring over at me, a decidedly concerned look marring his handsome features.

"Just come home, Julia. Please," she begged, quiet now with the hysteria expended. "Just... just get here."

And with that, the line went dead.

I would often wish that I could forget the moment. Disremember it. Cast it on a furnace and watch it burn. Curl into smoke and voyage on the breeze to a negligible size. Dissipate into the night.

My dad's body.

Prone at the bottom of the stairs. Lifeless.

Throwing open the front door, I saw her. My mum. Crouched at his side as if silently willing him back to life. Knowing it was futile deep within her but persisting. Clinging to any aqueous hope that it was all an illusion or a nightmare. A haunted, tormented dream from which she would wake.

That night passed in slow-motion. Black and white like some ancient film before technicolour was invented to bring monotony to life.

They would say it was accidental, a fall down the stairs. Incredibly tragic of course but just that; an accident. Unavoidable.

But I knew what they didn't.

It had been no accident.

It had been murder.

Whether the possibility would ever occur to my mum, I did not know.

Certainly not in the immediate aftermath. She was a shell of herself for weeks. So was I.

What hollowed me even more was the knowledge I carried in me, cohabiting with the grief and residing about as peacefully as a raucous tenant.

My uncle was back.

He had murdered my dad.

Murdered him in just the same way he had murdered Lorraine.

CHAPTER 8

Julia- 3 Months Later

What whisps of cloud there were paid only fleeting visits to the cerulean sky. Grass, luscious in its sheer quality, undulated carelessly over the hillside as it crested like the foamy sea to worship the copious sunlight. This landscape synonymised the ocean, just visible, playing host to a cataclysmic battle fought between the cantering white horses and their indiscernible riders. Out of sight, yet still making their presence felt in the callously stirring wind beginning to whip into a gale that would transform the serenity to pandemonium.

Three months and the grief remained excruciating. As aggressive, as unabating, yet more of a constant dull ache than the stabbing pain I had known at first.

The thing that, above all else, had buoyed me through that turbulent time, was the friendship of Jonathan Crookshank. He was at my side through it all.

Nodding encouragingly from the congregation as I stood at the pulpit, preparing to eulogise my father. Enfolding me in his arms as the coffin was lowered into the ground. Whispering words of encouragement as I navigated my university exams only a month after daddy's death.

Now, it was August and I had come to a decision: I was taking a year out from medicine in Trinity. It had been my mum's idea really and after a little persuasion I had agreed readily.

For years, I had intended to take a gap from studying in order to focus purely on writing. The time seemed provident. After enduring what I had, I needed a break from Medicine.

"You're only twenty-one, Julia," my mum had said. "It's just a year. Take the time and do something that you love. Allow yourself to grieve properly."

As we meandered through the grounds of Ardgillan Castle, a place that has long been a favourite of mine, Jonathan reiterated the sentiment now: "It's the right thing Julia, you deserve to take time to yourself you know."

Shielding my eyes against the sun, I stared blankly out at the sprawling suburb of Balbriggan below us, the labyrinthine maze of houses little more than pieces from a child's toy village at this distance.

"I think it is," I mumbled quietly.

"It is."

For a long moment silence reigned but, as always with him, it was not uncomfortable.

"I'm so lucky to have you, Johnny," I pondered almost to myself, turning towards him seriously. "I really mean it. Things have been bearable because of you."

He did not immediately reply but when he did, there was a conviction in his words. "The world needs more people like you, Julia. Honestly it does."

I laughed wryly. "There's plenty of people who wouldn't say that."

"Well, they're silly."

"Trust me, I'm quite hard to put up with."

"I can put up with you just fine. Honestly, I've never met anyone like you, Julia. And trust me, I've met a few characters in my line of work."

"I can imagine." I paused thoughtfully for a moment. "Sometimes I'm a bit jealous that I don't do your job."

"Really?"

"Yeah, a bit." We sat down on a bench, brown paint fluttering to the ground at our disturbance. "I think I'd be good at it. Like, I have this really awful habit."

"What's that?" The edges of his eyes crinkled as he smiled.

"Scrolling on property websites. Swiping left. *Sometimes* right." I shifted just a little closer to him.

"Have a type do you?" There was humour in the question. Curiosity too though.

"Oh, yes."

"Enlighten me."

"Blonde, handsome, funny, smart."

The grin still lingering, he said: "I meant in properties."

"What did I just describe?" My tone was laden with feigned confusion.

He looked at me long and hard. "And *that*, Julia, is why I like you so much."

"I believe you. Thousands wouldn't," I murmured with what I hoped was a provocative pout.

"Julia, I want to ask you something." He began the sentence in a rush, as if coaxing himself to say the words. "If you want to say no, it's absolutely fine. I get it. But I have a proposition."

"Okay..." I hesitated, mildly curious as to how he would proceed.

"You know the way we've been a person down in the office ever since Lorraine..."

"Yes, I... I know," I interjected, not wanting him to complete the phrase.

"Yes, well, we're beginning to struggle a bit..." The words petered out rather awkwardly.

"Right..."

"And I... I was thinking. Would you like to come and work for us? You'd still have plenty of time to write but you'd enjoy it I think..."

I was stupefied.

Unsure how to respond, I said slowly: "Johnny, I'm flattered that you'd even ask but... I'm not qualified. How could I walk in there and start selling houses?"

"You could because you're my Julia." He squeezed my arm. "And I have every faith in you. You'll learn as you go and I'll help you. I promise."

His profile was forming a shadow on the ground, the sidekick to my own. I looked at the silhouetted pair for a few seconds before turning back to his face.

Suddenly, I knew my answer

"Alright then," I intoned with confidence. "I'll come and work in Rockstar Real Estate."

CHAPTER 9

Julia

Before I was quite aware of it, my first day as an agent at Rockstar Real Estate was upon me in a whirlwind of anticipation, excitement and a slight sprinkling of nerves.

My feelings were tempered by a quiet assurance however. I understood the world of property well. It was something by which I had always been fascinated and through my secret hobby of spending hours scrolling on property websites (*not* dating websites), I had acquired a definite level of knowledge relating to it.

Dressed professionally in a powder blue linen suit, my hair was arranged in sultry blonde waves that I hoped would appeal to Jonathan. Not for any other reason other than to look professional of course.

Rockstar Real Estate occupied a prime location in the very centre of Dublin. Set in the middle of one of the city's main thoroughfares, it was a well-respected business amongst the populus. The agency's speciality was the luxury end of the real estate market and they were not afraid to flaunt it. I followed them on Facebook and enjoyed the property tour videos they made of the city's luxury housing. When the era of Celtic tiger ceased to roar and the market deflated, their ambition failing to receive the memo, still they persisted. With barren front windows and fertile fantasies of self-worth they had survived where so many had not. Now, with property prices soaring again, they represented the upper echelons of Dublin society. Jonathan, at least in my opinion, did not seem to be of the disposition that suited a career in sales. I wondered how he survived without being swallowed by the sharks. Perhaps he had a hidden side, I conceded.

After all, I did.

As you look upon a square, remember it might actually be a cube.

The office was decidedly more glamorous than any estate agent's I had previously visited (and trust me, I've seen a few). Blending a traditional office with a Renaissance living room, it was certainly an imposing premises. The windows boasted the stereotypical property advertisements while the desks were of oak and the wallpaper patterned in damask. In one corner, a suite of Winchester furniture was arranged and it was there that my prospective colleagues waited to greet me.

Jonathan leapt from his seat on the sofa the moment I came through the door and I was rewarded by noticing how his eyes involuntarily travelled over me, appreciating my flattering outfit. "Hi Julia, you look lovely," he greeted, kissing me. On the cheek. Obviously.

It was chaste but only just.

"Everyone," he began, placing an arm solicitously about my shoulders. "This is Julia Joyce, the newest member of our team."

"Morning, nice to meet you all," I smiled dazzlingly around at the assembled agents, lathering my words in the confidence I tended to use when introducing myself.

There were two men; one was approximately mid-fifties and the other likely late thirties. Beside them was a girl, of indeterminate age but probably several years older than me. It was she who spoke first.

"Nice to meet you, I'm Emily." Her introduction was made in a placid voice with an accent that, although not strong, was definitely north-side. She proffered a slim hand to shake mine and gave a pleasantly hospitable smile. My first impression assessment concluded that she was of an amiable if rather meek character. Nice but maybe a bit of a wallflower. The type who like to blend in. Cut to a length just below her shoulders, her hair was of a mousy brown and her features, fairly pretty, were accentuated by heavy makeup. She wore a plain floral dress and oversized blazer that seemed several sizes too large.

I glanced briefly at her left hand and, finding it without a ring, wondered if she was in any way attached. Could she have designs on Jonathan? No, I decided. They wouldn't suit each other. I, on the other hand, was exactly his type. Not that I was *actually* going to date him but you know...

Anyway, that's diverging from the topic.

Returning her handshake and smile warmly, I turned to the younger of the men as she resumed her seat.

He stood up and I noticed that his skin-tight trousers ended several inches above his ankles. Clearly, he thought this was trendy. The same motivation may have accounted for the short back and sides haircut streaked with varying shades of dye. "How ya, Julia. What's da' bleedin' story?" he said brightly, pumping my hand with aggression. "Welcome to Rockstar land. I'm Anto by the way." His air emitted warmth in that cheeky Dublinese way and I couldn't help but feel endeared to him immediately.

Finally, it was the turn of Eamon, the older gentleman who wore a neat suit and his silver hair in a peaked quiff. "How's it goin', Julia? What's the craic?" he questioned in an unmistakeable modulation: that of county Tyrone.

"If you're wondering why he speaks like that," Anton interjected, clapping Eamon on the back. "It's because he's from Norn Iron."

It was at that moment that a door at the back of the office space was flung open and a voice belonging to someone who I originally presumed was using a microphone assaulted our ears.

"Hey, hey Rockstars!" declared the orotund Frederick Featherington-Smythe. "Are we slacking or are we selling out here, lads?" Just as Jonathan had assured me was customary, at least two more buttons of his silk shirt were open than strictly necessary, the aviator sunglasses were perched on his nose and his hair was oiler than Saudi Arabia.

Suddenly noticing my presence, he halted in the middle of the floor and spread his arms wide. "Julia! How's my latest Rockstar?" he asked exuberantly. Without waiting for a reply, he strode across the room and gestured to the desk nearest the front door with a flourish.

"Make yourself at home. 'Cause you know, that's the biz 'round here." He delivered his customary smirk.

"Thank you, Mr. Featherington-Smythe. I'm sure I'll be very happy here," I answered politely, attempting valiantly not to burst out laughing. I was all too conscious of Jonathan pointing at the side of his head and making circular motions with his finger in the universal symbol for 'psycho.'

"Now, you'll all be so sad to hear I have to go out on a viewing, but," he did some sort of half pirouette, "just remember Julia: sell, sell and sell some more. Whatever it takes, just make those sales. Yeah? Remember that and you'll be a *Rockstar.*"

Sordidly sweeping us with a scintillating stare, he allowed his words to ring out, heavy with purpose.

"Right then, best be off. Money to make, people to please. You know how it is."

And with that, smirking yet again, he departed the office.

"Feckin' spanner," ejaculated Anto. "What a bleedin' tool."

Eamon muttered wryly: "Wouldn't get thon twat in Tyrone. It's good, honest dealings up there."

"Eamon likes to periodically remind us of all the things that happen here that apparently wouldn't in Tyrone," Jonathan whispered into my ear. "You'll get used to it."

Thoughtfully, I nodded around the office. "I rather suspect I will."

CHAPTER 10

Julia

The remainder of my inauguration passed in relative mundanity. The other agents duly accepted my presence as an inevitable fact of office life and within a few days I felt truly like one of them. They were all pleasant people in their own ways, if a little of an eclectic mix. Committed and dedicated to their jobs, they were intelligent and being in their company always proved interesting. I had never been one to fit in but I found that, at Rockstar Real Estate, I did. No one conformed there. I appreciated that immensely.

About a week after my arrival, conversation in the agency turned to the issue of an upcoming office party to celebrate four years of Mr. FFS's tenure as the owner of the business. It had previously been led by the original founder but he had taken over Rockstar Real Estate on their retirement and grown it to become the leading estate agency in Dublin. In spite of his theatrics, I had to admit he was capable.

Customarily, discussions regarding the party took place in his absence as actually spending time in the office did not appear to be of a priority to him. He was constantly making excuses that he had 'places to be.' The exact nature of aforementioned 'places' remained a mystery to us all.

"Doesn't it bother you that your boss is never here?" I questioned Jonathan as our glorious leader departed yet again.

He shrugged in response. "Dunno really. It's sort of a new thing. Since you came actually. Maybe you're scaring him off." This last was added with his devilish little grin that I had become rather accustomed to.

"Well, I *can* be rather scary," I admitted with a flirtatious hair toss.

We were interrupted then by Eamon, hollering across the room at us: "Weans, where do youse think we should have this do?"

'Weans' transpires to be a general term used in the north to describe young people and Eamon made a point of collectively referring to Jonathan and I by it. The two of us had become almost inseparable since I began work. I wouldn't have hesitated to call him my best friend. Usually, I struggled to trust people but I found being with Jonathan easy and our double act hadn't gone unnoticed to the others either. Something else strange was happening between us though. Occasionally, I'd find that when he looked at me, it wasn't the look of a friend to a friend. It pained me to admit it, but a spark of hope was ignited within me. Recently, my life had been so overshadowed by grief. Maybe it would be nice to be...loved by someone.

Not that I was encouraging the relationship in any way. I mean, me *flirting*? Never!

And yes, I am being sarcastic.

"Wherever we go," said Jonathan. "It better not be anywhere in Temple Bar."

"Aye, wile dear," concurred Eamon with feeling. "Tourist trap so it is."

"What he means is that it's a bleedin' rip-off." This was added by Anto in a rather chagrined voice, as if the atrocity that was our city's most famous drinking area caused him extensive personal suffering.

"Only thing is, Anto," Eamon piped up again, "there could be a few boys coming to us looking a re-mortgage if they buy enough drink in thon place!"

Anto actually hooted in glee. "Bleedin' right Eamon," the two high-fived like hyped up teenagers, "Get your clients locked, best business plan ever."

"What do you think Emily?" I asked her kindly. She was the shiest amongst us and rarely raised her voice.

"Oh, I don't mind, whatever you lot want," she mumbled.

"What about McDaids?" I suggested. "They have an upstairs that's great for parties. I think my dad knows the owner as well..." I trailed off. It was a mistake I had been making frequently; talking about my dad as if he was... still here.

If anyone noticed my error, they kindly didn't comment but seemed enthusiastic about the proposition. They were a considerate group in that way. Since beginning work there, the gnawing grief had been assuaged. A little anyway.

"Are you alright, Julia?" Jonathan's quiet words jolted me out of my thoughts. He rubbed my arm. "If... if you want to talk about anything you know I'm here. Don't you?"

My heart melted. "Thank you, Jonathan. I...do know that."

And I did. Truly.

"Here, Julia," Anto threw a question at me this time. "Are you working here on the black or wha'?"

I almost spluttered a mouthful of my Americano (Jonathan had thoughtfully brought it over from Bewley's just the way I like it; strictly black, absolutely *no* milk)across the paperwork on my desk.

"What do you mean, Anto?" I tried to keep my tone light-hearted but wondered how well I was succeeding in this endeavour. After all, you could argue that I have previously been involved in some activities potentially aligning to the description of 'on the black.'

But more on that later.

Anto arranged his features into a conspiratory guise and winked deliberately. "Like, you don't have a PSRA license, do yi'?"

Relieved that this was as much of my misdemeanours as Anto suspected, I said brightly: "Oh well, no, I don't. Not yet anyway. But hopefully soon. Technically, I'm here as an apprentice but I've started studying online for a real estate diploma so I should be able to apply for my license in about six months." I beamed around at my colleagues. "Honestly, this was only supposed to be a temporary thing after my dad..." I swallowed abruptly, "but I've loved working with you all so much. I'm getting the license so there'll always be an open door to make it a more permanent thing in the future."

"Auch Julia, we love you too wee pet," said Eamon. Eamon's always had a soft spot for me and I for him. I think it's because I have connections to Tyrone. "But you're not giving up medicine are you?"

I shook my head. "No, of course not. I'll go back next September. Good to have options."

Soon after this examination of how well I was abiding to Ireland's property laws, conversation turned to Maycroft Demesne. Automatically, my guard shot up. The sooner that place was sold and removed from the agency's books, the better. The investigation into Lorraine's death appeared to have petered out; my dad was in charge of it after all and without him, any leads they may have been exploring went cold.

What the Gardai didn't know was that I could have solved the mystery in an instant. But trust me; it's better that way.

Still though,for as long as there was interest in those four walls, my secret was in jeopardy. When it was sold, things would move on and the past would be replaced with someone else's story.

Everything would be forgotten.

"Emily, I reckon this one's for you," Anto said surprisingly seriously. "The rest of us all have big projects at the minute and we can't really deal with anymore so..."

"Oh so you think it's alright just to pass me the poisoned chalice do you?"

This enraged outburst was so violent we all were physically startled.

"No! Of course not, Emily. God, don't be silly. It's just... you have less on than the rest of us at the minute and I thought..." Anto stuttered uncertainly.

Hotly, Emily pushed back her chair and raised herself into a defiant stance. "I'm never as good as the rest of you. Am I? It's all about you 'Rockstars.'" She made air quotes with her fingers. "And I'm just the runt of the litter. So, of *course*, it's fine to let me deal with a house you know is never going to sell!"

"Now, Emily, hold on a second-"

"Just SHUT UP!"

It was following that parting term of endearment that she stormed incandescently from the office.

"Has she had a personality transplant or is it a certain time of the month?" Jonathan verbally pondered.

"Defo PMS talkin'," Anto muttered. "You should hear my missus when-"

"I'll do it," I exclaimed before I could think twice. "I'll take on Maycroft Demesne. I like a challenge," I finished resolutely.

"Aww Julia, are you sure? I know Emily got her knickers in a twist but that place is a handlin' waiting to happen after everything..." started Eamon.

"No, I'm sure. I want to do it," I said with certainty.

Jonathan piped up then. "I agree, Julia. There's no better woman," he beamed back at me and there was a definite... pride in the gesture. "You should have it. I know you'll manage."

Anto nodded too. "Knock yourself out. I don't want it anyway."

I felt illuminated. "That's settled then. Don't worry, I'll have it out of our hair in no time." At that moment, I was reminded of when I was at school, taking on a load of extra responsibility while secretly wondering when I would find the time to manage it all.

But I always did then.

And I would manage again now.

You see, if Maycroft Demesne was secure under my watchful gaze, I could control the narrative. Ensure nothing compromising came to light. It was the golden opportunity; too perfect to miss.

One thing you should know about me is that I can manipulate anything. Nobody messes with Julia Joyce.

I would sell that house if it was the last thing I did.

CHAPTER 11

Julia

About an hour had elapsed when Emily returned to the office, head hung low and eyes deliberately averting anyone else's. She didn't utter a syllable for the remainder of the afternoon and it was to my intense dismay that I found myself alone with her at the end of the day. Anto, Eamon and Jonathan had already left work but I was staying late to finish writing up the particulars for a new listing. I considered leaving the ball in her court and not speaking to her unless she spoke to me but as I was just preparing to finish up, I broke the silence.

"Emily?"

"Yeah?" Her sigh was laden as she raised her head reluctantly from her desk. I couldn't help noticing that the document she was supposedly perusing was upside down.

"You know that Anto... didn't mean anything earlier. He thought he was doing you a favour."

Her eyebrows crumpled like soiled tissues. "I do know that," she murmured quietly.

"Well, that's good then," I smiled encouragingly. "I just didn't want things to be awkward. See you on Monday."

Glad to evacuate the elephant in the office, I made to exit. Emily's words gave me pause however.

"Wait, Julia. Please!"

Surprised, I relinquished my hold on the door handle and faced her.

"What's going to happen with Maycroft Demesne?" There was trepidation in her question. "Will they change agency or something?"

Wearily, I sank down at my desk again. "I'll be managing the sale."

Upon hearing this, her complexion altered to adopt an ashen aspect.

"You're not serious?"

"Of course I'm serious. Why? Do you want it now or something?" I was mildly offended by her critical tone and retaliated rather harshly.

"Do I want it? Do I want to gouge my eyes out with spoons?"

"Okay, right. Seriously, what's really going on here? Why were you so opposed to dealing with the place?" Measuring my tone with patience, I fixed her with a sympathetic expression. "You can tell me, Emily," I said softly.

She couldn't know something could she? Surely not. If she did, I had to ascertain what. Immediately.

"I..." her speech faltered. "Well... it's obvious. My colleague died in that house! She was murdered! Nobody in their right mind would buy it so what's it going to do other than take up space in the window?"

"That's understandable," I conceded, "but not every buyer would be bothered by something like that. Not every buyer would even *know*. We were fortunate in the fact that Lorraine's death didn't actually get a lot of press. So, be honest with me here, Emily. What's the real reason? I know there's more to it than that."

"Alright then. I'll tell you." As she said this, it was as if a fire began to blaze in her veins while simultaneously all the aggression petered out. "You'd better know. Especially if you're going to be working here for a while."

What she said next was going to matter. Hugely.

I had to find out what she knew.

"Go on, Emily, tell me," I almost whispered.

So, she did.

CHAPTER 12

7 Years Previously

Maria has been different lately. In the beginning, it was only mere differentiations from her usual self that piqued Emily's interest. However, over the past few weeks, she has noticed her sister reverting to behaviour so uncharacteristic that the small seedling of concern within her has become a flourishing flower.

For a start, she is distracted. Distracted as in she seems to be permanently residing on another planet. Sometimes, when Emily attempts to make conversation with her, Maria just stares in reply. Blankly. Completely unresponsive.

Secondly, she is now obsessed by her weight. Unhealthily obsessed. To the extent that Emily cannot pinpoint the last time she saw her consume a substantial meal. The pounds have shed off her like discarded clothing, leaving her once generous figure a distant memory. Instead, she now appears thin, drawn and what frightens Emily more than anything: vulnerable.

Finally and perhaps most mysteriously, Maria is surgically attached to her phone. Her fingers skim the screen in incessant typing, communicating with some unknown being who is rendering her sister little more than a mere stranger off the street. Someone she no longer comprehends.

Trying to talk to Maria will be futile. Emily knows this. But there has to be another way. Her opportunity will come. She simply has to be patient.

When it does, it is on a night much like any other. Emily is camped out in the living room flicking aimlessly between the channels, her fingers hovering on the remote. The front door slams shut which indicates Maria's return from tennis practice. It is quickly followed by the pounding of footsteps on the staircase as she hurries to shower off the exercise. Before, Maria would have stopped with Emily before going upstairs. Asked how her day had been.

Answered the same question. Tonight, she doesn't.

Emily carefully replaces the remote on the coffee table and leans forward. She places her hands on her knees as she prepares to listen. The sound of running water greets her. This is her chance.

Stealthily, she exits the living room and ascends the stairs, sometimes taking two steps at a time to avoid those that creak. Maria is unlikely to hear her anyway over the noise of the shower. Not that with her current state of preoccupation, Emily could probably scream blue murder in her face and she wouldn't notice. When she reaches Maria's bedroom, she closes the door softly in her wake. Upon the bedside table is exactly what she has been seeking: Emily's phone.

Emily and Maria bear a significant resemblance to each other and therefore the facial recognition is fooled. The phone unlocks. With no hesitation. When it opens, it immediately reveals a WhatsApp chat and it does not take Sherlock Holmes to know its nature. This is messaging with... romantic intention. To put it mildly. Emily's eyes widen as they scan the words before her. There are pictures, too. God, Maria, how could you be so *stupid?* Emily ponders the question but an answer eludes her. She clicks on the profile picture and it fills the screen. A handsome man. A *very* handsome man. If she had to estimate his age, she would say early twenties. Maria is eighteen. At least he isn't some geriatric paedophile then. That said, these things can be faked nowadays. Catfishing is a pertinent threat in today's world. And based on the context of the messages, she has yet to meet this man in person. The discourse stretches back three months. That coincides with Maria's marked change of demeanour. The distraction, the desire to lose weight, the attachment to her phone. Suddenly, it all makes such glaringly obvious sense to Emily. The chat is entitled "Nick" and the name is followed by a red heart emoji. Of course. She is utterly infatuated.

At that moment, the folding doors to the ensuite are pushed open and Maria emerges into the room, her bathrobe drowning her willowy form. She is irate. Emily can practically envisage the tendrils of smoke emanating from her sister's ears.

"What the hell are you looking at?" she seethes through gritted teeth. "Give that back!" Violently, she snatches the mobile from Emily's grasp.

"Who. Is. Nick?" Emily separates each word into its own sentence and fixes her sister with a scintillating glare. There is silence.

"Answer me or I swear to good God, I'll go and tell mum and dad about this!"

"Okay, okay, look. He's just a guy." Her shrug is nonchalant. "And I like him. A lot."

"You *like* him? *A lot*? Have you ever even *met* him?"

Maria's expression is sheepish then. "No."

Emily cannot prevent herself from openly laughing. "You must actually be thick."

"Of course I'm not, Emily! You just don't understand what it's like to be in love."

She scoffs again. "Oh, so, we're in love with him now are we? That was quick."

Maria flops down onto the bed. "You don't get it."

"I don't get it? That's alright, Maria. Blame it on me, why don't you?"

"I'm not trying to blame it on you, Emily," she whispers repentantly.

"Jokes aside here. You sent him pictures. What if he leaks those? You could be ruined!"

"Nick and I have a *connection*, Emily." Maria's words are firm.

"How do you know that this connection isn't with some ninety-year -old dude in Nigeria?" Emily's words tremble.

"Why do you have to spoil everything?" Maria is now on the verge of tears.

"Trust me. The only person who's spoiling anything here is you."

"Why are you trying to deny me happiness?" she moans melodramatically.

Emily does not answer the question. "Promise me you won't meet up with him on your own. Let me come with you. I'll be discreet."

"You honestly think I would allow *you* to come on *my* date?"

"I won't disturb you in any way," Emily says it placidly, calmly. "But it's the safest way, Maria. It's to protect you."

"I don't need protection!" Maria screams this time, appearing slightly demonic with her soaked hair and bloodshot eyes. "I'm not a baby like you."

"Right, I'm going. I have better things to do than be insulted by you." Emily fills her features with hatred.

"Fine."

"Fine."

Discontented, Emily does leave then. What else can she do? Her greatest fear though is that telling Maria not to do something will make her want to do just that all the more. And she would be right.

CHAPTER 13

Maria has yet to do anything in life quite like what she will do tonight. Throughout her existence, she has been a generally obedient girl. Modest, unassuming, restrained. Nick, though, makes her feel worthy of note. Wanted. His compliments settle, butterfly kisses on her skin, golden fireflies that illuminate her person. He *is* her person. Of that, she is confident.

She will meet Nick tonight face to face for the first time. They have arranged their rendezvous in town; in Sinnotts on South King Street. Maria has not told either Emily or her parents where she is going, instead making the excuse that she is heading to her best friend's house for a study session that will likely result in her staying the night. It is a good lie, Maria reflects. After all, hopefully she *will* be staying the night. With Nick. Vaguely, she wonders whether they'll go back to his place or check into a hotel. Preferably the latter. Nick is a doctor and although he is only in his mid-twenties and likely recently qualified, even junior doctors earn good money. Don't they? Maria isn't sure but if the expensive clothing he wears in his social media pictures is anything to go by, the guy has cash.

For the occasion, Maria's garments of choice consist of a crushed white velvet mini-skirt that exposes her bronzed legs, toning with the sallow hue of her face she is attempting to accentuate with the application of some carefully selected cosmetics. The skirt would formerly not have required a belt but now it is making attempts to abscond down her legs and so she has secured it at her slender waist. She hitches it higher. Nick will like that, won't he? It is suggestive. Completing her image is a black halter neck top with a small slit which provides some shape to her flat chest. It isn't her...usual look but hopefully she will be rewarded when Nick sees her.

Pleased with her appearance, she glances at her bedside clock. Six p.m. She is in good time. Her train leaves Raheny station at 6:30 and is supposed to arrive in Pearse at 6:50, giving her ample time before she meets Nick at 7:30 in Sinnotts. As a last-minute thought, she seizes a long raincoat from the back of her bedroom door. Her parents may be suspicious if she goes downstairs clad as she is. It is hardly an outfit for hitting the books.

Maria pokes her head into the kitchen and bids her family a perfunctory goodnight. Her parents, who are both teachers, are marking papers at the table and barely afford her so much as a second look. Emily, though, wears a dubious expression. She is not deceived but thankfully, she remains silent.

Without further hindrance, Maria exits the house. One of many benefits of a location such as Raheny is the close proximity to the train station so the walk requires less than five minutes. Her tread along the footpath is leisurely, barely conscious of the steady release of rain from the laden nimbostratus overhead. To Maria, the world is bathed in a radiant light. Every droplet of water is an angel's caress. Leading her to her destiny.

As expected, she arrives with quarter of an hour to spare. She seeks refuge on the platform beneath an overhang and takes the opportunity to send Nick a text.

Can't wait to see you!

His reply is immediate.

Me too! xxx

Maria sighs contentedly. Is it even possible to be this lucky?

No, Maria, it is not.

Boarding the train, it is standing room only. A reasonable predicament for a Friday evening. Maria is sandwiched between a young man with headphones on his head and an older woman clinging to a toddler's hand. Step on a train in Dublin and you are immediately served a cross-section of urban life. A study in miniature spelling the stories of the city's populus. If you cast your eyes around the carriage, you will encounter those from all walks of life. Each with their own tale to tell and, most crucially, their own secrets to conceal.

Her journey terminates in Dublin Pearse. The voices of her fellow passengers merge in an eerie echo, voyaging upwards into the station's vaulted rafters. Maria negotiates her way through the throng and emerges into the perishing daylight of Westland Row. Bordering each side, the Georgian facades stretch skyward as she traverses the historic street. The stoic statue of Oscar Wilde presiding over the area sits cross-legged on the bench outside Kennedy's Pub, a staple of old Irish literary tradition. For a brief moment, Maria almost imagines that the inanimate man raises a finger off his walking stick in acknowledgement. Bidding her farewell.

She continues on through Lincoln Place, past Trinity College's Gate (where she hopes to begin studying next year) and down Nassau Street to the main thoroughfare of the city: Grafton Street. Approaching St. Stephen's Green Corner, she swerves right, the familiar outline of the Gaiety Theatre seeping into her vision. The pavement is crowded. A courtroom drama is playing and it appears to be pulling in the punters.

Raucous laughter perforates the air. Huddled groups congregate around the outside tables in front of Sinnotts that take the form of repurposed Guinness barrels. Maria pulls the heavy door open and enters the premises, descending the wide staircase to the underground establishment. At the bottom, she scans the room. Another watering hole central to the literary scene. The walls are adorned by countless prints and pictures of those whose pens have inked the essence of Irish cultural identity so superbly that centuries have failed to erode their vigour.

That is when she spots him. Nick. Her heart contracts. It is really him. He is seated at the bar, beneath the large television screen showing a rugby match that dominates the back of the space. Bodies press together, leaving little of a path but, somehow, she propels herself towards him. Not once do their eyes depart from each other. He has captured her. Utterly, completely.

"Maria," when she reaches him, he breathes the word like he is savouring the syllables. Nick rises in greeting and plants a kiss on her cheek. Far from chaste but respectful. For now. Retracting, he runs his gaze over her. "Even more beautiful in reality."

"I can't believe it's really you," Maria says quietly. Nick is, without question, the most attractive man she has seen in her life. Now that he is in front of her, she is struck by the fact that he is very...mature. This man is not in his twenties. More like thirties. Exactly what age he is impossible to say. But he is at least fifteen years her senior. Who cares though? Plenty of people in loving relationships have that age difference and are perfectly happy. Age is just a number. Despite this, what is sparking a minimal ignition of concern is the fact that any photos he imparted to her were definitely taken when he was younger. Not that intervening years have made him any less handsome; the opposite in fact. However, dishonesty occasions the first stirrings of disquiet.

She sits elegantly at the high bar stool, on top of the rain coat she removed so that her revealing attire is exhibited for Nick's benefit. It affords her great pleasure to notice the descent of his eyes first to her cleavage and then onwards to the skirt conveniently riding up her legs. A smirk twirls on his full lips as he slides a cocktail of unknown origin across the rutted surface of the bar top towards her.

"What's this?" she questions, hoping it doesn't appear pathetic that she is not exactly au fait with alcoholic beverages.

"Sex on the beach." This is said with a pointed wink. Something is telling Maria that he will not be playing the perfect gentleman for much longer. He is handsome, he is alluring, he is the epitome of masculine charm. This is what she wants. So why then, does she feel decidedly uncomfortable?

"You're a doctor, are you?" she says it to burst the bubble of tension that seems to have enveloped them.

"I am."

"Wh...what kind?"

"A psychiatrist." He wets his lips with his Guiness and lowers it again. "The study of the human condition is a most complex field, Maria."

"I'm sure it is.", she curses herself for failing to compile a more interesting reply. All of a sudden she feels extremely small in this cavernous space.

His gaze is intense, possessing a heat under which a white lily will wither. "Just when you think you've seen it all, you discover some other angle, some other outlook on life, that you did not previously comprehend."

There is some ulterior meaning to this assertion that Maria is certain she falls short of understanding. She does not understand *this man*. That is becoming clear as crystal.

She is only roused from her musings by his quizzical expression and she realises she has not responded.

"That's... very... true I'm sure, not that I really-"

A smile, almost sympathetic in nature, curls the corner of his mouth. He nods slowly, in the manner of a scientist who just reached the expected conclusion of an experiment.

"Yes-yes, you don't."

Maria experiences a strong urge to redeem herself but just how exactly she intends to accomplish this she is unaware.

"How long have you been a psychiatrist?" she offers confidently. Still, the inadequacy worries at her being.

He is momentarily surprised by the question but then shrugs. "A while." His demeanour droops then, the reluctance to tear his eyes from the pint in front of him conspicuous. Somehow, this question has shocked him. His movement is measured as he raises his eyes to hers once more. "Do you want to know something, Maria?"

"I do," she says slowly, wondering if this is some form of disguised test.

"You're the most beautiful woman I've ever met."

He intones the words steadily and something in them shows Maria that this is far from the first time he has deployed them on the female species.

In spite of herself though, she says: "Do you really think so?" There is that innate quality about Nick that demands the respect of the victim. Although she feels utterly at sea in this interaction, she is certain that she craves his approval.

"Oh, yes. Certain." For the first time, he reaches out to touch her with his arachnidian fingers. They trace the inside of her thigh.

She gulps.

"And I don't need to be a psychiatrist to know you find me attractive." The statement is casual.

With that, he leans forward and kisses her. She had expected.... butterflies or...fireworks. But there are none. Nothing. Nothing except the heavy stench of dread that coaxes itself into her nostrils and settles in her stomach as a tangible taste. The flavour of fear.

CHAPTER 14

She is not quite sure how she has found herself in this position.

Nick retracts his lips and scrutinises her features. "Did you like that, Maria?" he says softly. If she were to answer honestly, she would say no. She can't answer honestly though. It is his aura that tells her such a thing would not be wise.

"Yes. I... I did," she says simply.

He seems satisfied. Before she is quite aware of what is happening, he kisses her again. Intensely. And when he suggests they depart the bar, she does not argue.

They emerge onto the now darkened street together. The pavement is quiet, the crowd long since ensconced inside the theatre. Even the revellers at the outside tables are no longer anywhere to be seen.

"Where...where are we going?" she ventures timidly.

He winks at her again. "I was thinking we would go back to mine."

So no hotel then. That said, Maria's original intentions for the night have been altered. Suddenly, her only desire is to go home. Without Nick. However, she does not protest as he leads her through the gathering gloom of the night back towards Pearse Station. Apparently, he resides in Howth and his objective is that they will both go back to his place. What will occur when they reach this unspecified location, she is unaware. She can imagine though. And she is far from comfortable with it.

The platform is deserted. A solitary piece of litter, an abandoned tinfoil wrapper, dances across the concrete surface. It is buoyed by the wind; an invisible force that pushes the object to do its bidding. Nick's hand is secured on her waist. Sharp gusts of the increasing breeze assault them, Maria's hair whipping out behind her. It is then that Nick manoeuvres himself so that his body is pressed against hers. His hands are wandering, his lips firm on her mouth.

A train speeds past. Beneath its thunderous battle cry, her whispered pleas for him to cease perish.

"You're so wonderful, Maria," he breathes admiringly into the frigid air. He is an actor delivering his line with the perfect poise.

Maria says nothing.

Their train approaches and grinds to an abrupt halt. Nick places his arm around her and guides her across the gap, onto the vehicle and into a vacant corner. The seats are arranged two- facing- two so he positions himself directly across from her, his eyes alighting on hers periodically while he grasps her knee under the graffitied plastic of the table. In the carriage, the fluorescent light bathes the passengers mercilessly, skimming their skin as gently as hailstones. On the back of her right thigh, Maria is afflicted by a slight irritation. Looking downwards, she notices that the grimy fabric has been perforated and the stuffing is spilling out. Salivating for escape.

Conversation is elusive as they traverse the tracks, the train devouring them all too quickly. Fleeting streaks of light cavort beyond the glass as they trundle through the various suburbs and stations. They are poisoned darts as they pierce her vision, proprietors of a joviality depleted from her veins.

Monotonous is the voice that declares their arrival at Howth. What was once a mild concern has metamorphosed into sheer terror and it only increases as Nick snakes his hand around her arm yet again and they exit the train station into the carpark. Nick drives a large Range Rover jeep, an impressive car. Somehow she is not surprised. He holds the front passenger door open as she enters, fingers splayed on the small of her back.

"Almost there," he informs her as the car makes its way along a wide road overlooking Dublin Bay, the area punctuated by the comely glow emanating from the many surrounding properties. Maria knows this area to be an affluent one and many of the houses they pass are excessively grand. She cannot help but wonder where Nick calls home.

She does not know that when she crosses the threshold, she will never leave again.

"Oh my God! Nick, do you *live* here?" Momentarily, Maria abandons her trepidation. It is only natural when faced with the sight before her.

The house is truly magnificent. Crafted from sandstone, it is a thing hewn of inherent beauty. An aloof old mistress observing keenly the lethargically lapping waters below. The only light is afforded by the lampposts situated at intervals along the protracted driveway and due to the inky blackness of the night, the finer details of the landscape do not greet the gaze. But the ethereal enchantment of this place is something that must be appreciated. Under any circumstances.

"Ah sure, it's only an auld shack." Nick chortles deprecatingly.

Tonight, there is no gallant moonlight to illuminate the scene. Stepping from the jeep, Maria almost stumbles without the aid such a luxury would give. Her saviour is instead Nick. Grabbing her firmly, he murmurs still gently: "I've got you Maria." His whitened teeth glint. Like knife blades.

She is lead through the imposing doorway and into the entrance hall, legs moving forward of their own accord despite her commands to turn the other way. Run as fast as she can physically muster; as far away from this house as she can possibly get.

Maria does not.

Rather, she allows Nick to remove her coat and hang it upon a hook. Welcoming her home.

"Can I get you a drink?" he questions hospitably.

"N... no. I'm alright, thank you."

"You'll have something, won't you? It's a special night." He removes his own jacket and drapes it over the back of a low antique chair. "Go and sit down in the living room and I'll bring you a glass of something nice."

She complies with his wishes and meanders into the first room on the right. Much like the hallway, the place is burgeoning with antiques which strikes Maria as unusual for what is apparently a bachelor pad. All of this for one person. Did he inherit this estate? Purchase it himself? Surely not. Yes, she could see he had money but this, well, *this* is another level entirely. Perching on the precipice of a Winchester sofa, she awaits his return. He sweeps in carrying two tall glasses, the contents of which appear to be hissing and spitting with hellish intent as they catch the overhead cast of the crystal chandelier. "Now," he smiles as he places the glass into her hand. "Cheers. To us."

And she is barely even startled when, mere moments after she takes her first sip, darkness consumes her.

CHAPTER 15

Emily cannot sleep. She has tossed and turned for what must surely be hours, her pursuit of the elusive treasure that is slumber futile.

Maria did not listen to her warning. It shouldn't really come as such a surprise; after all, Emily is younger and lacking experience in the relationship department. But still. Maria is being completely foolhardy. She has never met this Nick person, yet she has convinced herself that she is in love with him. In *love* with him. How can you be in love with someone you've never met? Emily asks herself the question and cannot provide an answer.

Within her heart, she knows the truth: Maria has gone to meet Nick. Alone. A distinct sensation of nausea assaults her when she begins to consider the potential implications of this. There is a glaringly large possibility that he does not exist at all and is really some catfish with paedophilic tendencies. After all, everyone has heard the stories of such things doing the rounds lately.

If that is the case (and at this stage, she'd almost be surprised if it weren't) then where is her sister now? Many images jostle for admittance to her thought process but she simply will not afford them the real estate. At the unbidden picture of Maria being bundled into the back of a white van to be taken God only knows where, beads of freezing perspiration erupt on Emily's forehead. She sits up in the bed and breathes deeply. In and out. Somehow, this eventually succeeds in lulling her into a restless sleep that is not really sleep but a demonic purgatory between her conscious and unconscious mind. What she doesn't know is that pure hell awaits her when she rouses.

The faint murmur of voices rises upwards and greets her ears the moment she awakens. An early hour still, watery sunlight filtering through the roller blinds and pooling on the carpet. Rubbing her eyes warily, she coaxes herself from the covers and pads out on to the landing, straining as she does to hear the conversation ongoing below.

"... for a while now... struggling mentally... all becoming too much to handle," the words are said by someone unfamiliar to Emily.

"Yes, yes of course. We understand. Although it's all just such a *shock*" This comes from her mum.

"You can rest assured that we will take the very best care of her. Your daughter is in safe hands, Mrs. Wilson."

"Thank you, Doctor," her dad says quietly. "We appreciate you calling."

Emily's knuckle bones are visible through her gossamer skin. She clutches the banister. Clinging to life as she has known it.

Before she can convince herself to do otherwise, she pounds down the stairs and erupts into the kitchen. The sight before her steals her breath: Nick. He looks older than in the photo she saw but it is still undeniably him. Dread douses her body.

"What's going on here?" she blurts out, eyes darting between her parents and this mystery man.

"Emily, this is Doctor-"

"Where the hell is Maria?" The question bursts forth like liquid lava. "Tell me. Tell me now or else-"

"Calm down, Emily, pet. Maria is safe. There's nothing to worry about but there's just a little explaining we need to do. It will all make sense when-" her mum begins to placate her.

"Look, I'll leave you to it. I understand that it's hard to process this but you're assured of our every support. I can't reiterate that enough. Any questions you have, we will be more than happy to answer but of course we do request that she be given at least a fortnight to adjust to her new surroundings without visitors. Once that has passed, you will naturally be more than welcome." With a respectful nod, the man retires to the hallway and moves to the front door.

"Hold on a second," Emily starts again, "you can't just *leave* like that. I need to know what's going on here. This isn't fair!"

"Emily," Nick fixes her with a steely look that blends sympathy with condescension in a poisonous potion. "You parents are going to explain everything. All I can say is that your sister has been... finding life tough lately and I am helping her to heal. She is in the right place. Just know that. Good day, Mr and Mrs. Wilson."

Emily is just on the point of retaliating with a few pertinent asks as to why the man who was engaging in intimate online discourses with her sister is now calling himself a doctor 'healing' Maria of some anonymous disease but, before the sentence can be strung together, he opens the door and departs.

She executes a pivot on her heel, turning to look at her ashen faced parents. Her jaw falls but she cannot wheedle any words.

Her dad places a hand on her shoulder and guides her into the living room where he pushes her placidly onto the sofa. Trepidation colours the whites of her eyes as she gazes fearfully up into the mutually drawn expressions worn by her mum and dad. "Tell me what's going on, please," she murmurs barely audibly, all anger suddenly depleted.

Her mum sighs deeply, tugging insistently at a loose thread hanging from her blouse. "Maria's gone into rehab, Emily."

"Rehab?" echoes Emily incredulously. "What do you mean, *rehab*?"

"We've all seen that Maria has been acting a little... detached lately," her dad says hesitantly, the direction his speech is taking uncertain.

"You could say that."

"Yes," his brow furrows. "She's been finding things difficult. Her mental health has been suffering and she's ... she's become addicted to painkillers."

At this, her mum's composure crumbles and she bursts into a torrential flood of tears. "Why didn't she just talk to us and... and...

and tell us how she was feeling? We could have helped her, Mark!" Any coherent sound is drowned then.

"It's alright, Ashlene. There's nothing we could have done." Gruffly, he pats her on the back in his well-meaning but taciturn way. "She'll be fine. Nick will take good care of her."

"Nick?" This is ejaculated by Emily at a pitch capable of desecrating glass.

"Nick is a doctor. A psychiatric specialist at Serenity Springs Centre over in Howth. He's a complete gentleman. He took very good care of your mother a few years ago."

A few years ago. They generally tend to avoid 'a few years ago' as a topic of conversation. The fact that, following the dispersal of some utterly unwarranted (at least, so she claims) rumours in relation to Ashlene and a young male teacher in her department, she had an 'episode.' What could otherwise be referred to as a complete mental breakdown. Of course, it strikes Emily now, Nick was the psychiatrist who her mother attended back then. And who is credited in their household with performing the near miracle of putting Ashlene back on the straight and narrow. As a result, finding himself exalted to the beatific heights of a hero.

"Last night, he found Maria wandering around St. Anne's Park," continues Mark. "She didn't go to her friend's house like she said she was."

"Serenity Springs? The Loony Bin?" Emily abruptly jumps to her feet. "That man put Maria in a loony bin?"

"Emily, don't call it that!" Ashlene chastises. Her reprimand is half-hearted though. She is having the same thought.

"What am I supposed to call it then?" Deflated, she slumps back into a sitting position.

Neither of her parents answer.

It is Mark who breaks the silence first. "Maria had... taken quite a lot of tablets last night. She was in a bit of a state when Nick found her. If he hadn't come along when he did we could be in a very different position now. We owe him so much gratitude."

Emily should say it. Get it off her chest. Tell them about the messages. They'll ring the Guards then and Maria will be found. She will be brought home.

There is simply one problem: Ashlene and Mark trust Nick implicitly. He has proven himself worthy of their trust before, after all. The institution in which Maria is being kept appears of the highest calibre. Yes, there will be a fee for the treatment she receives but in return, it will be discreet. Emily has absolutely no proof whatsoever to the contrary of their beliefs. She might know what she saw, but they don't. In a matter of months Maria's addiction is expected to alleviate. No one need ever know of this 'obstacle.'

However, this is not an obstacle. For obstacles can be overcome. Resolved. Giving way to an open path than can be tread freely. The remainder of a lifetime.

In Maria's case, a bomb has detonated every remaining inch of that path.

CHAPTER 16

The world is indefinite at its edges, oblivion rapping insistently at the door even now. For a moment, Maria is completely unaware of her surroundings but slowly, like the gradual dawn of the sun at daybreak, reality seeps beneath the entryway and illuminates the room in which she sits.

Everything is white. Pearlescent white. The shade of white that assaults your vision and forces your eyes shut. A featureless white. Devoid of colour, yet replete with darkness in spite of its dazzling light.

Furnishings filling the space possess a minimalist, Scandinavian quality. It looks rather as if someone went on a shopping spree in Ikea and deposited their haul within these four walls. Odd, ponders Maria obscurely. The section of the house she was in earlier whispered of days gone by, the swish of the old gentry's fine garments still practically audible. Somewhere in her mind, she asks the question: how did they move her here? Casting her gaze downwards, she receives her answer. She is sitting in a wheelchair.

There are two men positioned across the pine surface of the desk. One of them is Nick and the other previously unencountered. He is older than Nick, hair tinged a silver hue that just might edge towards grey.

"Ah, Maria," he begins. His tone is almost paternal. "You have woken, pet"

She attempts to protest as his calling her 'pet' but finds herself incapable. Her windpipe has been sealed over, air alluding her lungs. Valiantly, she tries again and manages to feebly mutter: "Nick?"

"Don't worry, Maria. I'm here," he says placidly. The words are expressionless. And so are his features.

Suddenly, she jolts forward. "You took me on a date!"

Nick laughs and it is a dry, mirthless sound. "A *date*?" The chortling intensifies. "Don't be silly, Maria. Your dreams were obviously most vivid."

Confusion furrows her brow: "But... but you did, we met in Sinnotts and- "

"We did not go on a date, Maria." His words have gained no feeling. Her eyes are inexplicably drawn to the single painting hanging on the wall behind the two men's heads: three red dots set against an orange background. She becomes fixated on them. The difference between each circle negligible, the background bleeding in. Their circumferences snake amongst the block colour. An indescribable emotion fills Maria. Why did she think she had been on a date with Nick? Of course she hadn't. Such a thing would be ridiculous. She is wrong. He is right.

She swallows. Hard. "We didn't go on a date." She declares this as a simple statement of fact. Nick nods. He is satisfied.

"Precisely, Maria."

Somewhere, deep within Maria's mind, she knows the truth: Nick *did* take her out. He brought her back here, to his house. Although, is it *really* his house?

However, slowly but surely, the rational reasoning of which her brain was once capable is being eroded. Soon, it will cease to exist at all. Maria is powerless to resist the forces overtaking her. There is nothing she can do.

"Last night, Maria," it is the other man speaking this time, she still has not learned his name. "Nicholas here found you in St. Anne's Park. You were under the influence. The influence of painkillers. You have been addicted to them for a while now, haven't you?" Each word spirals downward into an incomprehensible abyss of oblivion. In the periphery of her sight, she observes the painting. Of course he is right. Why would she argue?

"Yes... yes, I have."

His nod mirrors Nick's. "Good girl, Maria," he says, satisfied.

"Now." Nick again. "As a result of this, we will be keeping you here for a while. In rehabilitation."

Nonchalantly, he lifts the ceramic cup placed on the desk in front of him to his lips and sips from it. "We have developed a treatment plan for you that will implemented over the coming weeks. It is going to help you, Maria. Help you to heal."

She does not speak.

"Nick is right Maria." The grey-haired man leans across the table and gazes deeply into her eyes. "Isn't he?"

"Yes, he is."

"That's it." He sits back in his chair, stretching his legs out and resting his hands on the back of his head. There is a decidedly smug expression on his face.

Nick pushes a small bottle towards her. "You will be taking these, Maria. They will produce a state of relaxation, allowing your mind the time it requires to repair." There is something so rehearsed in his speech. It is obvious he has delivered it many times before. To many unsuspecting girls just like Maria. She is far from the first and she will not be the last. "You must take two now."

Hand trembling, she lifts the bottle. It emits a quiet rattle that perforates the deafening silence. She shakes out two tablets into her cupped hand, raises them to her mouth and swallows them dry.

Both men afford her a superficial smile. "Dr. Winchester will take you to your room now, Maria," Nick says with a glance at his colleague. "I trust you'll be most comfortable there."

The Doctor's chair screeches alarmingly across the ground as he stands and crosses to Maria's side of the desk. "You have nothing to fear," he monotonously intones. Maria feels nothing. She is numb in every sense of the word. Without complaint or remonstrance, she permits him to wheel her from the room.

With one final look back over her shoulder, Maria assesses Nick's profile. It grows gradually smaller as she is borne away. Just before he dissipates from view, Maria sees the smile spread across his lips.

CHAPTER 17

Kneading her fingers together restlessly, Emily stares distractedly around the waiting room. It has been two weeks since Maria was admitted to Serenity Springs. Two agonising weeks of waiting, wondering, weeping in silent despair. Emily has never experienced trepidation quite like the feeling that is diffusing through her veins at this moment. She has attempted several times to address her concerns regarding Nick with her parents but on every occasion, before the tale makes it past her lips, courage deserts her. They wouldn't believe her anyway. Or at least that is what she says to content herself. To erode some of the guilt.

Now, the boreal surface of the plastic chair on which she is perched presses against her flushed skin. Uncomfortable. Everything about this experience is. There is no clock in the room and there is no window. Is that intentional? To have no method of telling the time. Not even by tracking the sun's progress through the sky. Her parents are similarly silent, surveying intently the ground at their feet.

After what surely must be hours, Dr. Nick appears in the doorway.

"Good morning, Mr and Mrs. Wilson, Emily," he nods gallantly at them all in turn. He really is an extremely attractive man. Anyone can see that.

"Morning," they all rather absently murmur.

"If you follow me, I'll take you to Maria. She's been looking forward to seeing you." He beams around them all with a smile like midday sunshine. He claps his hands together like the crack of midnight thunder.

Lethargically, the three of them rise from their seats and walk behind Nick down a seemingly interminable corridor. The floor is a beige parquet, the walls a neutral shade of cream. In many ways, this property could be a private house. Yes, the waiting room was clinical but aside from that, the place feels... inhabited.

Entering the hallway, every available surface appeared to be loaded with antiques. Tastefully so. Definitely not the typical décor of a mental institution or rehab centre or whatever the hell this place is supposed to be. All Emily knows for certain is that Maria was goaded here. And there is something suspicious about this house. The place reeks of it. Something, she is unsure what, does not add up.

Whenever they enter Maria's room, Emily is again presented with a conflicted picture. The room is small; miniscule in fact. She must concede though that it does not seem dismal. A vase of primrose yellow daffodils sits on a low coffee table. There are a few lamps from which a comely glow emanates. On the floor is a plush rug that the feet automatically sink into. Cheerful, homely.

However, there are other details of the space that ignite concern within Emily. To name a few: the solitary barred window which rations natural light, the harsh wrought iron bedframe that even *looks* uncomfortable and the apparent lack of reading material or indeed any other form of entertainment. Emily is aware that Maria is not permitted access to the internet; she has not been able to communicate with them since her arrival in Serenity Springs. It is deemed poisonous to the 'healing' mind to have contact with the outside world. In hindsight, Emily will often wonder how this did not trigger alarm bells in her parents sooner. Alas, it did not.

Maria is sitting up in the bed. Her dark brown hair is washed and her pyjamas are freshly cleaned. Yet, she has got even thinner than the last time Emily saw her and the pallor of her face is one characteristic only of death.

Nick tactfully withdraws, leaving Emily and her parents alone with Maria.

The moment the door shuts in his wake, Ashlene throws herself, sobbing hysterically, at her daughter.

"Oh, Maria. How are you, pet?" she chokes out, releasing her from the embrace and looking her up and down.

Maria's reply is a rather debilitated: "I'm fine, mam."

She is anything but. Emily can see that. Her parents probably can too.

For a short while then, nobody says anything. The situation is decidedly awkward.

"Are they treating you well, Maria?" Mark questions suddenly, sharply, soberly. He fixes her with an intense stare.

And that is when it happens: Maria begins to bawl. Hysterically. "Please, *please*, take me away from this place. Mam, I want to go home. I can't stay here any longer. It's awful. Honestly, you have no idea. They make me... make me take these... pills and ... and then I can't remember anything and-"at this point the almost illiterate torrent descends into completely incomprehensible wailing. An unreadable look passes between Ashlene and Mark, the sentiments it harbours unknown to Emily. Considering the gravity of what Maria has just claimed though, they are not appropriately alarmed.

That proves that these... *people* have succeeded. After all, there are only two ways to silence someone's voice. The first is to kill them. The second, well, that is even more deadly: to discredit them. Make everyone believe they are not of sound mind. Even their own parents.

"Maria, darling, I know it must be hard being away from home. But this is the right thing. Dr. Winchester and his team are taking good care of you. And when you're better, I promise you'll be back home before you know it." This is offered by Mark, who is shooting periodic glances at the door. He can't bare to see his daughter like this. It is a situation he cannot deal with and therefore, his only desire is to remove himself from it.

His wishes are granted in the form of Nick's reappearance. Maria's crying has subsided to unobtrusive sniffling sobs and she has slumped back in the bed, spent from the exertion. "Mr and Mrs. Wilson, I'm very sorry but I'm going to have to ask you to leave now. You'll understand that Maria's contact with visitors must be introduced gradually," Nick's words are compassionate. Emily looks at him and is filled with distrust.

"Yes, yes of course, Doctor." Ashlene clears her throat self-consciously before leaning down and kissing Maria goodbye hurriedly. "We'll be on our way. You rest now, Maria pet."

Ashlene and Mark depart the room alongside Nick but, for a moment, Emily lingers. The frustration coursing through her is nauseating. She wants to scream at her parents, tell them to listen to Maria. But they won't believe her. She knows that.

"Hang in there, Maria." Her words are negligible in this emotionless void. Still, she feels compelled to say something.

"Emily," rasps Maria hoarsely. "Don't trust anything they tell you. Please." With that, her voice perishes. Emily flees the room then too. The guilt that was previously lapping at her toes has swelled into a wave threatening to engulf her entire person. She has to escape.

"Are you alright, Emily?" She almost leaps straight out of her skin. It is Dr. Nick. He has been watching her from the corridor outside, having ushered her parents into a room further down it.

"Y...yes, Doctor," she stammers, swallowing hard.

"Good. Now go and join your parents in there." He gestures to the door through which they have just entered and she complies.

Their expressions stoic, her parents are taking up two rigid backed chairs in front of a simple pine desk. The room is barren, again jarring with the traditional introduction to the property. There is no decoration whatsoever, bar a painting of three dots on one wall. The same image with which Maria was faced when they inducted her into their hellish den.

Nick settles across from them and places his elbows on the desk, joining the tips of his fingers together. "I apologise for that. It must be challenging to see your daughter in such a way," he says sympathetically, looking each of them straight in the eyes. Emily has to hand it to him; he is a fabulous liar.

"It... certainly isn't easy," Mark says slowly. "But we're indebted to you and Dr. Winchester for all you've done for her."

Nick looks downwards modestly, at the desk's pristine surface. "It is simply our job, Mr. Wilson."

Emily seizes her opportunity to speak then, "She seems unhappy, Doctor," she is mindful to keep her tone polite and not accusatory even though the only thing she wants is to lunge at the man before her and squeeze every last iota of life from his veins. "There really isn't much to entertain her either..." she trails off uncertainly, sure he will not take her seriously.

Instead, he sighs deeply and raises his face upwards again. "Look, Maria's condition is a challenging one. She has responded well to the treatment but is rather... prone to delusions. Fantasies, as it were. Quiet contemplation is what she needs for now. Reading, TV, being online, all those things distract from the healing process."

To feck with this so called 'healing process', thinks Emily.

Her parents nod. Obediently.

Somewhere, in the recesses of her mind, Emily becomes apprised in that moment of the fact that she has lost forever not only Maria but her parents too.

CHAPTER 18

Nicholas Joyce shuts the door firmly behind the Wilsons and bolts it, securing himself within the confines of the office. An island in the midst of an ocean. A tentative glimmer of serenity in the midst of the malevolence swelling, swirling around him. Engulfing him. Ear pressed against the wood; he listens to the retreating sound of their footsteps along the corridor. Diminishing gradually, they fade from life.

Eventually, he retreats back into the room, moving towards the patch of light spilling through the bay window. Outside, normality is monarch. As he peers down the tarmacked driveway, a passing car disturbs the autumnal blanket of leaves littering the road, sending them into oblivion. Scattered into all directions.

He becomes reflective then. Seeing himself again a young medical student hanging the stethoscope about his neck for the very first time. He felt then the promise of the object, listening to the pulsating beat of potential just as easily as the human heart.

He felt also its power.

Nick wonders then, idly, what he would see if he looked within his own heart. Goodness, not evil. Virtue, not sin. Or a blurring of both; an amalgamation so natural. The chemicals reacting with each other to form a medicine unique to the individual. Side-effects unknown.

He crosses to the desk and sits, kneading his temples with fingers splayed. This was never what he wanted of life. Of his career. Sometimes, he wonders how it came to this. Monetary greed, he supposes. A greed that led him here, to Serenity Springs. Following orders and obeying the commands of Gerard Winchester.

It is then that he catches sight of the photograph. Taken last year, on holiday in New York, at the top of the Empire State Building. Just him and his girl. Niece really isn't a strong enough word. He takes her in. The sparkle of her smile so dazzling, it would rival the twinkle of the skyscrapers around them when bathed by the retiring sun. Her blonde hair falling about her shoulders, so like her mother's, definitely not inherited from his side of the family. He remembers the first time he held her in his arms, pressed his cheek to hers, his lips firm on the soft skin of her forehead. How her eyes laughed even when her lips could not and how he knew. How he knew his heart was tethered to hers. The pride ruminates in his soul for everything she was, everything that she is and everything that she will be.

And that is when he makes his decision.

Maria knows. She knows and she is capable of speaking out. It has begun already. They're not asking hard questions for now but they will. It is only a matter of time.

On this occasion, it has gone too far.

He has no choice but to increase her dosage of Winchester's drug. A drug that, if he is honest with himself (which he always tries to be), she does not require. A drug that does not possess even the merest smidge of a healing property.

As Nicholas Joyce draws the liquid into the syringe, his thoughts are not with Maria.

They are only with his girl.

They are *only* with Julia.

CHAPTER 19

There is a field. In the field there are flowers. Technicoloured flowers. Vibrant. The grass is coated in a gossamer dew. A dew that whispers of morning as clearly as the sun ascending the unblemished sky overhead. A pulsating orb that emits such a radiant glow, its rays could sustain the hearts of all those cast in the luminance of its shadow for eternity. It is in this field that she stands. Waiting. Waiting on her prince. And suddenly he is there. Cantering effortlessly towards her on a sable stallion. He jumps from its back with a dull thud and runs towards her, his face looming larger the closer he comes...

"Maria?" the word slices through her consciousness. Mercilessly, reality confronts her. It is the doctor.

The doorframe vibrates from the heavy slam. There is no field. There are no flowers. The handsome prince does not exist. Instead, she finds herself incarcerated in the same bleak corner in which she has lain for... well, she does not recall how long. Whitewashed walls, iron bed, a single steel seat at its side.

"How are you?" he asks her.

She does not reply.

"Have you taken your medication today?"

Barely audible, she utters: "He's coming to get me."

On the doctor's face, there is a flicker of mild amusement. "And who would that be?"

"My boyfriend," she says, like it is obvious.

The doctor assesses her soberly. "You don't have a boyfriend, Maria." A floorboard creaks beneath his tread as he steps closer to the edge of the bed.

"Where are my parents?" The question is ejaculated suddenly.

"They're not here."

Maria sees the shadows then. She sees shadows often now. Contorting shapes dancing sinuously over the walls, the floor. Twirling through her mind. Penumbras obliterating coherent thought.

"Does that mean we're alone?" For the first time, the beginnings of what could be trepidation infiltrate her voice.

"Yes, unless you've got someone under the bed," he laughs. Hoarsely. He is enjoying this, Maria surmises. His job is a game to him.

She is unsure of exactly why she does it but she swipes her arm impulsively, striking the waterglass on the pine bedside table. It is flung to the floor, shattering into a million shards that litter the ground.

The doctor gives a slight start of surprise. On the whole though, he is unaffected. Stealthily avoiding the angular pieces, he crosses to the solitary barred window, fixing his gaze to the outside world. The outside world. It is an unattainable thing. As much of a fantasy as the lands to which she voyages in the drug- induced dreams.

"You're really not helping yourself, you know." A shaft of light breaks through the bars and falls across his face. It roams across the ground. Like a long finger. Yet another shadow.

His back is turned and so Maria takes her opportunity. She rises shakily from the bed and pulls the curtain shut around her. However, he notices. He opens it once more. The curtain rings grate cuttingly against the pole.

Gradually, she backs away and perches on the bed again. Without permitting her eyes to depart from his face, she eases her legs beneath the coarse sheets and tugs them around her. Tightly.

"Maria, you and I need to have a little talk," he begins casually. Something in her snaps. She has to get out of there. She swings her legs sideways and again exits the bed, running for the curtain.

But he is blocking her way.

"You can't get past me."

She can't. Sheepish, she sits back on the bed. He descends into the chair.

"You've been rather disobedient lately."

"Have I?" her question displays disinterest.

"Yes," he places his hands on his knees. "You must know that what we do here is all for your own good."

She scoffs. "Yeah, right because this being locked up in a loony bin is *so* good for me."

Abruptly, he stands. "That's not what this is! You fail to recognise how fortunate you are."

"If I'm so fortunate, why do you make us take so many pills?"

"How dare you-"

"What's in them anyway? What exactly are they supposed to-"

"Stop it!" he screeches. "It is not your position to question our decisions. You do not have a medical degree."

"No, but I do have common sense."

Maria cannot prevent herself from saying it but the moment she does, she knows she is going to suffer.

He steps closer. There is no refuge. She is powerless. Vulnerable. The way he wants it.

And the speed of the swaying shadows increases. The wailing voices of protest are deafening. But only inside her mind.

Most often, the most frightening nightmares are when they are not nightmares at all.

CHAPTER 20

On the day they receive the news, Emily and her parents have just sat down to a hearty Sunday meal of succulent chicken, technicoloured vegetables and floury potatoes. The memory of last week's dismal visit to Serenity Springs has faded; the sharpness of its edges diminished to sepia tones. A solitary cloud scudding momentarily across the sky, it has now passed over. To be filed in the recesses of their minds and not thought of in times of ersatz joy such as these.

Mark attempts some form of joke and, although it is rather feeble, they all chortle. In defiance of reality. Kidding themselves into believing that all is as it should be. It is not. When the mobile phone begins to bleat, it serrates their laughter like it were tissue paper.

"Hello?" questions Ashlene, the last note of joviality in her tone echoing into the void that is promptly filled by the swelling of the voice at the other end of the line. Nick's voice.

"Hello, Mrs. Wilson. Is... is Mr. Wilson there with you?" he begins hesitantly.

Emily watches on, a palpable dread infiltrating her veins, as her mother's brow furrows. It adds at least a decade to her age. "Yes, yes we're all here, doctor," she responds briskly, concern all too evident.

He awkwardly clears his throat. "Good. I... I have some... some news regarding... well, regarding Maria. And I'm afraid it... it isn't positive." The admission of this fact is clearly expending a great deal of energy; the man can barely string two words together. This suave, sophisticated doctor is flustered. He appears to suck in a breath before he continues. "Look, I really think this conversation would be better had in person. If you... if you could get here. As soon as possible, please."

The fork in Mark's fingers that was suspended half way to his mouth now clatters to the plate with a clunk. The flavoursome food Emily has been chewing becomes as appetising as cardboard. Ashlene stands abruptly, the wooden chair screaming maliciously against the kitchen tiles.

"Of course," she stammers. "We're leaving now. Doctor, is it something serious? Is Maria alright? Is she..."

When Nick speaks again, he appears almost on the precipice of tears. "Just get here. Please."

And with that, the line goes dead.

The intervening period between that phone call and their arrival at Serenity Springs is one that Emily will scarcely remember. They abandon their plates at the table and hurry out of the house, the glacial air slamming against them like a brick wall.

Emily shifts discontentedly on the leather, her heart hammering in her chest. Thoughts cavorting down dismal alleyways, her fingers tug at a thread that has come loose from the leather's stitching. Anything to distract herself. In that moment, she watches the traffic zip by and pines for life as it used to be. As it never will be again. She knows even before she knows. Maria is gone.

Nick throws the door open the minute the car grinds to a halt in the middle of the expansive driveway. His figure is illuminated eerily in the overspilling hallway light. He shakes the hands of Ashlene and Mark and leads them down the familiar corridor to the jarringly modern office. The déjà vu almost swamps Emily as she resumes her seat in front of the desk.

The preamble to the pronouncement that will derail her very existence is succinct. She barely hears it anyway. She hears little but the rushing, gushing sound pushing relentlessly through her ears.

"Mr and Mrs. Wilson I... I regret to inform you that Maria overdosed this morning... on her treatment pills and-"

"Overdosed?" Ashlene's ask comes out an octave higher than normal. "And is she... she's okay isn't she?"

Nick fidgets uncomfortably. "I... I'm afraid there is no easy way to say this but... your daughter passed away this morning. I really am very sorry for your loss." Although his complexion bears a significant resemblance in colour to the crisp linen of his shirt, he has clearly delivered such news before. After all though, he is a doctor; it has likely been a part of his job.

Suddenly, there is absolute quiet. Time has paused. A distant car horn bleats obtrusively. A bird outside caterwauls plaintively. The painting of three dots seems to protrude from the wall. Garishly.

Emily is numb.

Then, the bomb detonates in their midst. Her mum is howling, sobbing the kind of tears that rack your body and appear primed to continue perpetually. Her dad is stoic but, gradually, a flush born of irate fury creeps over his skin, masking him in a veil of red. He leaps up in one sudden movement.

"We trusted you!" he yells at such a volume Emily is sure everyone in Dublin has heard the outburst. "You incompetent fool! And you call yourself a doctor? *How* could you have allowed this to happen? We allowed *our daughter* to be brought here to be healed, we paid you thousands and... and..." his torrent trails off as the full reality of the situation appears to assault him. Coming over limp, he sinks back down into his seat.

Meanwhile, Ashlene continues to bawl incessantly. Emily feels nothing. In some ways, this is the greatest shock she has ever received: her sister is dead. And in another manner, it feels uncannily like the inevitable fulfilment of prophecy.

As her tears begin to subside marginally, Ashlene manages to stutter: "Oh, Mark we.... We should have listened to her... she... she said she was being forced to take pills and that she wanted to come home and if we had just taken her home then she wouldn't be dead. Mark, Maria is *dead*!" The tears overtake her again.

Emily risks a glance at Nick. A thunderous expression is cast across his features. He is clearly not used to being doubted and the experience of such a phenomenon is disturbing him greatly. "I appreciate that this is the worst possible news a parent could receive but you must know that-"

"What if it was your daughter?" ejaculates Mark. Surprisingly, his statement produces a seemingly genuine effect on the man; an incomprehensible expression crosses his face and for the first time, Emily wonders what this man's story is. He may be twisted. He may be callous. He may be a murderer. But beneath it all, there is someone for whom he cares. Deeply.

"I... can only imagine how awful that would be," he says sincerely. Like a lone boat disturbing the serenity of a glass lake at dawn, a solitary tear caresses his cheek.

Mark suddenly lunges across the table at him, his eyes squarely on Nick's. "You better realise that you are going to suffer for this. I swear to good God; I will drag you through every court in this country if I have to. My little girl deserves justice and just believe that I will make sure she gets it."

Emily only wishes such a thing as justice were attainable.

CHAPTER 21

Maria's funeral has been and gone. The occasion was the most trying of Emily's existence yet she has not shed a single tear since the day they received the news of her death. They say everyone deals with grief in their own way and Emily wonders if adorning herself in this emotionless façade is simply a coping mechanism. However, she suspects there is more to it than that.

She tried to warn Maria. The moment she saw those messages on her phone; dread wove itself into her being and refused to relinquish its hold. When Nick showed up on their doorstep playing the hero to perfection, his disguise was invisible to her. She saw the true him. And, when she visited Maria in Serenity Springs, she knew that her concerns were more than valid. Although she knows it is wrong, her primary emotion is anger. Anger, of course, to the villainous Nick and, unspoken, anger towards Maria. For the utter stupidity that signed her own death warrant.

A few weeks have passed since the terrible event and as the stabbing grief recedes to a permanent, dull ache, her parent's thoughts have begun to turn to seeking justice for their daughter. Today, they have arranged a meeting with a solicitor to begin the legal proceedings against the staff of Serenity Springs for medical negligence. It isn't about seeking financial compensation. In fact, that is the last thing on their minds. Their aim is simple: to destroy the reputation of Dr. Nick. To make certain the fact that no other family will ever endure what they have.

Obviously, he isn't the only doctor working there. There are a few others, including that man called Dr. Winchester and apparently a matron too. The brunt of their fury however, is aimed primarily at Dr. Nick.

Emily is alone in the house. It is a Friday afternoon, the conclusion to her first week back at school since Maria's death. Utterly draining have been the last five days. Feigning normality. The weekend comes as a welcome respite. A slight trepidation is present, though. She is aware the battle her parents are about to begin to wage is one which will result in the exhuming of many unpleasant feelings. In an effort to divert her attention elsewhere, she flips half-heartedly through the pages of a book. Her thoughts remain only on death.

The doorbell hollers through her lethargic state. Why can't her parents let themselves in? Did they forget their key? It really would not surprise her; they've both been so absent lately. Sighing, she coaxes herself to her feet and stomps dismally downstairs. She opens the door. It is not her parents on the doorstep but a Guard.

Her immediate reaction is confusion. Probably the most natural sentiment given the unexpected arrival of law enforcement on your doorstep. When she notices the rather woebegone look on the male officer's face though, she greets again that one emotion that seems determined to be her constant companion: dread.

"Miss. Emily Wilson?" he questions heavily.

"Yes..." she begins hesitantly. "Is everything alright?

He does not answer the question. "Miss Wilson, would you mind if I came in?"

This places Emily rather on the backfoot. She had expected him to have accidentally arrived at the wrong house or, at worst, to ask if she'd witnessed anything that may provide a clue to some trivial nearby break-in.

"Of course," this is managed as politely as she can muster, a smile of wafer-thin consistency stretched across her lips.

"Thank you."

She leads him into the living room and he sits soberly in an armchair.

"How can I help you?"

"Miss. Wilson, I'm afraid I have some bad news." He fixates his eyes on the floor. A wave of nausea douses Emily. She has heard those words once before. And that was all too often.

"Your parents were involved in an accident, Miss. Wilson. The brakes of the vehicle in which they were travelling failed and... there was a collision with another car."

"What? No!" she screeches. "That... that can't be... not after..."

"Miss. Wilson, I'm very sorry but your parents... they didn't make it."

Reality recedes. Time is suspended. Life as she knows it is but a memory. She wants to cry but finds herself rendered incapable. She is trapped in a time warp, an almost identical conversation to that held in Nick's office at Serenity Springs occurring once again. The painting of dots glares at her from the wall. But it isn't there. Or is it? No. She doesn't know. The ceiling caves in. The dots are blinking, morphing, shaping. Her soul is splitting apart, flames licking through her heart.

The sound that she emits is feral.

The Guard is uttering platitudes. As he has clearly been trained to do. He tells her there was no pain. That it was immediate. That her parents had plans in place in case of such an event. That she will be looked after. That she has nothing to fear. That all will be well.

But he doesn't know any of that. Honestly? He doesn't care. At the end of his shift, he will walk away. Walk back to his life. A life that is foreign to tragedy and intimate with insouciance. That does not comprehend this earth-shattering injury. That does not know what it means to be all alone in the world.

CHAPTER 22

1 Year Later

Emily is not quite sure what to feel when Miss. Spencer requests that she stay behind after class. She can't be in trouble, that is for certain. Still though, she experiences an unusual... trepidation.

One year ago, shortly after her parent's deaths, Emily was packed off to New York. Her father's sister, Emily's closest living relative, resides there and the legal arrangement constructed by her parents stipulated that in the event of their deaths, this is where she should be sent. Emily has been fortunate. Her aunt is a most caring guardian and she wants for nothing. But, deep inside, she is hollow. She is only too aware that such a void can never be filled.

Life in Manhattan could not provide a starker contrast to her former existence in Raheny. Everything appears to be magnified ten-fold when compared to Ireland. Urban life in Dublin is no kin of this American metropolis. This isn't necessarily a fault. However, each night when darkness envelops the wilderness of concrete and steel, she yearns for the lush velvet fabric of the fields that spell home.

School here is enjoyable enough, admittedly different from Ireland on the surface but beneath the exterior, strangely much the same. Miss. Spencer, her English teacher, is from Dublin too. Like Emily, it is her first year here in Manhattan. Something in this provides a form of comfort.

Today, Miss. Spencer returned their last homework assignment: a personal essay on an experience that changed their life. It did not take long for Emily to decide on a subject matter. The recent events of her life form a ready-made soap opera in and of themselves.

As the last of her classmates depart the English room, she approaches her teacher's desk.

"Emily," she greets her with a mildly nervous smile. "I... just wanted to say that I... found your work very touching-" she halts dead in the middle of her sentence and casts her eyes downwards timidly.

"Thank you, Miss," Emily says slowly. Unsure of how to proceed, she scuffs her foot along the ground.

Miss. Spencer takes a long breath. "You're from Raheny, aren't you Emily?"

"Yes, Miss."

"I'm from Sutton, you know."

"Yes."

There is silence then. It is broken only when Miss. Spencer prepares herself to speak.

"Emily, was your sister Maria Wilson?"

In response to sheer shock, Emily almost stumbles backwards.

"She... she was." An instinct kicks in; a dubious suspicion. "Why do you ask?"

The amount of oxygen entering Emily's lungs is not adequate. Has she met this woman before? She scours her memory but she cannot elicit any remembrance of her.

"I knew her, Emily." These words sever the air. "From when she was in Serenity Springs."

"H...how?"

"Because I was in there too."

Emily almost vomits.

"*What?*"

Instead of a reply, Miss. Spencer walks around her desk until she is standing in front of it. She perches lightly on its corner. "It was Nick," she murmurs. "He lured me there. He lured us all there."

"There... there were others?"

At this, she throws her head back and laughs. "Others? Oh, Emily. There were dozens and not one in that whole Godforsaken institution had a genuine illness. The only people who were ill in the head were those doctors. And the nurse, she was as bad."

Emily toys distractedly with a strand of her hair. "That's terrible... I'm so sorry."

Miss. Spencer nods contemplatively. "You have no idea what they put us through you know."

Swallowing a lump in her throat, Emily ventures: "What do you mean?"

When she says them, her words are wry. "Abuse, Emily. Of many different kinds. Half of the time we were drugged. It left us completely out of it; we didn't even know our own names. Then, in between, you'd have moments of clarity. And that was nearly worse because it meant you knew what was going on. You felt the pain. The oblivion was... easier."

Now, Emily is sure the hammering of her heart will hurtle it straight out of her chest. "Did they... did they-" she cannot bring herself to form the words.

"They took advantage of us in every possible way, Emily."

Silence descends again.

"But then, they killed Maria."

Although Emily has known all along that is the truth, hearing someone else actually verbalise it hurts. Like hell.

"She wasn't responding properly to the drugs. The obedience drugs. She knew what was going on and she was outspoken about it. They didn't always work on me either," she stops to pick an imaginary speck of dirt from her skirt. "But I knew to hide how aware I was. We were allowed to socialise with each other briefly in a common room sometimes but within a few weeks of her being there, she was confined to her room. She tried to tell the rest of us the truth. It got through occasionally and some of us were beginning to question everything." She smiles an oxymoron of a smile. "They couldn't have that. So, they killed her."

Emily attempts speech but it fails her.

"I'm sorry for bringing this up to you, Emily. Please don't think that I'm trying to be inappropriate... or, well, you know- but I just, your writing brought it back to me. I knew immediately you had to be Maria's sister."

"No, of course not... I... I understand. It's just... hard." Emily swallows again. "And... and do you know if they're still operational?"

She shakes her head and when she speaks there is satisfaction in her words. "No, that's the thing. It's how I escaped. After they killed Maria, they announced we were being transferred. To a specialist unit in Spain apparently. In a place called La Campina, I think it's somewhere outside Seville. So, the next time my parents visited, I persuaded them to get me out. It cost them. Cost them significantly. But it meant I got away. With Maria's sudden death while under their care, they knew they could come under fire. And that was too much of a risk; they would all have been locked up." When she finishes the tale, she is breathless.

"But... but why didn't you say something... or go to the Guards, you had the proof, you *lived* it!"

Suddenly, a melancholic look creases her forehead. "I was afraid. Yes, they left the country but I was too scared of what they were capable of. If I tried to cause a scandal over the whole thing, I knew they'd find a way to silence me. So, I kept quiet and... tried to move on with my life. There was nothing else I could do." She shrugs helplessly.

"Like what happened to my parents," starts Emily. "They were killed in a car crash, apparently a brake failure but I... well... I think... there was more to it than that. They were starting legal proceedings against the staff of Serenity Springs and-" it is her turn to shrug as she trails off.

"I came out here to get away for a while. Staying in Ireland with it all so fresh was just... too much," Miss. Spencer says. "But I'll go back eventually and maybe try to get justice of some kind," this is said wistfully, her eyes glazed in youthful expectancy.

It is in that moment that Emily comes to a decision. Now seventeen, it will not be long before she is a fully independent adult. Soon, she will move back to Ireland and she will find a way to make them suffer. Suffer for what they did. Suffer for murdering her sister and her parents. Suffer for tearing her life and the lives of so many others into shreds.

CHAPTER 23

Julia

I could not give anything away.

"Emily... that's... oh my God that's absolutely awful. I'm so sorry," I said sincerely. I meant it. Everything that had occurred in that poor girl's life was despicable.

I had not chosen to play a part in it but sometimes in life you simply do not have a choice.

"It was a long time ago now." She gazed off into the distance, fixated on an invisible image. "Time doesn't heal all wounds but it certainly toughens the skin." Her laugh was droll.

Probe her. That was what I needed to do.

"You... you said you needed to tell me this because of the fact that I work here now," my tone was gentle, empathetic in every sense. "What did you mean by that, Emily?"

Swallowing, she took an interminably drawn-out breath. "I think Mr. Featherington-Smythe is a part of it. That group I mean."

Of all replies she could have made; this put me on the backfoot. "Why do you think that?"

"It's hard to explain but I just know. It's a... feeling. One day, a few months ago now, I saw this man come into the office. Mr. FFS took him straight into the back room but I got a glimpse of him. And I'm fairly certain it was Dr. Winchester."

"But... weren't they supposed to have gone to Spain?"

"Well, they were... Lord knows. Look, Julia. I don't know, alright? I don't know anything for sure. All I do know is that Rockstar Real Estate is not what it seems. There's something highly suspicious going on in this agency. *That* I do know." She paused for breath and I seized the opportunity to jump in again.

"What about the others? Jonathan, Anto, Eamon? You don't think they're involved too?"

This suggestion actually caused her to cackle. "God no! They're good lads, the three of them. Absolutely clueless about all of this. And you know Jonathan's crazy about you, don't you?"

Automatically, I began to blush. "No, he's not. We're just friends." I could have screeched at how cliched I sounded. "We care about each other. A lot. He's... like my brother."

"Right. If you were the sort of person into unapologetically flirting with your brother then I guess you probably could say that, yeah."

Ignoring this distraction, I persisted in my veiled interrogation. "So, what are you going to about it? I mean, it's unfortunate that you don't really have any evidence."

It was not unfortunate at all.

She drummed her fingers on the enamel surface of a coffee cup sitting atop the desk. "That's the thing. I don't have any evidence and because of that I can't do anything really. If I went to the Gardai they'd only laugh. Anyway, I'm fairly certain that they've protected them before. They wouldn't hesitate to do so again either I'd say."

Its freakish how scarily close to the truth she came with that statement.

"I'm glad I told you, Julia," she said then. "You needed to know. Especially if you're going to be managing the sale of that place. Don't underestimate how dangerous these people can be. I mean that. And if Featherington-Smythe is involved, the best thing we can do is to keep our heads bowed and say nothing." She bit down aggressively on her lip. "What happened to my sister... I don't want that to happen to me. Or you."

Little did she know.

"Thank you, Emily," I said, hoping the ratio of bewilderment, horror and fear in my voice was appropriately proportioned. "It means the world to me that you felt able to talk to me about that. I know... it can't have been easy."

Flippantly, she grimaced. "You needed to know, Julia."

She was right there at least. I did need to know. I needed to know to keep my guard up.

CHAPTER 24

Julia

That night, I made two decisions.

The first was that I was going to host an open house on Maycroft Demesne. Experience gleaned from a lifetime watching pretty much every property programme aired on television informed me it was a reasonable course of action. A challenging sale was potentially inevitable, after all.

The second was that I was going to invite Jonathan around to my house. Just to plan for the open. Clearly, *nothing* else was going to happen. It was essentially a business meeting for goodness sake.

My mum was on a night shift again so I had the place to myself. Ever since my dad's death, she had been taking on rather a lot of extra work. Perhaps it was her methodology of coping with the grief and I could hardly blame her for that.

In preparation for his arrival, I changed into a colourful kimono style dress that I felt rather accurately represented the more eccentric side of my personality. Just because it was comfortable though, not to try and *impress* him or anything idiotic like that. I also lit a few candles and removed a bottle of champagne from the wine fridge. It had been a hectic week in the office. We could both use a drink.

The doorbell rang and I answered eagerly, an anticipatory grin springing unbidden to my lips.

"Evening, Julia," he greeted me. As was now his custom, I received a gentle kiss on both cheeks. "Thanks for inviting me over."

Outside, the sky had spiralled into an ambiguous magenta as the lines between day and night blurred together. Two becoming one.

"Hello Johnny," I said, ushering him into the house. "I decided to pick on someone and thought it may as well be you."

I was barely conscious of what words made it past my mouth *Why* did he have to be so bloody handsome? Slung around his shoulders was a knitted wool jumper, his usual prisine shirt displaying just a nice amount of muscle. He obviously wasn't the sort of person who lived his life in the gym but he was certainly toned. I led him into the library, my personal domain, where I had set out the candles and champagne.

"I love this room," he praised as his gaze roved across the mahogany bookshelves and complimenting desk and cabinets. "It just screams you." This was said with a smile but not a typical smile. A smile of complete affection. A smile that reached right to his eyes.

"A Duchess needs her den," I purred almost sultrily. Stop Julia, I reprimanded myself.

It didn't work.

"Well, that's true." He laughed timidly. Taking in the champagne, he seemed to remember the bottle clutched in his right hand. "I brought this. But you seem prepared."

I accepted the gift graciously and as I did, discreetly assessed the label. "Moet Chandon, impressive Mr. Crookshank." I raised an eyebrow. "I think we'll put it to good use."

He seated himself in a leather armchair, eyes not leaving my face. "Some collection," he nodded around at the copious number of tomes lining the shelves. "Do you know how many exactly?"

"No, actually." I settled in the opposite chair and poured us a glass of champagne each. "I've never counted."

"You should." Silence descended as we each took a first sip from our glasses, the fire blazing in the grate sending miniscule sparks cavorting into the air.

"Well, if you've ever got a bit of time on your hands, maybe you could help me," I suggested.

Removing the jumper from around his neck, he said thoughtfully: "Mesmerising though, aren't they? Books, that is."

"Why do you think I write them?"

"Fair," he chuckled bashfully and looked up at me from hooded eyes. "Reading's my favourite thing too you know."

"I've seen you at it in work," I reached forward to top up his glass. "You think I don't notice but you're really not that subtle hiding the book behind your computer screen."

He placed his hand on his chest in feigned horror. "You expose me."

"I suppose I do. No judgement though," I added hurriedly. "Because I do the same myself."

"I'll blame you then. It's your bad influence."

That statement was highly ironic. Almost as if he knew how much he would come to be under my influence.

"Who's your favourite author?" I questioned with genuine interest. You can generally learn quite a lot about someone from the books they gravitate towards. If they read at all that is. Sadly, so many people don't these days.

He seemed to seriously consider his reply, deliberating with a curiously handsome contemplative expression. "She's looking at me," he murmured rather huskily.

I felt the blush attack my cheeks. "You don't have to say that. There's... plenty better than me."

With a deliberate movement, he leaned forward and seized my hand from where it was resting on the side of the chair. "No, not to me there's not." His stare locked onto mine with an eviscerating intensity. "*You* are my favourite. And you always will be." Slowly, he raised my hand to his lips and pressed them firmly against it.

"Thank you, Jonathan." Although I tried, I couldn't think of anything else coherent to say. I was rendered breathless. All I could see was that dashing face, that golden hair, those lips that were only centimetres from mine.

Perhaps it was the champagne, but I suddenly had an overwhelming urge to send this night in a *completely* different direction.

But I absolutely couldn't do that. Could I?

"I'm so glad I met you, Julia." He rose from the armchair and joined me on the sofa. "Even with... everything that's happened in the last few months, my life has been so much better with you in it."

The usual lump in my throat rose at the allusion to my dad's death but it was eased as Jonathan took my hand again and quietly squeezed it. "And I'm so glad you're working with us now. You're great at the job you know."

"Am I though?" I asked suddenly. "It's... sometimes I just feel like a bit of an imposter. I'm not trained in real estate and I just walk in and..."

"Julia," he silenced me. "There's nobody else who could do the job the way you're doing it. Honestly. I'm so proud of you."

I assessed him quizzically. "What's with all the praise? Do you want something, Johnny?"

"Yes, Julia. I... I do want something. I want you."

My heart rate rose to the level of tachycardia. Exactly how I did not snog the face off him right there and then will perpetually elude me.

This was real.

He wanted me. I wanted him. A mutual attraction. Straightforward, uncomplicated. Or at least it should have been.

I had to tell him.

Throughout my life, I have always believed in standing on my own two feet. Truly, I've never really trusted anyone. It almost killed me that I trusted him.

If there was going to be an 'us', if Jonathan and I were about to become more than friends, he deserved to go into it with his eyes wide open.

There was too much at stake to be selfish. He had to know the true me. The chaotic, complicated, not quite so perfect Julia Joyce.

Should he still want this when I divulged the tale, it would prove beyond any doubt what he really felt about me. And... well, if it frightened him off, then that was simply the way it would have to be.

But I owed him the opportunity to make that decision for himself.

"Jonathan," I began, breathing deeply. One hand had moved to my knee.

"Yes?" His free one was tracing the curve of my jawline. Possessively.

"Jonathan, you know the way I brought you here to talk about Maycroft Demesne?"

At this, a peculiar cast descended over his features. It probably did seem rather odd to unearth a work-related topic in the midst of a scenario that was poised to turn anything but professional.

"Yeah... uh, yeah, you did yes." He scratched his head.

"Well," I halted and cast my eyes downwards, uncertain of how to proceed. "Before we... if we... before whatever this is happens," I cajoled myself into meeting his eyes. "I have to tell you something."

And, in a torrent, the tale burst forth.

CHAPTER 25

7 Years Previously

On a Friday night in early December that is really much like any other, a fourteen-year-old girl sits at her desk. Before her, spread open, are a textbook and notepad and on the latter a pen scratches insistently. This sound is the only sound that shatters the otherwise complete stillness. Quiet, though, is comforting. In fact, it is necessary for working. Well, if she is honest, her homework was finished long ago but extra equations never hurt anyone. Outside, the breeze is brisk and the drizzle driving hard against the pavement: tonight is a night when no one should venture beyond the confines of home.

'Julia! Come down here a minute.'

She sighs wearily. Just then, she had been thinking about putting her revision away for the night and turning to the book. She's almost finished and there's just that one plotline that really needs-

"Julia! Earth to Julia, I need to talk to you pet!"

The voice is her uncle's, both her mum and dad are working nightshifts and he's come over to 'look after' her for the evening. Julia is quite capable of looking after herself and both her parents are well aware of the fact. The real reason uncle Nick has been dispatched is to make sure she doesn't spend *too* long studying.

With a quiet moan of frustration, Julia rises from her chair and thunders downstairs to the living room where her uncle has been surgically attached to back-to-back episodes of *Sun, Sea and Selling Houses* for the past three hours.

"Yes, Nick," she says, beaming a wide smile that reaches right to her eyes. For the most part, he is an attentive relative, generous with gifts and his time. However, when he has had a few glasses of wine, his inebriated conduct begins to adopt a rather alarming manner.

Nick pats the sofa beside him, inviting her to sit. "You're taking a break now, pet."

"Oh well, I could in a bit. It's just that I need to-"

"Julia, you've been up there for *hours*." He gestures at the TV. "Look, it's our programme." Eyeing her hopefully, he stretches out his arm. "Come on, I need hugs from my princess."

Failing to prevent a grin, she flops down beside him, cuddling into his side contentedly. House programmes are *their* thing. Her parent's laugh at them, watching them so religiously. But Nick and Julia simply don't care.

"Right, what's your estimate?" Nick leans forward now and presses pause on the remote just before the estate agent on screen reveals the value of a villa in Mojacar.

"Three-fifty," Julia says decisively. She turns to look at him. "You?"

"Three-forty." He resumes the programme and, as usual, Julia is revealed to be right. They erupt into their usual teasing, halted only by the ringtone of Nick's mobile.

"Hello?" he says slightly breathlessly, the last peal of laughter only just diminished from his lips.

The other side of the conversation reaches Julia's ears as nothing other than a rapid mumble. Something in Nick's expression though, causes her abdominal muscles to clench in anxiety.

He hangs up and takes a protracted breath.

"I'm really sorry pet but there's been a bit of an emergency at work,' he says. "I have to go and sort it out; you'll have to come with me and sit in the car. I'll try not to be too long."

This displeases Julia but she is polite and cheerful and never complains.

Her uncle, like his sister-in-law, Julia's mother, is a doctor. Only he is a psychiatrist who works in the local mental institution.

The journey is far from a leisurely one. Nick's Range Rover swallows the tarmac ahead, a salivating beast consuming its prey. Glancing across to the driver's seat, she can observe her uncle's jaw set in a firm, determined line. They make their way from Julia's house in Skerries to a secluded road on the outskirts of Howth. Even the entrance to the place is imposing, wrought iron gates thrown open.

Although the curtain of night has long since fallen, the sweeping gravel driveway is illuminated by lampposts spaced along it at equal intervals, each emanating a comely amber glow.

What waits at the end of the driveway, however, is another tale entirely. A cube of a mansion. Chalk-grey stone, barred windows and three towering chimneys. The picture as a whole resembles a crouching guard dog, preparing to pounce. It's body of stonework, eyes of windows and ears of chimneys.

Nick parks the car at the top of the drive and jumps out.

"Wait here," he tells her and approaches the door, ringing the bell.

The person who opens it does not enter her line of sight. Her uncle shakes hands with whoever it is and the door shuts once more in their wake.

For a few minutes, all is tranquil. Julia opens her well-thumbed copy of *Pride and Prejudice* and commences her chapter. She reads for about half an hour before the unmistakeable clamour of raised voices disturbs her. Closing her book, she sits up straighter and listens intently.

Most frustratingly, she is only capable of deciphering mere snatches of the heated conversation.

"Overdose..."

"Supposed to be the best..."

"Your fault entirely..."

"What are we supposed to tell the family?"

Intrigued, Julia exits the jeep. Careful to shut the door quietly behind her, it makes only a soft thud. Her feet tread lightly, carrying her towards the source of the commotion; a window in the right-hand wall of the house. Gripping the window sill, she crouches low and again prepares to listen.

"May I remind you Nicholas; she is dead and you killed her," intones another man's nasally voice, an irate sentiment dripping from each syllable.

An audible gasp escapes from Julia's lips. Who is dead and what can they mean Nick killed them?

Nick, kill someone? Surely not.

"I... I can't apologise enough. It was a strong sedative- you know she was becoming troublesome and I thought we needed to do something..."

Her uncle is stammering and even from her stooped position she can see his swinging arms as he paces to and from in front of the window.

"It is no great cause for concern," says a third voice, this one apparently female. "She was a liability; we were about to be exposed!"

"Quiet, Lorraine," snapped the nasally man. "Your opinion was not requested. The fact of the situation is that an inmate is dead. An overdose of drugs provided by you, Nicholas. The family will be suspicious; they were already asking questions thanks to her getting lippy on their visits. Before we know it, we'll have the Gardai and the health board knocking on the door demanding an explanation. Remaining here is too risky; we will need to leave Ireland. Arrangements are being made in Spain as we speak..."

Their voices diminish as they appear to move to the other side of the room. Julia stays crouched below the sill; ensures they have vacated the space directly in front of the window and eventually stands up. Peering in, she can see a dimly lit study. The walls are lined with bookcases filled with leather bound tomes. A wide desk stands in the middle of a cream carpeted floor and the room is expansive, Nick and the two others having transferred themselves to the far end. Her heart entwined in fear's unrelenting grasp, she backs away and scurries to the parked vehicle. She slides down the front seat, puts her head in her hands and feels tears abscond at the break of her and her uncle's bond.

The task of facing Nick is insurmountable so she feigns sleep on the journey home. When they reach the house, her uncle shakes her shoulder in his characteristically kind way. As he does, a poisoned dart of grief pierces her very soul and she knows that life as she knows it will never be the same again.

CHAPTER 26

Eve and Paul are celadon green. A decidedly sickly shade that appears to evidence a pallor characteristic of the betrayal, the agony, the utter disbelief they are experiencing.

Julia, exhausted from the effort of retelling the events to her parents, slumps against the sofa as something intangible wrestles with her heart like a prisoner attempting to abscond from their cell.

Paul swears.

Eve's head hangs low. "I can't believe this," she mumbles, enervated. "Nick... no, no, surely not. Paul, he's your brother. You know he couldn't have done this, don't you?"

"Nick..." he trails off, uncertain.

"Nick what?" questions Julia. "Daddy, I know what I saw."

"I know that, Julia. And I wouldn't put it past him."

"Come on, Paul. Nick couldn't kill a patient. He's a good doctor. He is!"

"He's a narcissist with White Knight syndrome, Eve. So don't protect him!" exclaims Paul with passion.

"I'm not protecting him; I'm just pointing out that there has to be some mistake here!"

"Mammy, it doesn't matter," Julia cuts in firmly. "I heard what I heard."

"Well, there's only one thing for it," Paul sighs, standing up. "We ask him to explain himself."

Eve glances at her watch. "But it's midnight, Paul."

"He's only away ten minutes; he'll not even be home yet. If he's any decency, he can come back here and tell us the truth. Not that he *has* any decency but-"

Julia is not surprised by this derisive comment. There has long been a certain sentiment felt between the brothers that she has never quite understood the origins of. It's like they're constantly skirting around, each trying to outdo the other.

Nick answers the call and agrees to come back to their house, mild confusion tempered by concern in his words. When he arrives, he sits down in the living room on the opposite sofa so that he is facing Julia, Eve and Paul directly.

It is Julia who begins the interrogation.

"Nick, who have you killed?"

The abruptness of her question confounds him. He opens his mouth to speak but the words evade his lips. As if as an afterthought, he clenches his jaw shut so that he is no longer gawping gormlessly.

"Wh... what do you mean? Is this a joke, Julia? Like that murder mystery party we did for your last birthday or something?" He attempts a laugh. The attempt fails.

"Nick, this is not a joke," Julia continues. "I overheard your conversation tonight. With your colleagues or whoever those other people are. I couldn't exactly help hearing, you weren't being quiet about it at all." She pauses to swallow. "And we need to know what the hell is going on. Because that was *not* some normal work issue."

One look at Nick and they can see; he is a defeated man. There is no point in pretending any longer. He has been caught red handed. By his fourteen- year -old niece.

"You weren't supposed to hear that Julia," he says gently.

"God, Nick, I'm not three!"

"No," he shakes his head, a small smile on his lips despite the situation. He looks up. "And in some ways, I don't think you ever were."

"Don't stall," Julia replies, her tone devoid of even a smidge of empathy.

The next ten minutes will alter Julia's life as she knows it. He tells them the tale. About Emily, about Maria, about their parents and all that he did.

About the perpetrators of this institution of abuse: Gerard Winchester and Lorraine Blackwood.

He tells them how he became a murderer.

At the conclusion of his tale, there is a deadpan silence. A silence that is shattered by Eve's exclamation of undiluted agony.

"Nick, no! No, Nick there has to be some mistake. This can't be true. It can't be!"

Whatever she says next is incoherent.

There is no sound explanation. Julia Joyce's uncle is a murderer.

But if there is one quality that Julia possesses, it is unwavering loyalty.

She and her parents come to a decision; they will protect Nick. Paul will not inform his colleagues in the Gardai. There will be no formal investigation.

True to his word, Nick leaves the country. That night is the last they lay eyes upon him. He promises them that one day he will return but when that day will be he does not know. If anyone inquires as to his whereabouts, they say Nick has got a job in Dubai and gone there for a year or two with his new girlfriend. After Dubai, it is Australia. And then New Zealand. After a while, people cease to ask. Cease to care. Julia could go around every country on the globe and one glaringly obvious fact will remain; Nick is gone and he is never coming back.

Or so at least, she thought.

She was wrong, as it would transpire.

But Julia will always love her uncle Nick. No matter where he may be. No matter what he may have done.

You see, there are many things in this life that Julia Joyce does not understand.

She doesn't understand how people would rather go to a disco than go to the theatre. She doesn't understand how people find maths boring. She doesn't understand how *someone* hasn't made men take their wives' surname and not the other way around.

But Julia understands why Nick did what he did. He did it to protect himself. He killed to cover his transgressions.

And honestly? Julia would have done the same herself.

CHAPTER 27

Julia

The room was quiet.

Absolutely quiet. The kind of quiet that had a life of its own and was capable of manipulating those ensnared within it. At the window, a curtain became slightly disturbed, meandering forward when buoyed by the persisting gusts. The pane itself moaned. Whether in protest at the assault from the elements or in a longing for the peace that came from within I did not know.

"So... what you're saying is... you think your uncle has come back... killed Lorraine and your dad and Emily thinks that... Mr. FFS is involved in it too. And Maycroft Demesne is Serenity Springs."

"I know it sounds crazy and it doesn't really make any sense but... yes."

"God," he lifted his glass again. "That hurts my head."

"Trust me, I don't understand it any more than you do."

I did not understand what happened next either.

Jonathan shifted closer to me on the sofa and simply looked at me. Like he was seeing me for the first time all over again. Amongst the silence, his breath came in a steady rhythm. Deep and intentional.

"Julia..." he murmured before his lips found mine.

Something exploded within me. A rush of heat and want and... and love. It surely wasn't supposed to feel like this, a simple respectful contact. But somehow it was everything. Overwhelmed, I gasped.

He pulled away and even in the semi-darkness I could see his blush. "I'm... so sorry Julia... I didn't mean to... to... oh God, I shouldn't have, I- "

Reaching out with a single finger, I placed it on his lips. Those lips that were now imprinted against mine. For all eternity.

"There's no need to be sorry, Jonathan."

"No... no there is... I imposed on you. That was unacceptable-"

"You can impose on me anytime you like."

The moon selected that moment to creep from behind a cloud. Such a gesture allowed a single shard of light to sidle through a chink in the curtains and reflect off the mirror glass on the other side of the room. It dispersed into a million different hues. Each one unique. Slightly flawed as the exact band of colour into which it fit was left undefined. Just like us.

He took one hand and tucked a stray strand of hair back behind my ear. "Do you... do you really mean that?"

"Of course I do," I whispered.

Slowly, his handsome features illuminated. In a smile.

Just when I felt silence may relapse, I summoned the courage to ask him a question: "Jonathan, what do you see in me?"

Shyly, he grasped my hand. "What do you mean?"

"I'm not a good person Jonathan, surely that's obvious to you now." I swallowed. Hard.

Something inexplicable flickered across his face. "You're perfect, Julia."

I laughed wryly. "Perfect? That's the last thing I am."

"You are." There was confidence in those two words that almost shattered my heart. Suddenly, I became excessively embarrassed. I swung my feet around and planted them firmly on the floor, drawing my arms around me.

"You're too good for me, Jonathan," I said slowly. "Whatever... this is... you could have this with someone normal. Somebody who wants normal things in life. Not someone like me."

Brow furrowing, he put his feet on the ground too. "Julia, normal is just a polite way of saying boring. You know that."

"Jonathan... you can still get out of this. Get away from *me* before it's too late."

I gazed into his eyes then. They were flickering, speckled with something unreadable. "It's already too late," he breathed barely audibly.

"Plus," I continued. "I'm not... pretty. There's so many other girls who look better than me..."

"Julia," he said, exasperated. "You're the most beautiful woman I've ever met. Other girls aren't you. They're just... not. I love the way you're different. I love how you don't care about... all that trivial, superficial stuff that they do. I love the way you're your own person. I... I love *you*, Julia."

His words almost winded me.

"I... I love you too, Jonathan."

This time, when he kissed me, I allowed it to linger. When he eventually retracted his lips, he said: "Did you... was that ok?"

"It... it was wonderful." I cast my eyes downwards. It is a rare thing for me to be timid but that night... I was. It felt like I was standing on a precipice, preparing to take the ultimate leap. Certain somehow, that when I did, I would fall into the arms of a man whom I had come to love. Against my better judgement, against all odds. Despite everything; I loved him. What was even further beyond belief was that he loved me in return. I had told him the truth about my secret. That was a thing I had never verbalised to anyone.

He took me as I was, as I am, as I always intend to be.

In a moment I believed may never cease, he continued to simply gaze at me. Visible in his eyes was something abstract, that I could not quite comprehend.

Although we were alone in the house, I rose quickly and closed the door to the library, hearing it shut with a click. Block the slight drought. Turning to face him again, I leant back against the wood. Waiting. Silent.

He rose. Deliberately, cautiously. He stood so close that his chest brushed mine, the musky scent of aftershave alighting on my skin. Half of his face fell into a murky shadow, half into the lethargic lunar light. The fire continued to smoulder in the grate. Gentle. Unobtrusive.

"Am I your girlfriend now?" The question was expelled suddenly, half in jest but meant to provoke an answer I genuinely craved.

"Of course you are," he said with a laugh. "That is, if you want to be."

"Well... I *might* think about it."

"Julia," a crease had appeared between his eyebrows, his tone serious again. "You know I don't care about... your past. Don't you?"

"I think I'm beginning to realise that." I smiled wanly, a grin that wavered like the tongues of fire dancing in the hearth. "And you can't begin to imagine how much I appreciate it."

For a second, there was stillness. Complete stillness. Undisturbed. Then his hand found my waist.

"Are you sure, Julia, about us?" he whispered quietly.

"Of course I am. With you, I'm always sure."

CHAPTER 28

Jonathan

Okay, I admit it.

I was shocked.

Gobsmacked, in fact.

But if you want the truth? I didn't care.

Should I have cared? Yes, I suppose I should. I mean, Julia's *uncle...* I'm not physically capable of articulating what he *did*. It was atrocious. Beyond words, it was atrocious.

I was not condoning that and neither was Julia.

Of course, I understand that she protected him to a degree. What else was she supposed to do though? She was protecting herself and her parents too. She had to do it. She didn't have a choice. Did she?

Above all else though, it proved one thing: Julia would do anything for someone she loves. That displayed more than anything could how passionate, how fierce, how loyal her love would be.

It took courage for me to make the first move as it were. What if I had read the whole thing wrong and she wasn't interested at all? She had most definitely been flirting a little but that's part of her personality. As it transpired, my fears were negligible. When she opened up to me that night, I saw *her*. The raw, unfiltered version. My only hope was that I would see it every day. Forever.

Like, before I met Julia, I thought *love* was something I felt for sportscars and champers... and... I don't know, seven figure listings?

But then... I met her.

It's the two of us now. No matter what.

The following evening was Saturday and that meant only one thing: the highly anticipated office party. Julia and I had arranged to meet on the corner of Balfe Street and Harry Street, outside The Westbury. Noticing her figure emerging from the crowd, I almost emitted an audible gasp. Unspooling like some thread of Grecian mythology, her cascading blonde hair fell about her shoulders, the pensive smile curving her rosebud lips a buoyant breeze that crept around me. She apparently noticed me then and looked up. The joy it brought to notice that enamoured expression spring to her features was a thing I did not quite deserve. As may be reasonably anticipated in the city centre on a Saturday night, the throng was of droves but as our eyes met, they dissipated. The world dissipated. Vigorously, she untangled herself from the web, bounding in burgeoning joy towards me. Quite oblivious to anyone who may have been observing us, she threw her arms around my neck, the puffed lilac sleeves of her satin gown synonymising the purple hue baptising the night. Overlaying the garment was a cream fur coat and stole. Her decidedly artistic aura was aided by the beret, also of satin, perched on her head.

"Well, Watson, aren't you going to tell me how gorgeous I am?"

"Watson?" I teased quizzically. "Is that my name now?"

"Yes. You're my boyfriend so I can call you whatever I want," she said smugly, pressing her nose against mine.

"Alright, Princess." I retaliated, sliding a stray strand of her hair between my fingers.

Mischievously, she waggled her eyebrows. "Where's my snog, then?"
Lacking the self-control to do otherwise, I kissed her tenderly, heedless of the rather public setting. We both became lost in the moment-

"How's it goin' weans, what's the craic?"

About as considerately as a chainsaw, Eamon's greeting split us apart. Springing backwards, I was met by the utterly stupefied face of our colleague. The ensuing five seconds were characterised only by an awkward clearing of my throat and our mutual inability to speak.

"How ya Eamon," I muttered eventually. "We were just..."

"Dear God... were you two... *snoggin'*?"

We shifted on the spot, enveloped by an uncomfortable quiet. Awaiting judgement.

"Auch weans, I'm delighted. I knew it, you know!" This was announced in a rather triumphant blurt. "I said to myself, Eamon, those two there have a wee thing for each other. So I did, right enough!"

"Look, Eamon," Julia began hurriedly. "Please don't tell the others about this. At the end of the day, we're colleagues and we probably shouldn't... well, you know but we feel so strongly for each other and-"

"Aww Julia pet, don't be worryin'. Sure, who would I be letting on ti'?"

"Letting on wha'?"

"Oh, hello Anto," said Julia, still blushing profusely, "what are you doing here?"

"Ehh... I'm here for the party. As in the office party? In McDaids." Brow furrowed in suspicion, he pointed across the street to the primrose yellow façade of the pub. Trimmed in a vibrant green, its gangly form blatantly opposed the quintessential red brick of Harry Street.

"Right, come on, let's go inside. It's Baltic out here," I declared, ushering the group towards the side entrance on Chatham Lane.

"But we have to wait for Emily and Mr. FFS," Anto protested, confusion still evident in his words. "And you haven't told me what was going on there."

Rather wearily, Julia sighed. "Right, we may as well tell you too.

But promise me that Mr. FFS won't get to hear about this."

"Okay..."

"Jonathan and I are... well, we're dating each other." In a protective gesture that somehow asserted our new found stance as a couple, I wound my arm around her waist as she proclaimed the announcement.

For a moment, I thought Anto wasn't going to respond but he then declared exuberantly: "Ah Jaysus! Spot the Durtbirds! Lads, it's Romeo and Julia!"

At this, he and Eamon began to fall about in hysterical cackles, their mirthful explosion not easily disbursed. Eventually, the giggles subsided as Anto turned to me with a wicked look that spoke of eminent teasing. "Right so, we want the details. How'd it happen? Who made the first move?"

From the periphery of my vision, I could sense Julia becoming shifty at my side. I knew how foreign this was for her. She'd never had a relationship before and the thought of our first intimate encounter being relayed to our colleagues was clearly disconcerting her a little. It disconcerted me too. Although I had a few casual relationships at university, I'd never known anything beyond a second or third date. The last time I went out with a girl, I was forced to endure an entire night of her ranting about the numerous trips she'd had to Turkey in order to facilitate cosmetic surgery on various parts of her anatomy. I don't know, maybe she thought I'd be into that or something. Let's just say I really wasn't.

"Well, I just... couldn't wait any longer," I began carefully. "Something told me Julia felt the same way and it turns out she did so... yeah, it happened. I've been in love with her from the second I met her."

"Auch, weans, that's wile nice," Eamon said so sincerely I thought he might cry.

Anto nodded thoughtfully and then continued: "Yeah, well, to be honest like, yis' really were being a bit obvious."

"What do you mean?" asked Julia.

"The flirting in the office-" Anto adopted a high- pitched squeak that was clearly meant to portray an impersonation of me, "*Oh Julia, she's so hard-working, she's so talented, I can't hide how much I want to snog her*, sound like anybody?" He winked.

I turned crimson.

"No offence like Julia, I think you're great and all but Jono does go a bit goggle eyed where you're concerned." He paused for breath. "Plus, yis' do be giving each other the mince pies."

"Ay?" pondered Eamon.

"The 'eyes', Eamon," Anto explained. "Of the suggestive variety."

"What's keeping Mr. FFS, I wonder?" interjected Julia in an obvious attempt to steer the conversation in an opposite direction before any more details regarding our relationship could be elicited. "He should be here by now."

I shrugged. "Probably won't show."

"Won't show? But it's his party!"

"We'd be better off without him," muttered Eamon darkly. "Remember the last Christmas party." This was added with a knowing look shared between Anto and I.

"I'd really rather not."

"Why? What happened?" Julia's curiosity had an almost humorous edge. Whatever the occurrence, if it involved our boss, it was sure to be... interesting.

Anto shook his head violently as if the memory pained him. "Well, he got absolutely locked out of his nut. Like, so locked he couldn't even find the key. We were up in Coppers Nightclub and you should have seen him throwing shapes. Making a complete eejit out of himself. Anyway, he snogged three women (the eldest was probably half his age) and then when it was closing time, he decided we were going to continue the party in one of our vacant properties."

"Sounds sensible," Julia remarked with a sideways glance at me.

"Yeah. There was a hot tub and he made us all get in."

"He *forced* you?"

"He literally insisted but I really didn't want to," I added, slightly worried Julia wouldn't exactly admire my involvement in such activities.

"Jono, lad. You were too busy driving the porcelain bus. Not very well either, you spewed all over the Sicilian marble!"

"That Guinness in the Coppers was dodgy," I muttered, feeling myself begin to resemble an over-ripe tomato. "It messed with my stomach."

"Aye and then one of the neighbours heard the racket and called the Guards!" Eamon exclaimed with passion. "Telling yi', wouldn't get thon in Tyrone. If a crowd o' stocious estate agents passed out in a hot tub, there'd be a bloody scandal!"

"Only Freddie was mates with the Guard and so we got away with it!" Anto was excessively triumphant.

It was only after this rather embarrassing anecdote that we eventually made it inside the pub through the lesser- known side door that leads directly on to what is quite potentially the narrowest and steepest staircase you will encounter in the course of your life.

"Sack the bleedin' architect," bemoaned Anto mournfully. "You should try going to the jax in this place." There at least, he does have a point. Should you find yourself in the unfortunate predicament of requiring use of the toilet while within the establishment, you can look forward to a precarious jaunt into a miniscule lavatory positioned perilously at the very top of the stairs. And after a few scoops? Deadly buzz alright.

"Now, Anto, that's what we call a period feature," I said, slapping him vigorously on the back. "As Mr. FFS would say; sell, sell, sell. Under any circumstances."

It was not until we reached the summit of the steps and made our way into the vaulted bar area that catastrophe struck.

For, arranged at a circular table in the right-hand corner, was the staff of Regal Residences.

Our main competitor.

"Well, would you look at thon-"Eamon started.

"Some feckin' neck," echoed Anto. "Ger' up outta me gaff."

His words clearly reached the ears of the Regal Residences head honcho because, a second later, he had risen from his seat and squared off to Anto.

"Anthony," he said through gritted teeth in an accent that screamed south of the Liffey more than a listing on Ailesbury Road. "Would you care to explain what exactly you're doing here?"

"It's a feckin' free country, Richard!" retaliated Anto with vigour. "And maybe *you* would care to talk about a certain property in Ballsbridge?"

"What about a certain property in Ballsbridge?"

"You gazumped me!"

"Hold on a second, *you* gazumped *me*!" screeched Richard in hyperbolised horror. "You do have an exceptionally short memory Anthony."

Suddenly sensing Julia at my side, I turned to her with a roll of my eyes. "Dopes the lot of them," I said. Then, lowering my voice a little, I whispered: "Fancy going over to the bar so we can have a minute alone?"

Wordlessly, she agreed and we detached ourselves from our

colleagues and competitors, moving towards the sparser populated bar.

"Watson," said Julia, gaze darting rapidly around the room. "Where's Emily?"

"Dunno. Haven't seen her. Maybe she's late." I shrugged dismissively. To be honest, I couldn't really have cared less. I found Emily a bit... well, tedious. I understood then obviously that she had been through some horrible things in her life. Still, she wasn't high up on the list of people I was desperate to spend time with.

"Anyway," I started again, "why do we need anyone else here? I'd rather it just be the two of us." Drawing her closer, I pecked her on the lips.

"Lads, yis' are hilarious, you know."

I groaned. Julia groaned. Seriously, not again.

This time it was Anto, seemingly having tired from his spate of sparring with Richard.

"You should have told us earlier," he chortled. "This is the best yet. A romance in the office. Never thought I'd see it, guys."

We both remained silent.

"Ah, chill out you two. You thought we wouldn't approve?"

"We didn't think you would, no," admitted Julia. "But Anto, we were also wondering... why isn't Emily here?"

"Oh, didn't I tell you? She's resigned with immediate effect."

This elicited a sharp intake of breath from the two of us, however, Anto spoke perfectly nonchalantly.

"Why?" The sound came, strangled, from my mouth.

"Didn't give a reason. Couldn't handle Rockstars like us probably. At least, that's what Mr. FFS said. Anyway, come on," our colleague wound an arm around both of our shoulders. "Let's go. We're having a Split the G competition against those bleedin' dopes," he gestured at the Regal Residences table. "And our reputation relies on us winning."

"Splitting the G's impossible," I grumbled. "I've never managed it before."

"Practice makes perfect, Jono." With this, he waved us over to the opposite corner where Eamon had sat down. He then ordered a round of drinks; Guinness for the three of us and wine for Julia.

"What's the craic with this splitting the G thing anyway?" questioned Eamon curiously. "I haven't a clue what you're on about, weans."

It was Anto who undertook the task of offering an explanation, enunciating his words with the air of someone calculating an extremely complex formula. "All you have to do is get the line between the black and white part of the pint," he pointed at his own to demonstrate, "exactly on the line of the 'G' on the Guiness glass." He looked around him victoriously. "And accuracy is essential. Not a millimetre off."

Eamon's expression was one of bewilderment.

"Why though? Sounds a wee bit silly in fairness."

"Excuse me, Eamon. Bit of respect please. It's a hallowed tradition around here." He settled at the table. "The last real estate conference I was at, Richard beat me." This was said as if he had been defeated at some World Championship. "So, we need to rectify that tonight."

"Wouldn't get thon in Tyrone," lamented Eamon.

"Welcome to The Pale, Eamon," said Anto, punching his arm. "Welcome to The Pale."

CHAPTER 29

Julia

I was highly discontented.

It made absolutely no sense. Why would she just resign? She *wouldn't* just resign.

You may call me cynical but consider; wasn't there something suspicious in her sudden decision to leave the office? Especially as it came only the day after confiding her suspicions about our boss.

Every instinct informed me her departure was no accident.

She had been removed.

The office party had been raucous, fuelled by the rivalry between the two agencies. Emerging from McDaid's into the early hours of the morning, lethargy gripped me.

"I'm hungry," I mumbled into Jonathan's shoulder as we meandered down Harry Street.

"Fancy a Supermacs then, darling?"

I acquiesced and we hug-walked companionably through the starlit city, the hollering of its nocturnal inhabitants unobtrusive as we took refuge in each-other's arms.

Entering the Temple Bar area, we continued on to Supermacs, settling at a booth in the corner after placing our order. It was after two in the morning and as a result we had the place to ourselves. Mingling in the air was the sound of silence and the delectable aroma of frying food.

"Guilty pleasure, this," I said, tucking into my chicken burger. "But so delicious."

Jonathan wiped his fingers on a napkin. "Best fast food in the world."

"Exactly." The smile fled from my face however, when I involuntarily thought of Emily. "Watson?"

"Yes, darling?"

"Don't you think it's strange about Emily?"

He appeared to consider the question. "Maybe talking to you made her think things over and she decided it was too risky to stay working for someone who might be involved in all that.... Stuff."

Swallowing a mouthful, I shook my head. "No, I don't think she would. She seemed fairly determined to just keep her head down, say nothing and try and get something on him. Something that might eventually allow justice to be done." I paused for breath. "I really don't think she would leave voluntarily."

"But why else would she go? I mean, for all its faults, Rockstar Real Estate isn't a bad place to work."

Looking up into his keen eyes, I forced myself to say it. "Jonathan... I think she was made to leave."

"Wh...what do you mean?" There was a tremor in his voice. "You... you don't think Freddie forced her to go, do you?"

Heavily, I sighed. "Well, I think given everything that's happened, it's the most likely possibility. She spills her suspicions to me yesterday and she's suddenly resigned her position today? Come on, you have to admit it stinks."

"It doesn't sound great, no." He grew pensive. "But how would Freddie even know she told you anything? You were on your own with her in the office."

"He would know if the office was bugged."

For a moment, I feared he might faint.

"No, no that's not possible. That would be illegal!"

I laughed wryly. "Do you honestly believe he would have any

qualms about installing a listening device in an office if he had a hand in the murders of several people?"

"Well...no." He trailed off. "Julia, do you think Emily could be in danger?" As he asked it, his demeanour was childish. That of a boy hoping to be informed there was in fact no monster under his bed.

The sad thing? There most definitely was.

"She could be," I said simply. "I don't know."

"Well... what do we do?"

Leaning across the table, I intoned my next sentence with purpose. "I'll tell you what we do, Watson: we figure it out."

CHAPTER 30

Julia

Featherington-Smythe had called an office meeting. I couldn't help but feel rather surprised at that if I was honest. He was an elusive presence. Whenever he deigned to actually spend time in the agency, he remained resolutely in his personal back office and did not emerge into the main workspace. Like a lethargic lion loyal to his lair.

That morning however, we were honoured by his presence, albeit over video call from the Galway office where he had been called off to for a few days in order to deal with a 'property emergency.'

There was a palpable sentiment of scepticism hovering amongst us as we congregated on the Winchester sofas that overlooked the bustling landscape of midmorning Dawson Street. We could not quite imagine why he wished to call us together. Usually, it was every man for himself in that place. Jonathan and I were intrigued but it was a fair summation to say that our colleagues were merely miffed at having their morning interrupted.

"Good morning, Rockstars!" Featherington-Smythe exclaimed jubilantly.

"Morning," came the lack lustre reply.

"Come on guys, let's have a bit more enthusiasm in the joint. I know yis' probably went a bit wild on Saturday and all but yis' look like I'm going to read yis' the last rights." He leered demonically round at us. I was seated beside Jonathan, who was grinding his teeth together from sheer frustration. Jonathan had always detested FFS. Everyone did really but no one more so than him.

On the other sofa were Anto and Eamon. The latter was gazing absently into space while Anto was furiously typing on his mobile phone, his movements so violent it seemed his finger might fracture the screen.

FFS cleared his throat before continuing, "Okay, so, I have an announcement to make."

"We never would have guessed," muttered Jonathan into my left ear.

"This," he gestured at the blank interactive board filling the screen behind him, "will alter the course of Rockstar Real Estate history forever."

I raised an eyebrow. Jonathan snorted. Anto continued typing. Eamon began extracting apparently used tissues from his pocket and concentrated on hurling them into the waste paper basket with excessive force considering it was two feet away from him.

My eyes remained firmly fixed on my boss though. Not for the first time, I was experiencing that intuition that I had seen this man somewhere before. He resembled a certain stereotype; pretentious, sleazy, verbally incontinent...you get the picture. Still though, my intuitions had a tendency to be accurate.

With a flourish, he pressed a button on the remote control in his hand and bold text appeared on the board. "**ROCKSTAR REAL ESTATE: INTERNATIONAL EXPANSION.**"

Suddenly, Anto and Eamon lost interest in the typing and tissues. Their heads snapped up. They were rapt.

"Expansion to where exactly?" I queried.

The sickening smirk spreading further across his face, he changed the slide. Two flags flashed across the screen: Spain and Cyprus.

"Now Rockstars," he began.

"Why can't he address us as normal human beings?" spat Jonathan to me.

"It has always been my ultimate goal to build a real estate empire and with your help I know we're going to conquer all markets and make me their emperor. Very simple, just three Ss: sun, sea and..." the pause extended just a few moments longer than necessary.

"Sales." A flash of light glinted off his aviators.

"Right..." I hesitated.

"We need to set ourselves apart from the competitors-"

"You mean Regal Residences," offered Anto.

"Aren't they already doing the whole Place in the Sun thing?" interjected Eamon.

"Well, yes but obvs, Rockstars, we are going to whip their backsides-"

"I swear to God if he says Rockstars one more time..." fumed Jonathan.

"Regal Residences are doing Portugal and only Portugal. They are basic so we are going to be *acidic!*"

Jonathan groaned.

"Now, saying as you lot lucked out with such a well-connected boss, we have the chance to acquire properties in Spain *and* Cyprus while establishing overseas branches there. This, Rockstars, is going to be epic but to get the show on the road, I'm going to be sending you all on a secret mission."

"Great, now he thinks he's James bloody Bond." Jonathan again.

"*You* are going to be property scouting overseas. Naturally, while you're there, I'll be expecting you to maintain an any means necessary approach."

Eamon suddenly began to look rather alarmed "Are we being conscripted?" he said to no one in particular.

"Precisely Eamon," FFS pointed at him like he'd just arrived at the right answer to a tricky question. "But don't fear, I lead with compassion."

"Compassion my bum," Anto mouthed.

"Firstly, the two Js. When you multiply Kirsty and Phil by Romeo and Juliet, what do you get? Julia and Jonathan!" Vigorously, he slapped the surface in front of him in delight at his own joke.

"Wait, so you lads are official now?" pried Anto.

"Look, Mr. Featherington-Smythe, would you mind leaving our personal life out of this?" My demand was polite but firm. How had he got to know about us anyway? But truly, I wasn't surprised; he had eyes and ears absolutely everywhere. I shifted uncomfortably at the thought I'd had about him bugging the office and covertly cast my eyes around the space, half-expecting the tell-tale blink of a camera's flashing light.

"Come on, Julia. Lighten up. You'd have to be blind not to see the soppy grins on your faces just because you're sitting-"

"You were saying, about the expansion?" I said pointedly.

"You're no fun."

"I assure you that I am plenty of fun. I was simply anxious to hear about your *wonderful* new venture."

He would not know sarcasm if it slapped him in the face.

"Right, Julia and Jonathan. Saying as I am so considerate, I'll be sending you two away together. You speak Spanish, don't you Julia?"

"Si."

"That's decided then. Julia and Jonathan are going to Espana. It's in my interests that the two of you go as Spain has the largest area to cover; namely the Costa del Sol. The most luxurious costa in the country."
"Why do you need to go to Spain to get a Costa? There's a sound one up the road you know."

"It means 'coast' Anto, you auld eejit. As in areas beside the sea," snorted Eamon derisively.

"Ohhh...right. Get you now."

"And we, Rockstars, are not limiting ourselves to the one area. *That* is the most common mistake made by incompetent idiots like Regal Residences. We're talking anywhere we can get our hands on. Be it Seville, Malaga, Murcia. So long as it's not Ballymun in the Sun (ergo, Benidorm.)" He guffawed grotesquely.

Jonathan's brow was so furrowed, it looked like he was hauling a wheelbarrow of bricks through the Sahara.

"So, what you're saying is you expect us to just fly off to Spain and... sell houses?"

"Hate to break it you, Jono, but you're an estate agent. It's what you do."

"Right but..."

"I have plenty of contacts," he paused to execute some kind of preen. "You know, have to tell them to join the queue."

"Delete. Mental. Image," huffed Jonathan.

"So I'll be organising meetings for you to liaise with local agents when you're out there. I'll need all of you to familiarise yourselves with the market-"

"But, Sir..."

"Zip it, Romeo or I'll put you on detention."

He supplied us with his customary smirk.

"Anto and Eamon, you're heading to Cyprus. Keep an eye on your e-mails because I'll be sending you all individual itineraries specifying exactly where you're to focus your search and the property types we need-"

"I don't speak Greek," objected Eamon.

"You don't need to speak the language; their English is good in Cyprus anyway. Stop trying to wangle out of this Eamon. Don't let

Julia make you feel worthless just by being a smarty-pants."

"Oi, that's my girlfriend you're talking about!" Jonathan exclaimed.

"Official now, are we?" sneered our boss.

"Just...just don't disrespect her like that."

I had never needed anyone to stand up for me but Jonathan being protective of me was... well...very becoming on him. This sort of thing was not in his nature and I knew it took effort.

"That's alright then," I said, rising from my seat. "I hear Regal Residences are recruiting. I might just apply for a position there and then I won't be making anyone here feel 'worthless.'"

That did the trick. I knew how to get around his type like the back of my hand. You manipulated their weaknesses, of which there was no shortage.

"Look, Julia, I'm sorry. That was a stupid comment and I... don't go near Regal Residences. They're a crowd of cowboys."

"And this place isn't?" Jonathan said under his breath.

"You're not seriously considering leaving yet are you, Julia? I need you on my team." For a moment then, he managed to sound almost genuine. Almost.

"I might think about sticking around, provided I am treated with the due courtesy I deserve." I swept my gaze across him.

"Whatever you need, Julia. Seriously. Just don't go. Please."

"What I need is my lunchbreak. Come on Johnny. Let's get out of here for a while."

Then, with those parting words, I sashayed out of the office as Jonathan followed in my wake.

CHAPTER 31

Julia

A few minutes later, Jonathan and I were perched at a miniscule mahogany table in the bowels of Bewley's coffee shop. The insistent whirring of the barista machines thrummed in the background and the cacophony of mundane chatter enshrouded the real substance of any singular conversation. It was the lunch time rush so the place was absolutely heaving, leaving Jonathan and I cramped in close proximity in the very back corner. Not that I was complaining. Jonathan had already downed a double shot espresso in an attempt to calm his nerves after the rather eventful morning meeting but I was perfectly composed, sipping my Americano (what can I say? I like my coffee strong and my men weak.)

"Who does he think he is?" Jonathan seethed, stirring his second coffee and sending it spitting over the beige napkins.

"I know how to deal with the likes of him Jonathan."

"You do, Julia," He stroked the back of my hand and for a moment I experienced a jolt of happiness so pure that nothing could overshadow it. Then though, it all came crashing back to me.

"This international property thing," continued Jonathan. "Are you...getting the same feeling that I am?"

"Foreboding? Yes. This proves it Jonathan: he has to be connected to... whatever this is. That's why he wants to sell Spanish property! He has contacts out there because of..." I could barely even bring myself to say it. "Something is seriously wrong Jonathan. I think that's obvious now."

"We'll figure it out, Julia. Together." A shy smile crept across his lips then and for a moment we lost ourselves in looking at each other. Until our phones buzzed simultaneously.

"Fecking FFS and his itinerary," moaned Jonathan glumly, opening the email.

I pulled my own phone from my handbag and perused the attached document. It was mostly as I had expected. We were to fly out for a fortnight and make a start on acquiring Spanish property. Our primary focus was to be on the Costa del Sol, particularly the area between Malaga and Marbella as well as the province of Seville.

"Julia, have...have you seen this?" Jonathan held up his phone. "The miser is putting us up in a two -star kip!"

"He wouldn't, Jonathan, this is Rockstar Real Estate we're talking about. We specialise in luxury."

"Yeah, but he thinks it's alright to skimp when it doesn't concern him. The twat."

Sure enough, the residence that was to be our abode in Malaga seemed to be trying to emulate the example of Faulty Towers. The entire premises needed multiple coats of paint and cleanliness was apparently far from a priority.

"We are *not* staying there." The statement came in unison from our mouths.

Okay, fine, I admit it; we're snobs.

"Well, I have an alternative base for our secret mission, Watson."

"Enlighten me."

"Very conveniently," I nonchalantly wet my lips with coffee. "I happen to own a villa in La Cala de Mijas, about half an hour's drive from Malaga."

"You're pulling my leg."

"When would I ever pull your leg?"

"Literally *all* of the time."

Scrolling through my camera roll, I selected a few photos of El Paraiso, our Andalusian abode, and handed my phone to Jonathan. The property had originally belonged to my mum's parents and had been passed down to her. Many memories had been made within its walls and I had a lot of affection for the place. Sharing it with Jonathan was right. It was an expansive villa and decidedly luxurious. I was assured of impressing him.

"Swanky gaff, Julia." He pinched the screen to zoom in on a photo. "The commission if I sold a place like that would be, like, I don't know-"

"Will it suffice?" I said to cut across his musings.

"Just about." He winked. "You're amazing."

"I know."

"Julia, I'm actually getting quite excited about this."

"Why would that be?"

"It'll be peaceful, relaxing. Just the two of us..."

His boyish face was lit like a lantern, eyes shimmering.

"That might not be wholly disagreeable." I could not prevent a smile.

"We'll be getting away from it all for a while," he said confidently.

If only we were to have known how wrong he was.

CHAPTER 32

Julia

The case was steadfastly refusing to shut. It was no surprise really; this was a predicament I faced virtually every time I travelled. I was an over-packer. Too many times in the past I had arrived at the airport exceeding the luggage weight limit and providing my parents no option but to pay for a few extra kilograms. Much to my dad's chagrin. It is a peculiar thing that I would have given anything for those remonstrances that I used to despise to grace my ears again. Seeing El Paraiso for the first time since my dad's death was going to be difficult. This, I had found, was one of the greatest afflictions of grief; whenever I ended up in a place or situation I had not been in since before it happened, a fresh torrent of memories tumbled through my brain. That said, it was beginning to ease a little. I shook myself. I had to focus on the future. The past was the past.

Although it was only a two-week trip, I had succeeded in stuffing the suitcase with a number of garments sufficient for about two years. There were evening dresses, casual dresses, my customary power suits (we were travelling for professional purposes after all), shorts, T-shirts, trousers, kaftans and just about every other item of clothing known to man. I've never been vain; it isn't that I disregard my appearance (quite the opposite in fact) but rather that larger and more pressing concerns have occupied the majority of my headspace for most of my life. Procuring straight As and publishing novels simply fulfilled me in a way hair straighteners and eyelash curlers never could. However, I have always afforded myself the credit of being fashionable (and yes, I am in possession of a penchant for designer brands). I would never call myself beautiful, but the word is firmly within Jonathan's vernacular where I am concerned.

I know what you're thinking; he's too good for me, too innocent. And maybe he is. But, well, I never asked him to fall for me. Did I?

A smile curved my lips upwards as I fingered the navy silk of the pyjamas he had bought me. The breast pocket had a curlicued gold 'J' embossed on the fabric. He had an identical pair; he thought we should match for the trip.

I know, we are *that* couple who coordinate our outfits. Laugh all you want; I won't be offended.

With one final Herculean effort, I sat down heavily on my luggage and tugged the zip closed around it. My Louis Vuitton carry on wasn't much better either. They both bulged ominously but would have to do.

Dragging the corpulent case behind me, I descended the stairs and glanced at my watch. Jonathan was collecting me at any minute. My heart fluttered within my chest. Yes, this was a business trip but it was a business trip with my boyfriend. Given everything that I had endured in the last months, I felt that I was deserving of enjoyment. We both were; Jonathan had not had it easy either.

I deposited my bags in the hall and crossed to the living room to wait on Jonathan. My head was resting against the glass of the bay window. As daylight perished, its surface adopted a reflective quality, meaning that while I could still look beyond the window pane, my gaze was also directed introspectively. At myself. Inside and outside in perfect equilibrium. Light and darkness. Sun and shadow. It seemed that, buried in me, was the innate knowledge of everything that was to come.

At that moment, the now familiar Porsche swung into the driveway and Jonathan bounded from the driver's seat. Just like every time I laid eyes on him, he was dashingly attired in clothing nearly as expensive as my own, today's brand of choice being Ralph Lauren. For both of us ironically. Most of all though, beneath the royal blue shirt and jumper that toned with his eyes, I knew that a heart so pure and good beat for me and me alone.

Sometimes, I almost feel guilty. Almost.

He rapped on the door then and I was jolted from my thoughts by the need to answer.

"Are you bringing the bricks to build a villa or what?" he remarked as he attempted to lift the case off the ground, wincing in authentication of my belief that physical labour was as foreign a concept to him as the phrase: "I would advise you not to purchase this property."

"It *has* got wheels you know."

"Of course I know, I'm not a total toolbox."

"That's debatable."

When we had finished sparring, we stored my luggage in the front boot and I locked up the house. Jonathan, being a gentleman as always, opened the passenger door for me before he jumped in at the other side.

He squeezed my hand.

"I honestly can't wait for this Julia. You need a break after... everything."

"I know." I reciprocated the squeeze, the smile on my lips belied by an ache that unbalanced the scales of emotion.

Traffic was relatively light as we made our way along the darkening M1 and before long the familiar line of sentry flags that indicated the entrance to Dublin airport came into view. Our flight was at nine o'clock which meant we would be landing late but Jonathan's allergy to a certain low-cost Irish airline had left us taking the last available Aer Lingus flight. I was beginning to regret the fact that I had entrusted Jonathan with booking the flights; there was a distinct possibility we did not have a seat on a plane at all.

"Why won't the poxy thing open?" Jonathan was staring at the electronic barrier to the carpark like it had spontaneously sprouted three heads.

"This is Express Green Jonathan. The ticket says Express Red."

"Crap, am I in the wrong place?"

"Uh, yes."

Jonathan emitted a shower of expletives. I giggled. "How many times have you flown out of this airport?"

"About a million."

"Spot the spanner."

"Come on, the carparks in this place are unnecessarily confusing."

"Or else you're just easily confused." I poked him playfully in the ribs. "Please tell me you actually got us flights?"

"I did better than get us just any old flights. I have a surprise for you Julia," he confided as we made a U-turn and headed for the correct carpark.

"You haven't sent us to the wrong country, have you?"

"No!"

"Just checking."

"We, my darling, are flying business class."

"Not a chance, we're only going to Spain!" I said incredulously.

Jonathan found a free space and put the Porsche in park. Then, he reached out and turned my face towards his own. "I want our first trip abroad together to be perfect and economy is the biggest buzz kill ever. Even if it's only for two and a half hours." A rather vexed shadow stretched across his forehead, icicles dripping over his eyes. "And you know the craic, there's always a feckin' screaming child in economy."

Unable to contain the horror such a prospect induced in me, I shuddered. "Don't even talk." If you hadn't already gathered as much, my maternal instincts are... lacking. In fact, I would say they're fairly non-existent.

"Well, fair is fair. You're letting me stay in your gaff."

"I hope Freddie's paying."

His irises ignited in glee. "All expensed to the company credit card, he can handle it."

"Didn't think the budget stretched that far."

"It'll be too late by the time he gets the bill," Jonathan said, like a naughty schoolboy. For someone who studied finance, he is quite potentially the least fiscally responsible person I have ever encountered. Sometimes, I wonder what sort of debts he'd wrack up if he didn't have my watchful eye hovering over him.

"You're so naughty."

"And you don't love that?"

I feigned a glowering expression. "You have your moments."

Although I'd never admit it to him, I was enveloped by contentment. Consumed by loss, I was hollow in so many ways but slowly I was allowing Jonathan's love to fill me again.

CHAPTER 33

Julia

A shuttle bus had mercifully appeared within a few minutes and we made it to the cavernous departures hall of Terminal 2 with minimal incident. It was sparsely populated at this time of night so our words echoed eerily through the vast space. Both sets of suitcase wheels trundled over the tiled floor with a constant sound that spoke the promise of adventure familiarly to us.

"Jonathan, can you read? That's the Emirates check-in queue, get out of it!"

"Oh yeah, sorry...d'you know they're like, the most luxurious airline in the world though?" He craned his neck to gaze down the length of the line as if expecting the plane to materialise then and there.

"Yes, but they only fly to Dubai and we're going to Spain so come on," I chastised, grabbing his arm and hauling him towards the Aer Lingus Business check-in.

Once our hold luggage had been checked in, the next hurdle to overcome was security. I made it through without occasioning the dreaded beeping but the same could not be said for Jonathan.

"Right bud, 'fraid we're going to have to frisk you." Jonathan was informed of the fact by a young officer who looked barely older than him. Something in the gleeful quality of his words made it clear this was the first time he had had the pleasure of conducting such an operation. "If you'll just follow me over here."

His wide eyes protruded from their sockets in sheer horror. The last occasion on which I saw him quite so alarmed was when he had to do a rental inspection in Coolock.

"Are you quite sure that's necessary?" asked Jonathan with a pointed sniff. "You do know I'm travelling in business class?"

"Always the posh knobs you have to watch." The officer snickered. Jonthan seethed.

Huffing, he reluctantly permitted himself to be led over to the side where the man proceeded to pat him down rather aggressively.

"Oi, watch!" exclaimed Jonathan. "Do you honestly think I've like... got an AK-47 down my cacks or something?"

He shrugged. "You never know these days. Travelling alone are you?"

"That's my girlfriend, not that it's any of your business," he gestured to where I watched on with an amused expression on my face. The pride in his words did warm my heart though.

"Romantic getaway is it?"

"We are travelling for *business* purposes," he grouchily muttered.

"What do you do?"

"I'm an estate agent." As he had a propensity to, he declared his profession with a vocal flourish.

"Ha, that explains the attitude."

"How dare you!"

"Come on, you know I'm right."

At this, I actually began to wonder if Jonathan was about to combust.

"I know that we're done here!" And with that, he stalked away, leaving the obnoxious officer chortling behind him.

"Prick," he mumbled to me.

"Don't mind him. It's just a power trip you know"

"Bet he's jealous of me because he wishes he got to take you away." His hand found mine as his fingers knotted around my palm.

"Like, he's no oil painting. The tide wouldn't even bring him out!"

"Bet it wouldn't even give him a wave," I said.

The world seemed to shine like polished glass as we wandered hand in hand through the retail area. Airports have always made me happy. Most people detest them for the droves of passengers, disappearing luggage, delays and deceptively pricey duty-free. However, standing there with Jonathan by my side, I watched the planes like elegant doves soar from the runway, framed by the rolling slopes of the Dublin mountains and knew that happiness was firmly within my grasp. It was a strange phenomenon indeed that this purgatory between home and somewhere beyond was exactly where I needed to be at that moment.

I forced Jonathan to suffer my obligatory inspection of WHSmith where I purchased two thriller novels and, while there, was rewarded by the sight of several people purchasing my own books. I used to spend so many nights dreaming that I'd witness such a thing. I'll always be grateful to myself for holding onto the fantasy until it was a fantasy no longer. Jonathan wanted to browse the whiskey collection then so I left him to it and wandered through the makeup stands without any real intentions of buying something. The scores of different shades began to diffuse into one another after a while and I had to exercise caution in finding a match for my porcelain pale complexion. There was a new range of lipsticks in the Clarins section though with a rose pink that seemed like something I would wear. I picked one up for a closer inspection and suddenly felt a pair of hands grab my waist.

"I want to wear your lipstick." It was Jonathan, winking sultrily.

"You sure about that?"

"Obviously."

"Ok then," I said as I removed the lid and smeared the fuchsia tint haphazardly across his lips.

"Julia!" he exclaimed.

"What? You asked for it."

"I wanted to kiss you!"

"Why didn't you just say that then?"

"Now I look like a clown."

"Maybe that's because you are."

He attempted to wipe it off with the back of his hand. It was futile and only succeeded in extending the colouring further up his cheek.

"I'm going to the jax to wash this off," he moaned, stomping out of the shop.

I giggled internally as I paid for the lipstick.

A few minutes later, Jonathan re-emerged from the gents with a clean face. He was smiling again.

"Sorry about that," I said.

"It's alright."

"Just so you know, you suit the pink. Bought it so I can put more on you later," I pouted and stalked ahead, leaving him snickering behind me.

We proceeded to the lounge in order to rectify Jonathan's apparent champagne withdrawals, as evidenced by his increasingly mournful laments of thirst. It would be an interesting (and potentially alarming) statistic if I were to ascertain exactly what percentage of Jonathan's headspace is occupied by champagne related thoughts. All I know is that the number would likely prove impossibly high.

We descended the escalator and traversed the long corridor towards the Airport Lounges, Jonathan now having moved on to deploring the fact that the British Airways lounges in Heathrow were superior to their Aer Lingus counterparts in Dublin. Personally, I found the Terminal 2 Lounge perfectly adequate. The walls were painted an emerald green; the floor was a grey parquet beneath the oak tables and the deep-seated chairs were comfortable. It was well-appointed (I have definitely mastered estate agent speak at this stage so I know that word lacks a particularly specific meaning) with a view across the airport runways, lit now with mathematically arranged edge lighting in the still deepening darkness.

"Look, it's our plane," Jonathan pointed through the glass as we sat watching the luggage being loaded on the hold, meanwhile sipping from two champagne flutes. "A330, usually only go to America so we were lucky to get it."

"So, what's the plan when we get there?" I asked.

"Well, we don't need to start working until Monday. It's up to you I suppose."

A thought struck me then. "Jonathan, I've been meaning to ask you... do you think we could meet up with your mum while we're in Spain? She is working there isn't she?"

Psychological studies have proven that, as humans, we are attracted to people who resemble our parents in some way. Sometimes, it's physical attributes or even personality traits. I have always been rather fascinated by that fact and I must concede that in many cases, I have observed the manifestation of it. Could I be in any way similar to Jonathan's mother? After all, Jonathan *was* reminiscent of my dad to an extent. Blonde, mild mannered, kind hearted and, at times, a bit of a coward.

His face suddenly became drawn. He barely ever spoke about her so I knew that deep down he was probably hurt by his childhood abandonment.

"She sent a card last Christmas from Cape Verde," he sighed heavily. "I don't know for sure but I think she might have left mainland Spain. Anyway, if she was in the villa beside us, I don't know if I'd bother to go and see her. It's not like she's ever cared about me."

I took his hand. "I'm sorry, I shouldn't have mentioned her. I was just being nosey. As always."

He gave me the ghost of a smile. "Don't worry, I understand Julia. But you're the only woman that I want in my life now."

And he was the only person that I could trust.

CHAPTER 34

Julia

Business class was barren. As luck would have it, we were the only people in the cabin. I shouldn't have been surprised; you had to be an exceptionally snobby individual to not cope with economy for two and half hours. Much to Jonathan's delight, we were each served a glass of complimentary Jean Pernet champagne as we settled in our spacious seats (although he did not fail to mention to me that Emirates did Moet Chandon.) Leg room was ample; the seats were fully reclinable with a wide middle arm rest that doubled as a table and there were in-flight entertainment television screens on the back of the seats in front.

Jonathan produced his phone and opened the camera. "Let's take a selfie," he suggested. "Saying as we're Rockstars and all."

"I thought you detested that description?"

"Well, sometimes the truth hurts."

"Alright," I conceded with an eye roll. He wound his arm around my shoulder and pulled me close to him. We took a selfie grinning pathetically that I would later see Jonathan had set as his profile picture on WhatsApp and Facebook. It used to be a photo of him and his Porche, so I was glad to see he at least had his priorities straightened out.

"You know, I used to want to be a pilot," said Jonathan thoughtfully.

"What made you become an estate agent?"

"Don't know really, I knew if I played my cards right the money would be good. Plus, I used to fantasise about driving a Porsche through the gates of some swanky joint and saying to a viewer 'Three mil and it's yours, pal.'"

"That dream *has* come true."

"I suppose." He seemed momentarily pensive. "Maybe I'll be able to work for myself one day. Not have to deal with old Freddie. Anyway, do you still have a bad feeling about... all this?"

I toyed with my manicured nails. "Well, it's just... with Emily suspecting Freddie is involved with the institution somehow and their connection to Spain and then suddenly he decides to sell houses there... it just seems suspicious."

Jonathan sighed. "Look, that's fair. And I really don't feel great about it all either. But loads of Irish people are interested in holiday homes in Spain so there is a genuine market. It could just be coincidence. We have to be vigilant but stay positive, too." He grinned devilishly in an obvious attempt to lift my spirits. "We have an excuse to be all alone for a few weeks. Just focus on that."

He was right. Wasn't he?

No, he wasn't.

My stomach swooped as it always did when the plane departed Irish ground, soaring steadily into the sky. The future was suspended like a feather in the clouds around us, its weightlessness making it seem so certain, so assured. But when all feathers fall, they greet the ground as a gentle teardrop.

CHAPTER 35

Julia

El Paraiso slumbers, contented. Hand in hand with sand where waves spill gently, it is nestled in the wake of watchful hills, their rugged terrain scarred by precipitous paths bleached the colour of milky moonbeams. Encircling the gated community within which this villa lies, a parliament of palm trees seeks longingly a handshake with the fringes of oblivion above, during summer mornings rendered cloudless blue, at twilight that tint of intangibility and in the recesses of night an impenetrable black. Its neighbour is the sea, like the God of the Old Testament, worshipped by so many and feared, too. Unrelentingly, it attacks the sandy shore with malicious whisper, a battle cry understood by all and comprehended by none. Further inland there is the town of La Cala de Mijas. Stereotypically Spanish, sweet sounds of the native tongue contort amongst its winding streets. A calming cacophony echoes from cobbled alleyways, from the wrought iron balconies that protrude barely a foot from the walls of stone, from the veranda hooded cafes where the aromatic arrangement of coffee beans tingles the tip of your nose like woodsmoke. Washing is strung, wall to wall, an asymmetrical bunting marking Mediterranean life in a similar way to the morning markets. Local produce and wares are sold from stalls; forming a kaleidoscope of colour. Fruit and vegetables, hand woven wicker products and the occasional counterfeit designer brand. Oh yes, we've all seen them.

It is amongst this corner of the province of Andalusia that I have spent many joyful times. We rarely came in the heart of summer, favouring the quieter points of the year when not quite such a multitude of tourists flocked to the Costa del Sol. Sometimes, if we found a cheap last-minute flight, we would even secrete ourselves there for a long weekend.

The villa itself is an eclectic mix of contemporary modern. Built in the late 70s, it was bought by my grandparents when my mum was a young child but has been renovated multiple times since. It is a substantial asset, consisting of four generous bedrooms, an open plan kitchen/ dining/living area, games room, private pool and outdoor seating area. The upstairs boasts a wrap-around glass balcony extending from the main bedroom which overlooks the sea, a mere minute's meander from the luscious rear garden. Although it is a private property, it belongs to a managed gated complex, providing housekeeping services as well as access to a gym, spa, golf course and tennis court. Really, it's like owning a hotel suite.

Jonathan and I emerged from the taxi outside El Paraiso shortly after two in the morning. Our flight had experienced no delays and we had landed punctually. As the arrival hall doors of Malaga Airport glided open before us, we were initiated into the quiet magic of a Spanish night. A familiar sense of ease enveloped me like an embrace; due to the reigning of winter, the air was far from the muggy heat associated with the country. It was barely warmer than home actually and I reflected that my purchase of several bikinis had likely been unnecessary. I couldn't bring myself to care though. What attracted me to Spain had never been the endless sunshine but rather the culture and atmosphere that pulsated at its heart.

"My God, Julia, talk about a classy joint!" exclaimed Jonathan excitedly. He was like a child on Christmas morning, inspecting each and every room with the trained estate agent's eye. Jonathan has a few great loves; Champers, luxury airlines, luxury hotels, luxury cars and luxury properties. And me, of course. I, however, am luxury on an entirely different level.

"I trust you're impressed."

"Impressed? Julia, why didn't you tell me about this place before now?" he said, running his fingers reverently along the marble kitchen countertop.

"Have to keep things interesting."

"Well, that's true." For a moment, he was quiet. Interesting was certainly one way to describe our relationship thus far.

I left the kitchen and retraced my steps to where we had discarded the luggage at the front door, more as an occupation to abate the sudden resurgence of grief than anything. Returning to El Paraiso, the backdrop to the sun dappled gaiety of my youth, riled the sadness within me. Each time I rounded a corner or heard the slightest noise, I convinced myself he would appear. That I would hear his laughter, be assuaged in his arms. And suddenly he was there; cooking dinner on the hob, its delectably enticing aroma filling the house. Chasing me into the pool, laughter on his lips and happiness in his eyes. Enfolding me in his arms as the dancing light of the outdoor firepit reflected the joy of our hearts

I could barely believe those days had died forever.

"Jonathan!" I called as I walked back towards the kitchen lugging my case. "Some help please?"

There was no reply.

"Jonathan! Are you messing with me?"

Still, the silence remained, devoid of an answer.

Expelling a deep sigh, I headed for the stairs and trudged upwards, yelling his name as I went. When I arrived on the landing I began craning my head through the door of each room. That was when I found him.

"Making yourself comfortable, are you?" I questioned.

Jonathan was in my bedroom. That said, it had been my parent's bedroom for as long as I could remember but clearly it was ours now. He had propped himself against the headboard and was reclining with a book in his hands. Falling across his forehead, his hair was tousled from the travelling. The pair of navy monogrammed pyjamas had replaced the chinos, shirt and jumper.

"I thought I may as well."

Briefly, I did not reply but entered the room fully and pulled the door shut behind me. I crossed to the vanity table and sat down, crossing my legs and fixing him with a dubious expression. Suddenly, though, something akin to self-consciousness assaulted me.

"So we're taking this room then?"

At the question, he openly laughed. "What was your alternative?"

"There's three other bedrooms."

"And? This is the main."

Swallowing, I shrugged. "Sorry, it's just... new I suppose. This was always my parents'."

There was silence for a moment as he continued to assess me contemplatively. When he spoke, his words were low. "Julia, you don't have to be sorry." The bed emitted only a gentle creak as he rose and came to place his hands on my waist. I stood from the chair and permitted him to hug me. Not feeling anything. Simply... numb.

"Julia, I can tell something's bothering you; what is it?" With an empathetic air, he stroked my cheek. "Tell me."

Although I pleaded that they wouldn't, salty needles began to prick my eyes. "I'm sorry, Watson," I said through the sobs, sinking onto the end of the bed. "But us being here... it just feels like betrayal."

"Betrayal? What do you mean?" He sank down at my side. "What's so wrong about this?"

I shook my head and sighed in frustration. "There's nothing wrong with it, Jonathan but that's just it. It's being back here... without daddy."

His jaw visibly clenched. "Julia..." he began hesitantly. "I know that it's hard. But you're allowed to move on. Don't guilt trip yourself. *Please.*" Reaching up, he brushed at a falling tear. "Your dad would be happy knowing that you're happy. Honestly, he would."

Through the film coating my eyes, I nodded. "He would," I said more confidently than I felt. "He would."

"Moving on isn't forgetting, Julia. It's just committing it to memory."

Stilled by their beauty, the words melted something within me. "Thank you Jonathan... that was lovely."

Suddenly exhausted by the emotion, I pulled on my own silk pyjamas and crept beneath the covers. However, sleep became a petulant child, darting behind corners and secreting itself into any available nook or cranny simply to avoid my possession. To diffuse the frustration, I opened my laptop and wrote for a while, losing myself in the lives of my characters until serenity settled upon me like the balmy night mooring the galaxies of stars to their stations in the velvet of the early morning sky. The insistent clicking of the keys eventually roused Jonathan though and my peace was disturbed.

"You still awake?"

"Can't sleep," I shrugged. "This helps. Anyway, I have my best ideas in the middle of the night."

He shook his head, a curvature springing to his lip. "You're a workaholic, you know."

"Somebody has to make up for you."

"Oi!" With that exclamation, he tugged the laptop from my grasp and began to page up and down through the document. "Anything about me in here?"

I wrenched it back into my arms. "For me to know and you to find out, nosey. If you're good, I *might* let you be the first to read it. Maybe."

More gently this time, he reached across me, saved the document and shut the lid. "You need to sleep, Julia," he said quietly. "You're exhausted." Timidly, he brought a hand out and drew me closer.

I lay snug against him and relaxed my eyes shut. In the last few moments before slumber claimed me, I felt myself almost detach from the present, observe while hovering outside of my own body. A harmonious image. Two figures. A young man and woman. Intimately close, asleep in each other's arms. Safe in their paradise. And I knew one thing for certain. Evil was alive. It was living, it was breathing, it was dormant while awaiting its hour. Slithering silent, creeping closer. Seeking admittance to its home; to the Garden of Eden.

CHAPTER 36

Julia

Awakening the following morning, I experienced that peculiar sensation of rousing and feeling temporarily unsure of where I was. However, as I unpasted my eyelashes from the sleep-flushed skin of my cheeks, a pleasant realisation dawned. Dappled beams of morning light filtered through the Venetian blinds that swayed scarcely discernibly, obscuring the door leading to the balcony overlooking the Mediterranean. The room was light; airy. Marble tiles, floor to ceiling glass doors, walls panelled with wood slats, low divan bed. The Spanish villa straight from the cover of a glossy real estate brochure.

Jonathan was already sitting up and on his phone, frantically firing off emails despite the early hour.

"Morning," he powered the phone off and flung it to the end of the bed. "Clients. Penthouse in Foxrock." This got an eye roll and chagrined expression. "Hard to stick before a morning dose of caffeine."

We went downstairs and sat at the island, sipping coffee. The cupboards were bare as it was months since anyone had been in the house but the bag of coffee beans that permanently resided along with our barista machine was providing our morning sustenance.

"We'll have to go to the supermarket and get a few essentials," I said, setting my cup down with a clink.

"Are you planning on cooking?" Jonathan asked sceptically. "No offence, Julia, you know I trust you with my life and all but I would prefer to keep you out of the kitchen."

Trust me with his life? Unwise, Johnny.

For once, I couldn't argue with him. My culinary abilities consist of the ability to microwave a ready- meal, toast bread, throw together a salad, make tea or coffee and order in a restaurant. But come on, I've survived twenty-one years, haven't I?

"What are restaurants for? Plenty around here." I got up and crossed to the patio doors to take in the view. Outside, a light rain shower had interrupted the radiant sunshine, its residue greeting the ground as doleful droplets dripping from the ferns of the palm trees. The sea shimmered across the beach; a gift wrapped in the haze of distance.

"Suitable for Rockstars like us?"

"You mean satisfactory for toffs like you?"

"Come on, you're equally bad as me," he countered, placing his drained mug in the dishwasher. He appeared to give something a moment's thought. "We're nice toffs though, not pretentious cows like Mr. FFS."

"Whatever helps you sleep at night-"

Just then, my sentence was severed by the soft melodic chime of the front door bell, the sound so unfamiliar I was temporarily stupefied as to its origins.

"Who's that?" questioned Jonathan, ears pricked comically like an over-eager labrador's.

"My Spanish boyfriend." The marble tiles reverberated beneath me, my footsteps a harmonious tune as I crossed into the hallway. "He's here to assess the competition." Rather cheekily, I pulled my face into a clown's mask of teasing, his warm lilt of retaliatory laughter tinkling into the air.

"I meant seriously, who is it?"

"No idea, probably Jose. He's the complex manager. He sometimes calls around whenever we arrive to see if we want anything."

Twisting the key in the lock, I seized the silvered handle and pulled the door open.

And my jaw almost made contact with the ground.

"Anto? Eamon? What on earth are you doing here?" This exclamation was proclaimed rather incredulously as my vision was filled with the unexpected sight of my two colleagues standing motionless on the doorstep. Together, they cut a forlorn image, woebegone expressions frozen in a pitiful poise clearly orchestrated to invite sympathy. They were both laden with luggage; two squat companions in the form of overstuffed wheelie suitcases at their sides and glutted rucksacks forcing their posture into a stoop. Mutually perspiring, a sheen of sweat lacquered their brows and, at least in Eamon's case, had dissolved into droplets that were chasing each other down the slope of his nose. In contrast to the very humidity that occasioned them, it struck me that they bore a humorous resemblance to skiers zipping down a snowy hillside. The silence was broken then as, all reserve of strength expended, the valiant seams of one case forfeited their battle and the contents spilled out into a shallow pool around Anto's ankles with a dull thud.

"How ya." Anto's mumbled greeting fought to be heard beneath its coating of fatigue. "Sorry for the surprise."

"How's it goin', Julia," Eamon managed with a feeble smirk. "Bet you weren't expecting us crowd."

I giggled slightly nervously. "N...no I wasn't. I thought you were supposed to be in Cyprus?"

"Naw," Eamon began as he reached up to wipe his forehead. "Change of plan. FFS decided he needed more bodies out here because apparently Spain's the focus for the minute. He sent us over to help you weans, so he did."

"Oh, right, so..."

"He has to stay in the Dublin office or else he'd have landed as well. God, if eejits were scarce he'd make a dozen, make you want ti' boke, so he would. You want ti' have heard him yesterday, going on like a hand bell about..."

"Look, Julia, I'm in a jocker here. Can we please come in?" pleaded Anto mournfully. He seemed a few seconds away from falling to his knees and straight up begging.

"Yes, of course, come on in," I stepped aside and allowed the two of them to trail through the hallway to the back of the house. "Jonathan's in the kitchen."

"Alright, Jono," said Eamon, depositing his bags in an unceremonious heap in the centre of the floor. "Sorry for barging in like this."

Jonathan's expression was one that lay at some unspecified point between bewilderment, incomprehension and horror. He almost stumbled backwards against the sink as his freshly washed hands dripped dark stains onto his cream slacks.

"Hi, Eamon..." Uncertain, he cast his gaze at me, the question in his eyes instead of on his lips.

"Freddie's change of plan. He wants more bodies to kickstart the office in Marbella. Anto and Eamon just got here," I provided by way of explanation.

"Lads, you look like you've been dragged through a bush backways," Jonathan diagnosed, assessing them with a voyaging glance.

"May as well have been," Anto moaned. "Guess what airline we had the pleasure of?"

Jonathan visibly shuddered. "My condolences."

The four of us settled then on the sofas in the living area attached to the kitchen, Jonathan and I facing Anto and Eamon on the opposite couch.

"Aye, left us outside foundering on the runway for an hour before they even let us on the plane. I was near froze!" Eamon shook his head in confoundment. "And then, after all that, we'd no rental car when we got here."

"Yeah, because that bleedin' toolbox," Anto gestured at Eamon, "booked it from Alicante Airport and not Malaga."

"Jaysus, Eamon, how'd you manage that one," Jonathan cackled in exasperation. "Bit of a difference, no?"

"Website was confusing," he muttered barely comprehensibly. "Clicked the wrong button."

"So then anyway, we managed to get a jam jar, drove to the hotel and long story short, it was complete kipville. Like, absolutely *manky*. Place *stank*. Remember that flat in Finglas last year, Jono? We had to do the inspection after yer wan moved out-"

"Please, please don't remind me. I've still got PTSD over that." Jonathan cringed behind his hand.

"Well, this joint would make that place look like The Westbury," Anto concluded, leaning back in his seat with the triumphant air of one who has just imparted an exceedingly entertaining narrative.

"And there were ants," said Eamon, obviously keen to join the conversation again. "A rake o' them. I reckon they're a bit laid back now on the whole cleanliness side o' things."

"Laid back?" Anto blurted this in a fit of crazed vigour. "They're bloody horizontal!"

"Aye, well, I'd say that's fair enough." Eamon nodded sagely. "But here, weans, we need ti' ask youse a favour."

"Go on..." I started.

"Can we stay here? With you like, in your gaff Julia?" Anto was practically breathless.

Before I could summon the words to reply, Jonathan had blustered: "Hold on a second, how did you even *find* us?"

Eamon threw him an oddly quizzical look, as if it were obvious. "Julia showed us photos of the place. There's not too many El Paraisos about. We just told thon boy, Jose he was called, that we were friends of Julia Joyce and he let us in to the compound."

"That's okay, thought you were stalking us for a minute there," muttered Jonathan gruffly.

"And, weans," Eamon began to laugh at the thought he was forming, "while we're here, we can be your chaperones! Never know what you two'd be up ti' unsupervised!"

He and Anto jibed each other in the ribs, reciprocally pleased with the joke at our expense.

We were silent.

"Of course you can stay," I said evenly when they had recovered from their explosion of merriment, "wouldn't want to feed you to the ants."

"Auch Julia, you're wile good." To reinforce the magnitude of his gratitude, Eamon rose and ensconced me in a tight bear hug, kissing my cheek. "I thought we were homeless for a while there."

Anto attacked Jonathan with a clap on the shoulder. "Nice one, lad."

Jonathan's smile was infirm.

Our guests then announced that, exhausted by their eventful journey, they were going to settle into their rooms and have a few hours rest. Together, they bundled the heap of discarded luggage into their arms and waddled upstairs, various garments absconding from their grasp as they did.

When they were out of earshot Jonathan said quietly; "Darling, do we really have to let them stay? What happened to us having some time alone?"

"They won't be here for the full two weeks. Freddie can't spare them from Dublin for that long," I reassured him with a squeeze on the arm. "They're good fun, we can put up with them fine for a while. And I've booked us dinner out tonight so we'll be away all evening."

"Ohh, date night." He perked up visibly then, grin that of a placated child.

Jonathan duly followed the others upstairs to unpack his own suitcase while I sat at the island and opened my laptop, preparing to write. I thought idly of all the occasions on which I had written here, ever since I adopted the authorial profession in my early teens. El Paraiso itself had been a constant source of inspiration, threading itself through much of my work. From my perch, I had the perfect vantage point of the ocean. Simmering like golden lines of static, the sun's sweet kisses fondled its surface, leaving love marks in their wake. Somewhere far on the horizon line, a ship scudded by. Its shadow lingered, throwing a smoky breath across the blue...

"Anto," hollered Jonathan suddenly. "You left six pairs of your jocks on the doorstep. Come on down and get them, ya Durtbird."

"Ah....lads...Eamon, you go and get them."

"Not a mission am I getting your filthy underpants, Anto. D'you think I'm stupid or something?"

Oh well. What can I say? Dubs and Tyronians.

CHAPTER 37

Julia

That afternoon, we left Anto and Eamon to sleep off the travelling and made our way into La Cala to familiarise Jonathan with the area. Strolling hand in hand out of the gated complex and making our way towards the town centre to collect the rental car I had arranged, the temperature was elevated slightly and the persistent purr of a sea breeze catcalled around us. It sent my linen skirt billowing around my legs, fanning out in an elegant pirouette when buoyed by the pleasant gust of heat. So why then, was a chill seeping through me?

Suddenly, I stopped short in the middle of the footpath. The hairs on the back of my neck were erect. Soldiers on guard.

"Jonathan, do you feel that?" I said, panic edging into my voice.

"Feel what?" His brow crinkled in confusion, head darting from left to right as he took in the deserted street. In the distance, someone shouted in Spanish, sounding suspiciously like a curse. A door slammed a few yards down the cobbles. A cat slunk out from behind a Cypress tree, twitching its whiskers and eyeing us with venom.

"It's like... we're being watched."

"Julia," he grasped my hand tighter. "I know it's hard after everything you've been through but you can relax now. You're safe." He smiled kindly. "You're with me."

I attempted a nod. But sharp swallow rippling wavelike through my throat was perceptible.

"Darling, I can't stand to see you upset. It hurts me." Tapping his chest, he cupped my face in his hand, his finger leaving an imprint on my skin. "But I promise you you're safe."

"Okay," I murmured. "I'm sorry for worrying you, Jonathan."

"Julia, it's fine. If you're worried, you tell me."

Trying to distract myself, I pointed out various establishments that were traditional haunts of ours to Jonathan, ranging from restaurants, bars and shops. I left him outside while I entered an understated, traditionally Spanish shopfront that hosted one of my favourite bakeries in La Cala. The golden aroma of freshly baked bread wafted from the kitchens and their products, the glazed cakes and pastries lining the display cases, glinted up at me tantalisingly. Selecting a few, I brought them outside to Jonathan. He was preoccupied peering through the window of one of the local estate agencies, commenting derisively on their lack lustre listings and dated office décor. I persuaded him to desist and we made our way down to the wooden boardwalk that serves the focal point of La Cala. It stretches for six kilometres, connecting the town to nearby Cabopino. "I've so many memories here, Jonathan," I mused. "It's... tough being back without daddy." I made a circular motion on the planks with my foot. They emitted a slight groan as I shifted closer to him.

"I know, darling," he placed his hand on the small of my back and pulled me into his arms. "And I can't replace your daddy. Ever. But I promise to always be here for you. For the rest of my life." Then, he dipped his lips to meet mine and kissed me. At that moment, a shaft of sunlight broke through the misty morning, anointing our skin with a radiant glow. Above us, amongst the clouds, swallows caterwauled sweetly. And there beneath the still waterlogged palms, I turned my face towards the light.

CHAPTER 38

Julia

We returned to El Paraiso just as dusk was sweeping the skyline, only to find a note from Anto and Eamon informing us Freddie had sent them to some kind of networking conference in Cadiz. They would probably have to stay the night but would be back in the morning.

"At least he made them go and not us," said Jonathan drily, balling up the note in his fist. "The last time I was at one of those things, it was a *nightmare*. Just an excuse for some passive aggression from drunk competitors. By eight o'clock, everybody was acting like a crowd of drunk uncles at a wedding."

"Well," I swung around on the dressing table stool where I was fixing a pair of pearl earrings into my ears, "aren't you lucky you get a night of passive aggression from me instead?" I gave a simpering smile which he knew, coming from me, lacked all the sweetness of which it was indicative.

He paused in buttoning his crisp dress shirt and kissed the top of my head. "Coming from you, it's just aggressive aggression, Julia."

I intended to take Jonathan to DaBruno's, an Italian restaurant a few miles outside of La Cala as a conclusion to what had been the most idyllic day. We had both altered our attire to evening wear and once ready, called an Uber for the short journey as a means of enabling us to (Jonathan's words, not mine) 'have a few scoops.'

The restaurant was almost deserted and as we meandered down the gentle slope towards the sunken building illuminated by strings of gleaming gold lightbulbs, it seemed this night was fabricated purely for our benefit. Jonathan requested a bottle of Chardonnay before we ordered our meal from the wooden shuttered menus; a delectable three courses of caprese salad drizzled in oil, succulent calzone and moist cheesecake. Gently crooning Spanish music wafted from a corner of the restaurant, almost hypnotic in its soothing quality. It settled over us, a silken shroud clinging to the gingham clad table-top.

"Cheers," said Jonathan, raising his wine glass. "To our unchaperoned evening."

I touched my own glass to his with a clink. "Thanks to FFS. Maybe he's not as chauvinistic as we thought."

Jonathan speared a piece of mozzarella with his fork, exerting just a little more force than was strictly necessary. "Wouldn't go that far. Anyway, last time, Eamon had conked out halfway through the first keynote speech. He won't be suffering."

To our left, the neighbouring table was filled as a couple sat down, effusing rapidly in the native tongue. "D'you speak any Spanish?" I questioned him.

"Not that much, did German at school. But I do know a bit," He leant forward and brushed my cheek with his thumb. "Preciosa."

Our mains arrived and we tucked in ravenously. We spent the next hour or two simply talking; what I love most about Jonathan is his ability to discuss any topic. His conversation is intelligent, articulate and insightful and although the common-sense levels sometimes reside at zero, tackling anything from literature to politics is easy with him. I was barely conscious of his hailing the waiter for another bottle of wine (succeeded by yet another) and before long I suddenly began to feel rather...relaxed.

"God, I'm exhausted," admitted Jonathan, downing the last slug of his wine.

"I wonder why." Upon the table, the three empty bottles evidenced our overindulgence. I was far from intoxicated but maybe just a *little* tipsy. "Come on, we'd better go."

Arriving home, we crashed through the door in a hysterical heap, mirth falling from our lips like soft raindrops. After a little effort, I succeeded in dissuading Jonathan from going midnight skinny dipping in the pool (it wouldn't have been the first time someone had, let's just say El Paraiso has witnessed the occasional exuberant party) but I didn't want to risk a contretemps to his career should his antics result in some unwanted neighbourly attention.

"Johnny, I think I'm a little bit drunk," I mumbled as we eventually reached the landing after a rather perilous ascension of the stairs.

"Well," stumbling slightly, he reached out for the landing wall and plastered himself against it. "We did have rather a lot of wi-"

Then came the crash.

It resounded through the villa, the terminating thump of a drum. The indisputable sound of shattering glass.

"What the hell was that?" Jonathan cried. We leapt apart, electrocuted by undulated terror.

"Th... that sounded... Jonathan, I think that was a window smashing." My voice was like saturated tissue paper. Air fought to coax itself past my windpipe and into my lungs. The diaphanous mist that had enshrouded us fell away.

"And that would insinuate... a person smashing the window in?" Jonathan asked.

"Yes, it would." I gulped. "Jonathan, listen to me now. Stay very still and keep your voice down. We can't let whoever it is know exactly where we are."

Possibilities crowded my brain. Few of them positive. Someone was breaking into El Paraiso. Was it a random burglary? Or was it something more sinister? Something connected to my dad's death? To the agency? To *the institution*? No, no, it couldn't be.

Footsteps came from downstairs. There was someone in the kitchen.

"Julia, should we lock ourselves in the bedroom? They're going to find us!"

“That’s not a good idea. We shouldn’t back ourselves into a corner Jonathan.”

“But Julia...”

“Stay there.” I commanded. “Let me handle this.”

“Julia, you are *not* going downstairs. They could... they might...”

I paid no heed but tiptoed across the landing to the gold framed picture hanging on the back wall. It was an artist’s impression of El Paraiso, dated from when it had first been built and etched in aqueous watercolour. Sliding the pad of my finger into an indentation in the side of the frame, I tugged it forward and it swung away from the wall to reveal the safe concealed behind it. I punched in the code. It opened. I slid my hand into the far recesses and emerged with the object I had been seeking. The gun.

Jonathan’s jaw parted. “Oh my God...Julia...what?”

Gripping the handle securely in my palm, it caught the light and glinted. An elegant, sleek pistol. Outwardly, it appeared petite, insignificant, decorative. Harmless. It wasn’t harmless. One pull of the trigger and it could change your world. I cocked it.

“Stay behind me” I instructed Jonathan. “And follow.”

He gulped and gave a faint nod.

Cautiously, I began to make my way downstairs, the gun proffered at arm’s length before me. The ground floor was in near darkness, brightened only by two small lamps situated on the sideboard in the hall. I reached the foot of the steps and continued in the direction of the kitchen, from where the sounds of someone’s intrusion still emanated. Stopping short in front of the double doors that led out of the entrance way, I listened intently. Were they searching the cupboards? Lying in wait? Why hadn’t they emerged from the kitchen? Jonathan’s breath was coming in ragged gasps, caressing the nape of my neck.

“What if they’re armed too Julia? His voice trembled violently.

"We have the element of surprise," I whispered more confidently than I felt. I wasn't sure whether I was attempting to convince him or me.

Before I could persuade myself otherwise, I pushed open the doors and emerged into the kitchen. As I switched on the fluorescent lights, I revealed the product of nightmares. A solitary figure, crouched behind the island in a futile attempt to conceal itself.

In that moment, the rotation of the world seemed to simultaneously speed up and cease entirely. An anonymous beast roared in my ears. My vision tunnelled. Nothing existed other than me and whoever lay behind the ghoulish white mask and black tracksuit. A person. In my kitchen. I supposed from their build that they were male.

"Put your hands up where I can see them!" I screeched. My words were demonic. Much to my intense relief, the absence of a weapon was revealed and without complaint, the man stretched his hands high above his head. Some of the all -consuming terror seeped from my skin. The adrenalin subsided.

"Take. It. Off."

"Your boyfriend on board with that?" The words were a snarl laced with condescension in heavily accented yet perfect English. A local. Who had obviously forgotten that he was against an armed opponent.

I was really not in the mood to tolerate innuendo from an intruder in my house in the middle of the night. Should he require a reminder, I stepped closer and brandished the gun mere inches from his throat.

"Who are you and more importantly, WHAT THE HELL ARE YOU DOING ON MY PROPERTY?" His cool resolve faltered. I could see it. When I am supplied with sufficient provocation, no one toys with me. And I mean, *no one*.

"Hey, hey. Just put the gun down senorita." Even when masked by the disconcerting white plastic, the sleazy charm greased his words to a level that was nothing but sickening. Reminiscent, actually, of my boss. Well, that was nothing beyond my capabilities.

"Don't you dare call me Senorita." Each syllable was an icicle. It brought me intense pleasure to see the gulp that rattled his Adam's Apple like a tennis ball in his throat. "Now, we have two options here. Either, I call the police immediately or you remove the mask and start talking. About what exactly your deal is."

"What she said!" echoed Jonathan vehemently. His voice was croaky. Whether from terror or lack of use I wasn't quite aware. I love him dearly but as it transpires, he can be a bit of a wimp on occasion.

"Alright, alright, alright," the intruder began. "Take a chill pill, Blondie. It's not like I'm trying to murder you in your bed."

"Oh, I do apologise," I said in faux contrition. "There was only an uninvited masked man in my kitchen at one in the morning but I was *so* silly to assume he meant me harm."

Suddenly, Jonathan's larynx was ignited. "You mess with my girlfriend and you are going to *pay*, buddy. Do you hear me?" He jabbed a finger at the still concealed face and squared his shoulders in a way that evidenced just how nicely he can fill that suit jacket. For all that he can be a coward, I am confident in the knowledge that when it counts, he would never allow me to come to harm.

"Because take it from me, she is a bloody demon." Despite the situation, Jonathan flashed me that glance of pure pride that told me all I needed to know.

The man snorted. "You let that little thing scare you?" Misogynism oozed from his every pore. Then something happened that completely deprived me of breath. Jonathan, in one fluid motion that was measured, controlled and aware of its intentions, ripped the pathetic covering from his face and drove his fist into the smug smirk illuminating the smarmy features. With a crunch.

CHAPTER 39

Julia

There was blood quite literally everywhere. Massacres have seen less burgundy liquid than the copious quantities that were spouting like an elegant fountain from the nasal passage of the man before us. After the iteration of numerous curses and instructing Jonathan to perform an impossible anatomical act on himself, he succeeded in sufficiently stemming the flow enough to remove the stained sleeve of his tracksuit from his face.

"Any more funny business and you, mate, and this fella," Jonathan shook his fist, "will be going in for Round Two."

"And don't forget about this either." I ran my forefinger swiftly over the trigger of the pistol to once again highlight its presence.

"You people are sick."

"Says the guy who goes breaking into villas in the small hours of the morning."

"Fine, touché."

Momentarily, a palpable silence hovered. To me, it was unbearable.

"Right, start explaining who you are and why you're here or else I call the police now."

Although it pained me to admit it, involving the police had become a less appealing option. I was fairly confident that the injury Jonathan had just inflicted could be classed as GBH and while the victim may have broken and entered and caused damage to the property, he was unarmed. That could make the self-defence card difficult to play (especially coupled with the fact that I was in possession of a firearm.) Plus, a foreign police force was more likely to sympathise with one of their own than two blow ins like us. It was better to at least attempt to deal with this ourselves.

And honestly? I didn't trust law enforcement of any kind.

"Right, look, I will, but just put the gun down. Please," he added, seemingly as an afterthought brought on by my withering gaze.

"Not a hope in hell-"

"It's alright Jonathan, I know what I'm doing." My fingers brushed his in reassurance.

I complied then and placed the pistol on the cold surface of the tiles at my feet. If he would just start talking...

"Okay, I'm not trying to do anyone any harm." He attempted a grin but it morphed into a leer. Clearly, he held himself in high regard. Tan skin and greasy, inky black curls reaching to his shoulders lent him an appearance many women may have swooned over. Not me, though. I can detect a sleaze a mile off. Not even Jonathan leaves me completely weak at the knees.

"I was sent here. Just to give you two a bit of a scare. No violence," he shrugged like he had innocently confessed to popping to the shop for a pint of milk.

"Sent here?" In unison, we were incredulous, the words emerging an octave higher than normal.

"By whom?"

"Afraid I can't say."

At that, I lifted the gun. "Talk," I said simply. "Or else."

"A woman." He shrugged again, as if that description didn't apply to fifty percent of the population.

"Well, who the- "Jonathan swore, "was it?"

"My client."

"And your client is?" I prompted; my patience threadbare.

"One of you property people."

"That's real estate professional to you!" Jonathan angled his body into an aggressive stance, waggling his eyebrows.

"Missing the point here, Watson." The breathy whisper did not reach his ears.

"Look, she hired me, alright? Said some of her competitors were in town looking for listings. She wanted me to come here, smash a window, mess a few things about but never anything about hurting anybody. She knows the passcode for the main gates because she has other villas in this complex currently on her books and she told me it. I was to scare you off, apparently. I watched the villa and saw you go out earlier. I was going to do it then but I...had another job to do."

I didn't force the issue. There were some things better left unsaid. The feeling I had had that we were being watched that morning now made sense though. He had been following us.

"So, I had to come back later and I didn't realise you had returned." Something like realisation dawned on his face then and he started to laugh. Nauseatingly. "Oh sorry, man," he said, turning to Jonathan. "Was I interrupting something? You know, she's not bad looking if you're into that amount of brains and feistiness in a female."

That earned him a knee from Jonathan in a place where I suspected it was going to ache considerably.

"Kindly refrain from the nonsense and insults unless you want to regret it." Jonathan's tone was one that dripped disdain and I reflected that I had taught him something at least.

"So, do people hire you for these...services often?" I asked.

"None of your business, lady."

"Remember, we're being transparent here." Intoning my words purposefully, I displayed the pistol yet again.

He sighed, growing tired of the charade. It was old to him now. "I just do as I'm told, alright? I don't ask for any details. She *was* very intense though. A bit of healthy competition, no?" He chortled even though it was not humorous.

"What was her name?" I probed. "Where does she work?"

"Good God, I don't know. I told you; I don't ask for details. She called herself Mrs. J."

I could see Jonathan holding in a snort at the mention of another 'J.' Was she mocking us? It was possible.

"What does she look like?"

"I never met her in person. Discretion is my speciality."

"You better not be lying."

"I'm not!"

"Prove it."

"How am I supposed to do that?" There was fear now brightening his dark eyes.

"She must have paid you. A bank transfer would suffice."

"I get paid in cash. She left it in a secure location. No trail and all that." At the warning furrow of my brow, he hastily added: "I have a text message with your address."

"Show me," I hissed.

He made to lower his hands, likely to take a mobile phone from his pocket, but you could not be too vigilant.

"Jonathan will get it. Which pocket?"

"Top left." His sigh was weary as he raised his hands to their original position.

Placing the gun again almost intimate to his jugular, I watched as

Jonathan retrieved an iPhone from the pocket of his tracksuit bottoms and set it into his hands. The latest model. Criminality was clearly lucrative.

He unlocked the screen and pulled up a chat titled 'Mrs. J'. There was only one message, a simple statement of my Spanish address. "Satisfied now?"

"Yes." I wasn't really; it was far from infallible fact but it would have to do.

"*Please* let me go." It was the politest he had been all night, almost begging.

"Okay. I'll show you out but don't even *think* about coming back. Ever."

Relief visibly doused his bloodied visage as I pushed him forward out of the kitchen and along the hall to the front door, all the while pointing the gun at his back lest he should have any last-minute ideas.

"Goodnight. I take it you can find your own way from here." Before he could reply, I practically shoved him out of the door and into the night, his shadow merging with the countless others it held.

CHAPTER 40

Julia

Jonathan appeared in danger of becoming reacquainted with his dinner when I came back into the kitchen. He had collapsed on the sofa and was bent forwards with his head placed in his hands.

"Please tell me I'm just absolutely wasted and imagined all that."

"I'm afraid not," I replied weakly. Every last inch of stamina I had in reserve had been depleted. If I didn't sit down, my legs were not going to effectively support me any longer.

"What did we witness?" Jonathan's question was seemingly directed at the atmosphere in general.

"I don't know," I said, turning my face towards the ceiling.

Jonathan jumped up then and began pacing up and down restlessly. "What sort of psycho hires a hitman because their business has got a bit of competition? Anyway, there's more than one estate agency around here. Why us?" He was gesticulating violently, his arms a swinging see-waw. The ornaments on the sideboard were in jeopardy. "And how did the female dog even know this is where we were staying?"

"I don't know," I repeated. All I felt at that moment was a rush of pure melancholy. It seemed my life was destined to pertain to nothing other than impending danger. Our day had been perfect and I had finally thought the clouds were clearing. Alas, no. That was too much to hope for.

"We have to ring Featherington-Smythe first thing in the morning and let him know about this. Maybe he'll even have an idea about who she is. Could be some old scorned lover of his," Jonathan suggested.

"Wouldn't narrow it down much." That got a titter in spite of the situation.

"Fair," he conceded.

"But Jonathan," I said, serious again. "How do we know that he isn't involved in it all? There's every possibility he could be Mrs. J!"

"Yeah, it's the drag persona," he winked.

"Jonathan!" I reprimanded him with my eyes.

"Sorry, darling." He shook himself, obviously attempting to invite logical reasoning. "If it was him, it still wouldn't explain how he knew the exact address. You didn't tell him, did you?"

"No of course not but Jonathan... I think it could be something to do with the institution."

If possible, he paled even further.

"You're not serious, Julia?"

"Think about it," I said, rising myself and beginning to pace. "We're in Spain and we know they have a strong hold here. We're fairly certain Featherington-Smythe is in bed with them; they centre a lot of their dealings around real estate. And...and Jonathan- Uncle Nick would know the address."

Those final words were coins falling down a well between us. Jonathan seemed about to protest but thought better of it. We both knew it was as likely as anything. I crumbled then, the emotion spilling over like Guiness from a pint glass.

"Jonathan, he killed my dad and now he's trying to kill me too. Maybe both of us! Oh God, oh God..." I stumbled backwards only to be caught by the couch. Howling, I tried to speak further but was rendered incapable by the knot of nameless feelings germinating inside me.

"Shh...shh... it's ok Julia, it's alright," Jonathan soothed. "Look, this might have nothing to do with any of that. It could just be some jealous woman afraid we're going to start stealing her commissions. You also don't know that Nick killed your dad-"

"But *they* did Jonathan. Those evil shower of pricks did. I just know it. He's a part of that, even if it wasn't him who actually... did it." I swallowed and bit down on a frown.

Jonathan wordlessly drew me still closer to him. The gesture spoke of so many things that could never be said. It stretched on pleasantly for a while before he eventually spoke; "Remember, he was told not to harm us, Julia. So, whoever or whatever is perpetrating this isn't planning on anything physical."

Well, let's just say that he was wrong.

CHAPTER 41

Julia

The following morning, the alcohol of the previous evening eventually caught up with Jonathan and he woke in a self-professed 'jockball.' We had both succumbed to sleep on the sofa, drained by the surprise encounter. Besides that though, going upstairs with a gaping hole left in the window conjured rather unpleasant images in my mind. A repeat of earlier and I was not quite sure I would survive.

Ignoring Jonathan's hungover groans emanating from the couch, I rose (consuming two paracetamol tablets in an effort to abate the undeniable ache in my own head) and placed a call organising for someone to fix the window. Then, I made myself a black coffee which I downed in two gulps, prepared one for Jonathan and shook him gently.

"Up you get, Watson," I ordered firmly but not unkindly.

He murmured something unintelligible.

"Right, okay, time for a bucket of cold water." I had a feeling that would have the desired effect.

"No, no, don't do that, Julia," he cried, sitting bolt upright. "I'm getting up now."

I smirked in spite of myself.

"You know, I had the most frightful nightmare last night, Julia." A faraway look glazed his eyes. "But then some toolbox broke into the villa and you pointed a gun at him and then I even threw a punch and kneed him in the...you know and..."

"Jonathan," I interrupted. "We've been over this. It wasn't a dream. It happened."

"Oh, Christ. So it did." Some of the cobwebs appeared to

disintegrate as he took in the shattered window. “Crap.”

Promptly, the company arrived to perform the emergency window repair and once a fresh pane of glass had been instated, normality began to feel slightly more tangible. We spent the rest of the morning relaxing (or trying to do so and failing miserably) before I grew frustrated and suggested we run an internet search for other properties for sale in the compound to see who the agents were. That, however, proved a fruitless exercise, when we wielded results in the form of at least ten listings all with different companies. Some of those companies in turn had dozens of employees. By the end of it all, my mind was a canvas splattered haphazardly with mugshots of estate agents whom we had trawled through on websites. Jonathan recognised a few from various conferences and networking events but none who he knew well. In short, Mrs. J could have been any of them.

At about midday, Anto and Eamon arrived back at the villa, rather bleary-eyed and marginally dazed. Together, Jonathan and I had made the decision not to inform them of our antics last night. Ignorance is bliss after all. The four of us then spent a few hours outside on the terrace, Eamon regaling us with a tale about some Cork based agents who got into a brawl and a Belfast man who murdered an R.E.M song at karaoke. I managed to do a few hours work, polishing off a solid three chapters, and afterwards turned my attention to my real estate textbook and the topic of valuation methods.

As the youthful age of the day progressed towards the advent of nightfall, my thoughts began to turn to our tasks for tomorrow. Jonathan was being dispatched to a new development of villas still under construction near Seville while I was to meet with an agent in Marbella, who was apparently an old colleague of FFS’s. She was Irish but had been living in Spain for many years. Our boss claimed she would prove a useful contact through whom we could acquire listings but I was beginning to feel distinctly uneasy.

“Watson,” I began as we were lying in bed that night, his head buried in a book and mine in my laptop. “What if your one I have to meet tomorrow is Mrs. J?”

He put his book down and grazed my cheek. "She's trying to help us Julia, if she was that greedy, she wouldn't be meeting with you."

I sighed for what seemed like the millionth time in the last twenty-four hours. A sigh that I dragged from the depths of my being like it was laced with lead. "I know, I'm just thinking of everything."

Soon after, we switched off the light and (after much tossing and turning on my part at least), escaped what had been a hellish day of meandering the labyrinthine warren of questions jostling in our minds.

I awoke to the tranquilising patter of running water. Jonathan was already up and in the shower, leaving an unoccupied space at my side that occasioned a start within me despite the newness of our cohabitation. My weary limbs resisted the instructions I gave them and I flopped back on to the pillows, watching with one eye shut and one open as Jonathan emerged from the en suite with a pristine white towel wrapped around his waist. He began to style his hair with his customary pedantic precision, ordering every follicle to attention. I lay in a pleasant paralysis, smiling to myself at his vanity.

"Very handsome," it was more a thought than something I had intended to verbalise but it escaped as the dawning of consciousness arrived. When he heard, his face illuminated though and he sat down on the edge of the bed, brushing my hair from my face.

"Thanks. Feel any better today?"

"Alright, I suppose. Still worried sick but probably as good as I can be," I replied, burrowing back down into the sheets. "I dreamt we were broken into again."

"Well," standing, he pulled his 'sales suit' jacket from its hanger, "it turns out you're pretty good with a gun and I'm fairly good with a punch so I'd like to see him try." Knotting his tie and securing it at the neck, he stalled before he spoke again. "Julia, why *do* you keep a gun in your safe?"

"Comes in useful." I abandoned the duvet before rising to my feet. "Don't be asking any questions and you'll be told no lies."

He laughed.

But he also fell silent.

Once dressed in a luxuriously cut Chanel suit, I kissed Jonathan goodbye before calling an Uber for myself, Anto and Eamon. They were going to be spending the day in the new office, organising the decoration and commencing interviews for the staff recruitment while I was to meet with FFS's old colleague.

"See you later, Darling. Miss you already," he called as he drove off in the rental car.

When I recall that morning, I ponder how ironic it was that he could soon have been missing me perennially.

CHAPTER 42

Julia

Usually, I possess the ability to ascertain my opinion of someone I meet within the first few seconds of our acquaintance. This time was no exception. The woman perched with feline elegance on the wicker chair across from me exuded an aura of austerity that lent a sour flavour to the very air entering my lungs. Her features were obscured by a pair of excessively large sunglasses that only served to increase her cat-like appearance and her angular cheekbones were framed by a glossy casing of bobbed hair such a shade of black that its origins were revealed as being from a bottle. The vermillion v-necked, figure-hugging dress adorning her slim build uttered a quiet yearning for the days when her age would have rendered the thought of wearing the garment not quite so ridiculous. All this was offset by a Louis Vuitton scarf draped across her shoulders, combatting the slight tendrils of iciness stealing beneath the veranda of the seafront café in which we sat. No detail eluded me though. If you were to inspect that scarf closer, I had a suspicion you would find it a fraud. The irregularity in the intervals between the logos told me some valuable information. That and her shoes. You should always observe a person's shoes. They tell you things there is no other method to discover. Scuff marks from unbridled wear on her Jimmy Choo heels dated their lifespan as stretching to the latter half of a second decade. Bought in the boom. When copious amounts of Irish people found themselves in the fortunate financial position to acquire second homes on foreign shores. Now though, those days a distant remembrance, the footwear completed the picture not of Celtic Tiger but something more akin to Celtic Kitten.

"Julia, isn't it?" The vice like grip in which she secured my palm was utterly devoid of hospitality.

"Yes, a pleasure to meet you Celia," I curved my lips in a well-practised pretence of a smile. Easier for me to apply than lip liner. "Thank you for taking the time to meet with me today."

"That's no issue." A note of sincerity entered her tone. "I would do *anything* for Frederick. He's a most dear old friend."

Also known as an old flame. What is it about greasy hair and pearlescent teeth that has such a profound effect on some woman?

"I hope you don't mind that I've ordered," she supplied with a sniff as I scanned the menu in front of me.

"Not at all." My mind was well and truly made up: I did not like this woman.

"I would highly recommend the Chicken stir-fry. Delectable *and* light on the calories," Celia trilled, gesturing towards her own dish.

Somehow, I doubted this woman would know a calorie if it hopped up and began to waltz on the ceramic.

"Unfortunately, I can't. Nut satay; I'm allergic."

"That's no problem, ma'am. We will remove it for you. I will inform the kitchen." The interruption stemmed from a hovering aproned waiter.

I offered a perfunctory nod of gratitude and assented. Although I had skipped breakfast due to our late lie in and despite the temptation to order a slightly more carbohydrate heavy pasta dish, I was unwilling to afford this woman the satisfaction.

"So, I believe you're on a sabbatical from your medical studies with a sojourn into real estate." It was phrased as an ask but it obviously wasn't. With that one solitary statement, she managed to inject her words with a poison that deprecated any individual except herself who practised either profession. Or maybe it was just directed at me.

"You're well informed."

"My dear, it pays to be well informed in this business. If you wish to survive, that is." She cackled even though it was not humorous and took a sip from the demitasse in front of her, ignoring the still untouched food. Her lipstick imprinted a carmine stain on the rim.

She transpired to be the proprietor of Prestige Realty; an agency based in Marbella who specialise in the Golden Mile. We discussed the dynamics of the Spanish property market for a while then, particularly the Costa Del Sol.

"The sunshine coast is where you want to be, Julia. Think of it as the Saint-Tropez of Spain." She shrugged. "It's high-end real estate central around here. Seven of the most expensive residential streets in the country lie within my remit. Gourmet cuisine, yachting, golf. We have it all."

She halted as the waiter placed a plate in front of me and silence reigned until he moved away.

"And at what price?" I countered. "All that glitters is rarely gold. Especially in the real estate industry. I have enough personal experience in this line of things to know that."

Raising one perfectly crafted eyebrow, she took another sip of coffee. "You're familiar with this area?"

"I assure you that I am. Intimately."

In what manner, I was not certain but I knew that I had rattled her. She contemplated me silently. A player considering their next move on the chessboard.

"You're a feisty one."

"I am."

"You know, it's strange... you're really not what I expected..." Those words were mumbled half to herself.

"I hope I do not disappoint." I lifted a forkful of food to my mouth.

She chortled again. "In many ways, Julia, I have the distinct feeling you and I could get along like a house on fire. If houses on fire weren't an occupational hazard."

At that moment, my phone began to vibrate in my handbag. I unclasped the article, pulled out my mobile and glanced at the screen. Jonathan. What could he want?

"Excuse me, I need to take this."

"Duty calls." She snickered. "It always does." Her eyelashes brushed the tan skin of her cheek in a gesture that held some semblance of a wink. The swish of a curtain at a play's final act.

Feeling uncharacteristically disturbed, I crossed the stretch of road beyond the café's façade to lean on the wooden fence overlooking the marina. I pressed my finger on the green button to answer the call. I watched the gentle lap of the current below. I gazed at a swallow soaring overhead.

I did not see Celia switch the plates.

"Julia, Darling, is that you?" Jonathan's voice crackled like a hearth through the line.

"Yes, Watson, of course it is. What's the matter?" I demanded a tad impatiently.

"Oh, my God, you're never going to believe what's just happened to me. It's been the most frightful morning Julia-"At that point, my ears were assaulted by the sound of static. His words became unintelligible.

"You're breaking up, Jonathan. Is everything alright?"

"So, I went to view the villas and the lead developer met me. I was waiting for him to show me around but then I noticed-" His words were obliterated again.

"Hello?" I said, increasingly concerned.

"- threatened me!" The phrase burst through the haze.

"Who threatened you, Jonathan? What did they say?"

Before he could answer, the line perished completely.

Horror handling my heart in its grasp, I phoned him again. But the call refused to connect.

Swearing beneath my breath, I reluctantly returned to the table and plastered on an ersatz smile once more. "My colleague," I said by way of explanation.

She moved her head in a negligible sign of understanding.

I took a mouthful of stir-fry.

She started to speak again.

And that was when it took hold: the allergic reaction.

I didn't require my medical training to know what was capturing me in its trap. It had happened before; the reaction that, at the age of ten, almost cost me my life and lead to an eventual diagnosis of a nut allergy. That feeling. That indescribable feeling. Impossible to explain to someone who has not experienced it. That realisation. That crushing realisation. A pressing need for water. How it always started. Before my tongue tingled and turned to lead in my mouth. Stars illuminated in the daylight above me. The world tilted on its axis. I gasped desperately but was denied air. My throat was closing. Anaphylaxis. I knew what I needed to do. Before it was too late. Without conscious thought, I swiped the epi-pen from my handbag and, as I had trained for so many times, hitched my skirt aside and drove it hard into my thigh.

CHAPTER 43

Jonathan

The place was a desert. When I say desert, I don't mean undulating sand dunes and cerulean sky. I mean a barren landscape devoid of colour but serrated by chalky roads and interspersed with the occasional tumbleweed. Long story short, you would have to have been out of your box to buy in that place.

I might be an estate agent and therefore it is naturally ingrained in me to showcase properties to their best advantage but this location was challenging even my ample bull crapping abilities. Making my way along the final stretch of road towards the spot where, according to my GPS, the development I was to assess for 'Rockstar suitability' (Freddie's words, not mine) was located, I could practically feel the prospect of a commission from this joint dissipating rapidly. To distract myself, I thought about Julia instead.

Julia... she was made for me. Really, she was. I suppose you could say I almost *crave* her. As completely pathetic as that sounds. It's like...well, it's like the world is a carpark full of Ladas and Julia is that one Porsche sitting in the middle of them. Or every other woman is cheap prosecco and she's champers. That's not a wonderful way to put it but she's just *her*. My Julia. Those last few nights that she had lain in bed beside me, I'd watched her when she was sleeping. I simply absorbed her. The way her chest rose and fell, the way her hair fanned out on the pillow, the way she curled in on herself as she slept. I'm not much taller than Julia but when she lies like that, I can envelop her fully in my arms.

I can at least dare to hope that she will be mine forever.

I can dare to hope that I know all her secrets.

Anyway, I proceeded further along the dirt track willing the journey to end. The whole driving-on-the-other-side-of-the-road thing had taken it out of me a bit and my hopes of making a few spondos were not improving greatly. These villas would need to be something spectacular to tempt clients out into the middle of the Andalusian wilderness, miles from a shop, beach or general civilisation. The city of Seville was apparently less than half an hour's drive away but there was little evidence of such a metropolis. Surveying the road ahead, a sign caught my eye. It was familiar somehow... when it hit me, I experienced that jolt akin to when you miss a step walking downstairs. La Campina. Emblazoned in garish white letters that reflected the early afternoon sunlight. I knew where I'd heard of that place before. When Julia told me about the institution. What worried me more than anything though, was that I was heading in its direction. This couldn't be good.

Sooner than I had expected, the turnoff for the development came upon me. Yet another twisty track that culminated in a site still in the heart of its construction. Towards the rear of the area, there were several villas apparently completed. They seemed rather incongruous to their surroundings, featureless white cubes jarring with the arid backdrop straight from a western. I half expected John Wayne to pull up in a Maserati.

It was eerily silent. As I stepped out of the car and surveyed around me, I was met with nothing. No whirring of pneumatic drills, no thumping of hammers, no building site banter. A void. Had Freddie been on the lash when he decided to send me here? Unsure of what else to do, I strolled tentatively across the dusty space and meandered up and down in front of the line of villas. Stereotypical in style. Little character. I was unimpressed. Yes, they were sleek. Modern. Desirable to a certain type of buyer: a South-Sider with notions probably. What was degrading them significantly though was the location. And it's all about the location in this business. When people imagine a second home in this part of the world, they want access to amenities. The sea on their doorstep. Bars. Restaurants. This place had none of that.

I was jolted from my reverie by the unmistakeable sound of raised voices. Emanating from the villa at the end of the row. Stealing towards the origin of the noise, I began to listen intently.

"How many times do you have to be told? How many?" The deep booming words were irate, fury threading each syllable. "Do you *dare* to disobey me?"

"No...no... I'm sorry...I just..." I could almost see the trembling owner of the high-pitched squeak.

Both accents were Irish. That was strange. Maybe not if they were here for the same purpose as I was. Although the ongoing discourse did not appear indicative of that.

Remaining tight to the front wall of the house, I peered around it to the source of the argument. An Armani suited middle-aged man held a girl by the collar and was shaking her. Roughly.

What was I supposed to do? Run at him and tell him to stop? Stay where I was? The latter was infinitely more appealing if I was honest. I mean, it was hardly my place. Was it? If it had been my Julia he was doing that to, I would have danced on his noggin. I would do *anything* for Julia. But it wasn't her. So, rather embarrassingly, my wimpy ways won out. She did seem terrified though. Not only that; she seemed unwell. Ashen faced, eyes sunken, skeletally thin.

There was no reasonable explanation for this. Or if there was it was alluding me. Could it be something to do with *them*? Whatever it was, I had just walked right into the middle of it.

Crap.

At that moment, the man looked up and saw me. He relinquished his grasp on the girl, her skin a hot coal.

"Go back inside now. We'll discuss this later," he said to her stoically, clearing his throat.

She scarpered. No need to be told twice.

"Sorry about that," he attempted a mirthful noise. "An inside joke is all. I'm Luke, the developer."

I shook his proffered hand. It was ice cold.

"Jonathan Crookshank. Rockstar Real Estate," I managed to introduce myself somehow, all the while swallowing the burgeoning lump in my throat.

"Ah yes. Frederick has told me much about you. A promising young agent by all accounts."

I smiled. Thinly.

He beckoned for me to follow him inside the villa, through an oak front door painted black and into a lofty entrance hall. It was benefitted by an open plan layout that conducted a current of light through the interior. I couldn't hold it any longer. The floodgates opened.

"What was going on back there?" The question popped like a pimple.

For a second, I thought he wasn't going to respond. He just stood there. Staring. Before his eyes narrowed into slits that spat acid at me. A beast preparing to pounce.

"You want to know, do you?"

"Yes. Yes, I do." My hands balled into fists.

"Very well," he stepped closer to me. Again, there was quiet.

Executing a pivot on his heel, he strode down the hall and into the kitchen. I followed. I didn't want to, but I did. Involuntarily.

It happened in a split second. With a swish of his suit jacket, he pulled a knife from a block on the island, slammed me against the wall and placed its tip at my throat.

A vein throbbed in his temple. My heart throbbed in my chest.

"Does this answer your question?"

No words made it past my mouth. My lips flailed ineffectually.

I nodded. He removed the knife and pushed me away from him.

"Now *get out of my sight*!" Not once did he raise his voice and somehow, that rendered it a million times more frightening.

I bolted. Just when my hand was on the door handle, he spoke again.

"And Jonathan?" Perfectly placid, like this was a social call.

"Don't you dare say a word to anyone about this. Not if you don't want a bullet through your girlfriend's pretty little head."

CHAPTER 44

Jonathan

My feet somehow carried me back to the car without me being aware of them doing so. Blood pounded through my veins, a rapid over rocks. Thoughts, barely coherent, battled in my brain for attention like a crowd of riotous rugby spectators. What had just happened to me? I had been held at knife point. Knife point. The words pierced the fabric of my being in the way their literal inaction would have pierced my skin. I wasn't confident of much in that moment, but I knew one thing: I had to get out of there. Posthaste.

Settling on the soothing cream leather, I thrust my foot on the accelerator and sped forwards. I had to execute a rather skilful multiple point turn in order to face the exit and as I did so, I cast my eyes for one final glance at the grotesque, gaudy, gloom-inspiring villas. Their linear structure and mathematical symmetry formed the impression not of sophistication but of something sinister and suspect. Simply sad. Looking at them, I reflected how the front panel of glass that extended along the breadth of the properties' faces seemed to so successfully shield the sun. Block out the light. The very antithesis of its purpose. Or was it? What I noticed then topped everything. Late night intrusions were as negligible as creaking pipes, threats at knife point like jokes in jest. For at the window, surveying the scene before her with an expression equally as desiccated as the surrounding fields, was a female figure. It was challenging indeed from this distance to ascertain the words she was mouthing. Soon, though, they became abundantly clear. "Help me." Horrifying. Yet still not as horrifying as the fact that the person mouthing them was Emily.

Right, if you've lost all respect for me at this stage maybe I shouldn't blame you, but I am going to try and explain. I drove on.

I saw her, I recognised her, I knew it proved undeniably that something was afoot. However, I did nothing. Maybe I am a wimp. My dad tells me all the time that I need to man- up (although he might phrase it differently if you get my drift.) That isn't totally unfair. It's just that developer dude, like, put a knife at my throat. Nobody in their right mind would have stopped the car, got out and kicked up a fuss about what exactly their former colleague was doing trapped quite obviously against their will in a half-finished villa in the middle of nowhere. Would they?

It was a struggle to keep my eyes trained on the road ahead. Fruitlessly, I was trying to form a hypothesis as to what was going on in that estate. Emily. What was she doing there? If I was honest, I had a strong inkling. It was excessive coincidence that she revealed her suspicions about the agency to Julia and then suddenly disappeared. It was totally and completely ludicrous that she mysteriously disappeared and then ended up here. In the middle of Andalusian nowhere. In a development Featherington-Smythe had sent me to. There was no point in denying it anymore. He was involved. Emily knew too much. And so, she had been disposed of. Cancelled out. An unwanted variable.

Still, the car continued to guzzle the tar before me. Droplets of rain began to caress the windscreen, released from the ominously laden clouds hovering overhead. They fell freely. Freely fell. Pieces into place. We could be next. Our boss knows that Julia really shouldn't be reckoned with; she's been with us two months and already made five sales for God's sake. She takes none of his verbal diarrhoea. I know self-praise is no praise but I'm not stupid myself. We're a team, Julia and me. An indestructible team. And we were on to him. I was becoming increasingly afraid though that he was aware of that. Emily was a liability, and, in many ways, we were too.

A bolt of lightning severed the sky. Thunder was a wailing, ailing animal. On the steering wheel, my hands were slicked in sweat. I had to pull over. Finding a lay-by, I halted the vehicle and composed myself. My breaths were ragged. My mind in disarray. My limbs waning in strength. Julia. Julia could be in danger. What if this woman she was meeting was involved in this too? When I considered it, it was highly possible. She *could* be Mrs. J. Who was to say that Mrs.J was only one person though, what if she was the whole lot of the sickos put together? Julia had been right. She always is. Scrambling for my phone, I called her number.

The connection was about as reliable as my profession's honesty. Eventually, her words met my ears. They were weak. Enervated. In that moment, all I wanted was to be with her. Never let her go. For as long as I lived. God, I could have done with a glass of champers just then. I know, I know; priorities and all that.

I started to explain the events of the morning but the line perished. I managed to content myself a little though; at least she had been able to answer.

Mildly placated, I gained the road once more and continued my journey homewards. It stretched on for a while. Uneventful. Until my phone rang again.

CHAPTER 45

Julia

Although my skin was flushed, my core was glacial. The avalanche of adrenalin coursed through my veins with a valiant intensity, battling the swelling of my airways and counteracting the rotating of my consciousness. With the jolt the medication occasioned, I collapsed backwards onto the cushioned wicker bench, my body reeling. Voices bombarded me. At the beginning, they were little more than distant echoes traversing the interminable length of a tunnel. Soon though, as I was propelled back towards reality, the distinct words became fireworks shooting through my brain.

"Are you alright, ma'am? Ma'am?" the question, tempered with compassion, was uttered in Spanish by the head waiter hunkered by my side. His already gnarled forehead was crinkled in concern.

"She's had an allergic reaction. She must have injected herself with an Epi-pen." This was offered by an indeterminate personage amongst the gathering crowd behind the waiter.

Employing herculean effort, I coaxed myself upright into a partially sitting position, mindful to leave my legs stretched out in front of me.

"Was she here with anyone?" A different voice this time. "Do you think she's alright?"

"She doesn't look it," muttered yet another.

"I... I'm fine... thank you," I managed to assert hoarsely, which occasioned a collective sigh of relief from the spectators. How grateful I was for my proficiency in the native language. My eyes darted hurriedly from one side of the huddled pack to the other, barely absorbing any detail except the one that confirmed my greatest fear: Celia was gone.

"Okay, let's give the girl a bit of space," ordered the waiter.

"The woman who was with me, you need to find her. Someone go after her quickly. She did this to me!" I choked out, my heartrate increasing not only from the chemical with which I had injected myself but from undiluted fear.

"What woman?" The lines reappeared on his face. "Ma'am, are you quite sure you're well?"

At that moment, I caught sight of the younger man who had served us. "You... you saw her... didn't you? The woman who was with me?"

"Yes, I did, Ma'am," he answered, words trembling. "Can I please assure you that I specifically informed the kitchen-"

"Don't worry," I interrupted him curtly. "I know that. It was her. She switched the dishes."

If the situation had not been quite so dire, I may have taken a second to appreciate how comically cartoonish the terrified expressions worn by both waiters were.

"I saw her!" hollered someone from the rear of the crush. "She just got into a taxi out front!"

She had gotten away. The news hurtled into me like a bullet train. Suddenly excessively weary, I slumped against the latticed wicker once more.

"Ma'am, are you sure you don't want me to call an ambulance?"

"No, no. Honestly, I'll be fine if I rest for a while," I managed to reassure him, bringing a feeble curvature to my lips.

Obviously realising that I wasn't to be persuaded, he nodded, dispersed the crowd and left me alone.

I had to contact Jonathan and let him know what had happened. He could come and collect me then. The adrenaline was wearing off and I seemed to be returning to myself but I still was far from enamoured by the prospect of a taxi journey with a stranger. I had just been poisoned. As good as, anyway. My reactions were speedy and that is the only reason I was not lying there a cold corpse. The severity of my allergy means death unless action is taken immediately. So in that moment, I was only too aware that someone wanted me silenced.

CHAPTER 46

Jonathan

I almost cracked the car's touchscreen in my haste to answer the call.

"Hello, Darling. Can you hear me any better now?"

"Jonathan?" her tone was strained, gossamer light. Horror accosted me. I could practically see her long eyelashes blinking rapidly, attempting to abate the tears.

"What's the matter, Julia? Are you okay?" Bile rose in my throat. I had just known something heinous was going to happen. She emitted a shaky breath in an attempt to compose herself. "Jonathan, I've had an allergic reaction."

The car swerved abruptly, earning me a cacophony of irate horn honking. "You... you what?"

"I injected myself with the Epi-pen immediately and I'm fine. Almost back to myself but-"

"What? You had to use the Epi-pen, Julia? How did it...what did you...?" I trailed off. "Are you in hospital?" "No, I'm still in the café in Marbella. Jonathan, you're not going to believe this. She switched the plates to poison me. We ordered the same dish and it came with nut satay but I asked the kitchen to remove it from mine. When you rang me, I got up from the table to answer my phone and when my back was turned, she must have passed her plate over to my side."

"Are you absolutely certain, couldn't the kitchen have made a mistake?"

"No," she started, this time the emotion overwhelming her. "You see, whenever I collapsed there was a commotion and she fled the scene in the middle of it all. One of the waiters saw her get into a taxi and be driven off."

I was at a loss for words. All I could muster was a rather plaintive, "Oh, Julia."

"Jonathan, can you come and collect me? I hate asking you but I just don't fancy getting an Uber home after... you know."

"Of course I will, Julia. Why would you hate asking me? I'm on my way back anyway so I'll reroute."

She gave me the name of the café and then seemed to remember.

"You were saying earlier... Jonathan, did something happen to *you* today?" her words were laced with anxiety again.

"Never mind that now, I'll tell you everything later. I promise. You just stay where you are and rest until I get there." I prayed that my instructions were soothing. After what she had endured, I feared tipping her over the edge completely.

Before hanging up, I told her I loved her about a hundred times and, the moment I disconnected, began to bawl pathetically. I cried and cried and cried some more, unable to contain myself. A filmy veil pasted itself across my eyes and rendered focussing on the road even more of an exertion than it had previously been. It was my fault. Due to the fact that she had had to answer my call, that cow got her opportunity. Julia had an intuition and I had not listened to her. Shouldn't I have known by now to trust her intuition? Apparently, I hadn't. And that utter stupidity had almost cost my girlfriend her life.

CHAPTER 47

Julia

I am terribly impatient. It really is a great fault of mine; I'll be the first to admit that. Never, though, had an interlude appeared so incessant. As I sat there, overlooking the iridescent tapestry of sea and sky marred by the yacht masts overlaying it, I was oddly reminded of how I used to feel in school when I'd finished my work and had nothing left to do.

Just when I was beginning to fret Jonathan would never make an appearance, I was rewarded by the glorious sight of him winding his way among the outdoor tables towards me.

"Julia," he gasped, entwining his arms around me and kissing me in a way that was not quite publicly decent. " I swear to good God, I'm never letting you out of my sight again."

"That," I held his shoulders and regarded him at arm's length, "is incredibly possessive, Watson."

He bundled me into his embrace and we remained like that for a minute until one of the watching waiters pointedly cleared his throat. Clearly, I had more than outstayed my welcome.

We gladly made our exit and the short return journey to El Paraiso. It passed in silence, neither of us quite capable of mustering a coherent sentence. The moment the front door slammed in our wake, Jonathan pulled me into his arms and kissed me deeply again. Unwillingly, I squeezed his hand and retracted. "I'm going to have a shower, I feel all sweaty," I admitted.

Hand trembling, I turned on the water and slipped beneath the frigid torrent cascading from the showerhead. It was only then that I permitted the salty droplets to abscond from my eyes, the harsh reality of the day's events to secure me in their grasp and submerge me in the icy lake of realisation. What no one tells you about having an allergic reaction is that it is traumatising. At ten, having it occur for the first time, I hadn't known what was happening to me. I thought I was dying. That sickening sensation of my tongue tingling in my mouth had remained with me ever since. Sometimes, I had nightmares about it. And that nightmare had once more become a reality. My tears merged with the water. They became as one. So similar and so different. One born of evil, the other of innocence. Yet when combined, there was no way to know one from the other. Evil and innocence. Together, co-existing. The lines between them hazy as morning mist.

The temperature gradually increased until it became almost unbearably hot. However, it produced no effect on me. Allowing the water to assault my skin, needles of flame licking every pore. An unforgiving caress.

When I had washed, I emerged from the condensation ridden en-suite with a large fluffy towel clutched around me to combat the sudden chill of the bedroom. Hurriedly, I dried myself and changed into my silk pyjamas, the luxurious fabric whispering against me. I sat on the end of the bed and began to comb out my hair, running the brush through it absentmindedly. A rap on the door startled me.

"Oh, Jonathan. Hi."

He was leaning against the doorframe, hands in pockets, sleeves of his white shirt rolled up to his elbows with top button opened.

"Hi," he said. "I came to check on you."

"That's very sweet," I mumbled quietly. "Do you want to come in?"

Without reply, he crossed to the bed, sat beside me and took my hand in his. "Are you definitely okay, Julia?"

"I am."

"Aren't you supposed to go to hospital after...?"

I blew out a shaky sigh that stuck in my throat, leaving the debris of misery behind. "Well, yes but I caught it early and I'm fully back to normal. There's no need."

"You know, I don't think I've ever been as afraid as when you phoned to tell me... just the thought that anything could have happened to you. I would *never* forgive myself. And... and I feel like it's all my fault because she switched the plates when you were talking to me and-"

"Jonathan, it's not your fault but I am concerned about the villas earlier. Did something happen? You sounded really strange."

I noticed his features falling as he took my hands again. "Do you really want to talk about that tonight, darling?" There was a pleading look in his eyes that begged me to let the subject rest.

"I want to know, Watson."

He confided in me. The whole harrowing tale. My heart sank like a pebble with every detail. I wanted to discuss it, talk it through like we had each new piece of information that had come to light. Formulate a solution. Doing that with him somehow made even the most outlandish occurrences appear rational to some degree. Jonathan though, said we should attempt to forget it temporarily and take at least one night of our time away together to enjoy ourselves. If he didn't want to dwell on the fact he had a knife held at his throat, who was I to blame him?

"Please don't let this ruin tonight, Julia. I promise I'm okay."

I swallowed. Hard. Miraculously, I summoned a nod. But the beginnings of another thought were beginning to blossom in my mind. "Jonathan?"

"Yeah?"

"I think... I think we need to tell Anto and Eamon."

With his front tooth, he bit down on his lower lip, discomfort seeping into his pores. "About... today?"

"Not just today." Placing my hands on my knees, I coaxed myself to stand. “About everything. We start at the very beginning and tell them the truth.”

“Julia...” his words stalled, catching on his tongue and curling it in his mouth. “Is that really a good idea? Plus, it would mean telling them about... your... involvement.” He uttered the word like it were a prohibited curse.

Tentatively, I mused: “I... I think they’ll understand. And... after the break-in and now today, I’m really beginning to fear that someone means business. To *silence* us, Jonathan.” I twisted on the balls of my feet in agitation. “After Emily disappearing like that and then showing up... *there,”* I struggled to form the idea. “We know Rockstar Real Estate and FFS are at the root of everything here.”

Argument delivered, I plopped down on the bed again. “That means this affects them too. They deserve to know.”

Still appearing relatively unconvinced, he nonetheless agreed with a debilitated: “Okay...”

Smiling, I pecked him quickly on the lips before he could say anything else. “Thank you Johnny. I know you always understand.”

Whether to hide anxiety, regret at my decision or a flirtation of both I was not aware but he cast his eyes downwards. He exuded an agitated energy that betrayed how truly disconcerted by the day’s happenings he was.

“Come on,” he suggested eventually. “We’d better go down; the boys will be back soon.”

And, as if they had read his mind, the doorbell bleated below us.

CHAPTER 48

Jonathan

Whenever Julia went upstairs to shower, I decided I had to call Freddie. I debated whether or not to tell him about what had happened in the development but in the end reached the conclusion that it was best to omit that section of events. Luke's parting threat was still ringing in my ears. What I did plan to tell him though, was that Julia had an allergic reaction. As Julia was often keen to remind me, we didn't know if we could trust him. In fact, it was quite likely that we couldn't. It would be interesting to gauge how he took it.

"How ya, Jono," greeted the unctuous tones of my boss. "Story?"

"Hello Mr. Featherington-Smythe, sorry to disturb you but there's something I have to tell you-" Not surprisingly, he was barely listening.

"How's your mott? Sure there's loads of work going on over there, Romeo. Just remember I am paying you a wage. A *very* substantial wage." He cackled at himself. "Oh, and I hear you got a few surprise visitors to join the party as well."

"Look, Sir-"

"How did it go today with Luke? Cracking joint, bit far inland maybe but the right client and we're talking-"

"Julia had an allergic reaction!" I blurted abruptly. "She had to inject herself with an epi-pen. She could have *died*. It was that woman you sent her to meet, whatever the hell her name was. They ordered the same dish but obviously Julia's was supposed to be nut free. That woman swapped the plates and Julia got the one with nut satay and..."

There was a deadpan silence.

"What?"

"You heard me."

"Is she alright? Was it anaphylaxis? Is she there? Can I speak to her?" For once, our glorious leader had bona fide disquiet in his words. Miracles never cease as they say.

"She's in the shower but yes; she's fine," I said coldly.

"Well, that's... that's good. I mean to say... Julia's a lovely girl. I have a lot of respect for her."

Respect? Freddie actually respected someone without a Y chromosome?

"How well do you know that woman you sent her to meet?" My demand was firm. I was learning to stand up for myself. And my girlfriend.

When he spoke, his words were stilted. "Well, Celia is an old friend and colleague. I know her intimately and she would never do something like that... I... I'm sure of it. How do you know it wasn't an accident?"

He knew her intimately. Fecking Durtbird.

"She had been eating the meal and nothing happened but then she got up to answer a phone call, came back and had a reaction. Your Celia clearly switched the plates. Plus, she hightailed it out of there when Julia got ill." Threadbare was my patience. To hell with the obnoxious twat.

He did not reply. Momentarily, I thought he had hung up.

"I really am glad she's okay you know," he said surprisingly humanly.

"Yeah, well, it was a close call. I could have lost her today." There was little I could do to prevent the crack in my voice. "I need to go now. I want to spend some time with Julia."

"Jonathan?"

"Yeah?"

"You're a very lucky young man."

"What do you mean?" I asked.

"Julia is a special girl. You couldn't do any better. Always remember that." He cleared his throat. Was Freddie actually getting emotional? "And...and promise me that you'll take care of her. She'd hate me saying that, you know how she is, but... just... just... be very grateful that you have her."

With that, he terminated the conversation. I slowly lowered the phone from my ear and assessed it suspiciously. Frederick Featherington-Smythe, the world's smarmiest slimiest sleaze (Julia's description) had been... nice to me. About Julia. Affectionate, even. It did prove one thing: he hadn't been responsible for her reaction. However he was involved in this whole sorry mess, he didn't mean Julia harm. I was sure of that. Why though? He must have been lusting after her, I decided. Not that I could judge him for that exactly but, like, she's *my* girlfriend so I'm allowed to. He's not. I was puzzled though. Julia wasn't his type; he went after bimbos. Women who lack an appropriate amount of clothing and/or brain cells. Not strong, intelligent women. Anyway, if he so much as laid a finger on my little angel, he could look forward to a trip to the Dublin Mountains in the back of a transit van with a few sales boards in tow so that I could batter the bleedin' head off him.

The next problem I faced was telling Julia about what I witnessed at the villas. I wanted to be truthful with her but I would have to curate the tale in a way that didn't make me look like the big girl's blouse I was.

Yeah, I know. Quite the task.

When I went upstairs to check on her and saw her sitting there, uncharacteristically glum, my heart almost bled. Julia hates to be pitied but... well, she was deserving of it. She'd never admit it (probably not even to herself) but she'd been *struggling* recently and I think that's partially why I was so shocked when she suggested we impart knowledge of the recent goings on to Anto and Eamon. And, I have to admit, a little uncomfortable. They're sound lads, don't get me wrong. I trust them well enough but.... I don't know really, it just felt secure keeping it between us. Like if we secreted it from the outside world, nothing was real somehow. It helped me to detach from it, I suppose.

Julia went to sit down in the front living room while I answered the door to our colleagues, fresh from a day of overseeing operations in the new Marbella branch of Rockstar Real Estate. "Any craic, Jono?" Eamon questioned as he barged past me into the kitchen. "I'm starved so I am." Without seeking permission, he threw open the fridge with a flourish and began feasting ravenously on the cut of Spanish ham Julia had purchased the previous day. Anto collapsed into the embrace of a high leather stool and started to knead his temples, as if the vigour would erode his frustration. "Christ, I think I need to go on the lash," he declared. "We had the plumber in the office sorting the jax and he just packs up at two in the afternoon and says he's going for a siesta!"

"Aye, I says to him, 'Where do you think you're going boy?' and the auld fecker just looked at me and says 'Mañana, mañana!'" Eamon visibly ground his teeth together. "The cheek o' him!"

"Mañana, me hole," Anto grumbled.

"The eejit didn't even do the job properly either. As soon as he left the bloody thing leaked. Telling yi', the last time I saw that much water I was about Fermanagh!"

For a moment there was silence, as the two of them shook their heads in united frustration. It was only when Anto looked up and observed the glum cast still clinging to my features that he spoke seriously: "Jono? Why do you look more depressed than a Man United fan?"

If the circumstances had been ordinary, I would have laughed.

But the circumstances were not ordinary.

"Lads, Julia and I need to have a chat with you. Some things happened today... it's a really long story but you have to hear it. Julia could have died... it's been really stressful," the feeble explanation tumbled from my lips, broken and incoherent. I gripped the edge of the island, trying to compose myself even marginally.

"Julia could have *died*?" repeated Eamon, swallowing the piece of ham abruptly. "What do you mean, Jono? Is she alright?" His brow crinkled, forming parenthetical curves around his eyes.

"Yeah, yeah, she's alright now but... feck, I think I've had better craic telling clients a sale fell through," I moaned. "Today's just been... crap."

"Well, can we see her?" Anto jumped up from his seat as though he had been electrocuted. "Where is she?"

"She's waiting on you in the living room," I proceeded to usher them into the more formal reception area, their posture indicative of prisoners being brought to trial.

"Julia!" exclaimed Eamon, practically tumbling on top of her. "Auch, wee pet, what happened ti' yi?"

"Allergic reaction," mumbled Julia into the fabric of Eamon's blazer that was tenderly suffocating her. "I'm okay."

Anto shoved Eamon aside then and hugged her too, "Don't scare us like that again, Julia," he chastised fondly, kissing her forehead. "Jono had us thinking you were a near goner for a second there."

"You blokes done snogging my girlfriend?" I said good humouredly in an attempt to lighten the mood that fell rather flat as I sat beside her on the mint green circular love seat. Anto and Eamon took the vacant sofa, the latter toying distractedly with the tassels on a scatter cushion.

An awkward silence descended over us then, stealing beneath our skin and writhing uncomfortably. It gave my gut an excuse to somersault in my abdomen, flip-flopping so violently I thought the enzymes in my stomach were having a tennis match.

"So, what was it you wanted to tell us weans?" Eamon's tone was dressed in a casual costume but the clothing was tattered, exposing the anxiety beneath.

Julia sat forward, considering her reply carefully. "It's a long story... and one that requires some Dutch courage. Johnny, there's a Rioja in the wine fridge, would you get it please?"

When I returned, the bottle of burgundy liquid clutched under my arm, Julia had produced four bulbous crystal glasses from a corner cupboard and I deposited a generous serving in each.

"En vino veritas," proclaimed Julia, clinking her glass against mine. "The only way."

CHAPTER 49

Julia

We began at the beginning, succeeding in imparting our story fairly chronologically. Jonathan and I alternated the narrative between us and in the periods we weren't speaking, sipped satiating drags of the sweetly spiced Rioja. When I reached the section of the tale that denoted my involvement, the amazement and shock on our colleagues' faces definitely multiplied but to my relief, they did not appear completely horrified. Conclusion reached, everyone fell momentarily silent.

"Well, my God," said Eamon, fracturing the stillness. "I knew I should never have left the Gortin Glen Property Gurus. Wouldn't get thon there, so you wouldn't."

"Jaysus," concurred Anto, draining his glass and gazing at it with a quizzical expression, as if expecting it to magically replenish. "But sure, we always knew FFS was as crooked as a ram's horn."

"I think this lot are more crooked than the roads in Tyrone," bemoaned Eamon, half to his remaining serving of alcohol and half to the room at large.

"What are we like," Jonathan snorted helplessly. "Working for the most corrupt business in Ireland."

Eamon wrung his hands together. "Aye, well, when I was working in Tyrone, we had this competitor. He'd have been from the Sperrin Sales Specialists, so he was. Wile jealous. Anyway, I was trying ti' sell this house out in the middle o' the country and there was this big farm right behind it. Kept spreading manure every time I brought a client out and I got sick o' it so I went to the farmer and told him there was to be no more manure when I was doing my viewings. But as it turned out, this competitor o' ours was paying the farmer to spread the stuff every time I came out. Just to put the clients off so they'd go ti him instead!"

"Have to hand it to him, that was a *smart* plan," marvelled Anto.

"Ehh-" interjected Jonathan. "Was there a point to all that Eamon?"

"Aye, I'm just saying like, yi' can't let your enemies get ti' yi'."

"I still can't believe what you saw today," I said, turning to Jonathan in an effort to put the conversation back on track. "The abuse that those girls must have been through. It's sick."

"It is," he mumbled, melancholic in demeanour. "Poor Emily, she doesn't deserve this. Not that anyone does."

"But what are supposed to do?" Anto was now slumped sideways, in a universal gesture of submission to something he could not control.

"It's Freddie!" Eamon soberly declared. "That blade's rotten to the core."

"I think we can all agree there." I pursed my lips as I swirled the liquid in my glass and took the final gulp, enjoying the sting of the alcohol on the back of my throat.

Jonathan made an admission then: "Meant to say, I rang him earlier."

Surprised, I asked: "Why?"

"I didn't tell him about what happened to me obviously but I did tell him about your reaction. Julia, he was concerned. Like, genuinely worried about you. He didn't have anything to do with that at least. I know it."

"Well, maybe not personally but all of this is connected. Mrs. J, Celia, Luke, they're all involved with the institution in some way. They want us to back off. More than back off; they want me dead. My dad was killed because he knew too much. Lorraine was killed because she knew too much. Emily was captured and brought out here *because she knew too much.* Whatever we do from now on, Jonathan, we have to be extremely vigilant. Let them *think* they've scared us off. If we don't, we could be in serious danger."

"God but it all makes you want to go on the pints, doesn't it?" said Anto, tipping his head backwards.

"What about Celia? If she really is an estate agent, one of you might know her," I said to the three of them.

"Never heard the name but it's worth a try." Jonathan fished his phone from his pocket and opened the search engine. "Where did you say she worked?"

"Prestige Realty in Marbella, apparently."

The movement of his fingers on the letters emitted a harmonious click, forming the phrase 'Celia Prestige Realty' in the search bar. He pressed enter.

And his faced morphed into an expression so wholly unique to anything I have ever witnessed, it would be unreliable to even attempt a description of it.

"Julia," he said, breath coming in short gasps as he placed the phone into my hands. "I do know her."

I accepted the device and studied the headshot image on the screen. Celia. My would-be assailant. It was then he proclaimed those three earth shattering words.

"She's my mother."

CHAPTER 50

Julia

Jonathan's *mother*.

My boyfriend's mother (who I've never met, by the way) tried to kill me.

And very nearly succeeded.

"I'm so sorry, Julia." The words came, unobtrusive as his tread, as he slid the glass doors open and passed from the bedroom onto the balcony. A few hours had been and gone since his revelation, deepest throes of darkness circumscribing the palm trees' fronds, faltering in exuberant salutation of the celestial granules scattered like glitter upon velvet. They were every shape, every pattern, every dimension. Some spiralled. Some waltzed lethargically in undefined motion. Some were harried commuters who paid perfunctory visits to our eyes.

Resolute, my gaze was trained on the abyss before me. This tenuous hour, where sea and sky ruminated, no clear definition between them. The small firepit that denoted the centre of the outside space had been stoked earlier, a few tentative flames cutting the night. They were diminished now; petered out. The only light the trifling glint provided when the sporadic bursts of moonshine caught my sclera. Appearing and disappearing, synonymising the tides.

He laid his hands on the balcony's glass surround and was quiet.

"It's not your fault."

The quietude relapsed. It persisted, apparently perpetual. It struck me that we were as strangers then, unapprised of the other's thoughts. Considering carefully but only within the confines of our own consciousness. Little to guide us in how to approach our next words. Both fearing what emotion we would disturb in the other.

“Did you ever resent her? Growing up, I mean.” I forced the question from my mouth, the syllables unwilling to come of their own accord.

Again, he was quiet and I felt sure he wasn’t going to respond.

“Yes,” he said eventually with conviction. “Yes, I did. More than you can ever imagine.”

Again, silence relapsed.

“Sit down.” His imperative startled me, causing an involuntary ruction in my staring match with oblivion as I finally turned to face him. He had perched lightly on the outdoor sofa, his hand patting the space at his side in unspoken invitation.

I complied, although harbouring the foreign emotion of discomfort in his presence.

“I used to fool myself,” he shook his head sadly, the memory clearly paining him. “That she was just... away temporarily. That she would come *home*. Because she loved me really, didn’t she?” This was addressed to himself, or at least the secondary voice within him. The voice that lies within us all; to taunt, to guide, to punish. I could see the years peeling back then, layers of an onion, Jonathan returning to his childhood a reluctant visitor.

“Every birthday, every Christmas, every *bloody* occasion.” The gasp he emitted was a mating of misconstrued mirth and unspeakable pain. “I thought she’d come. But she never did.” His voice fractured, slicing his sentence. In that moment, as he looked at me, I saw not the young man I fell in love with but the child. Languidly, a dainty curl had fallen onto his forehead, escaping the perfectly styled blonde waves. An exception to the rule. He was again a little boy without his mother.

And strangely, I loved him still.

“You know,” he began again, turning his face to the stars. “She only ever bought me one thing, I think it was for my first birthday. A teddy bear. Mr. Snuggles I called him, still have him now." We both tittered then, a sound of contrast. "And Mr. Snuggles and I, we were *inseparable*. All those times when she didn't show, I'd hold him tight and tell him it was okay. That... that..." I grasped his hand. As tight as I could muster. "That mammy was coming home."

"Oh, Watson..." I was unable to speak.

"Julia?"

"Yes?"

"You asked me why I became an estate agent. And... and I said it was for the money, the glamour," he paused again, preparing himself to continue. "But it wasn't. It was because.... well, it was because I wanted to bring people home. Because my mum," he choked a final time. "I never managed to bring her home."

Voice at the peak of weakness, he said: "And then, after all that, it turns out she's a fecking estate agent herself." The laugh was wry and he seemed to consider the fact. "I knew she owned a business but I never knew what kind. Honestly, I didn't, Julia. You have to believe me."

"I do believe you Watson." My voice was tender, soothing. For once, you might say.

"I don't know why she'd try to kill you Julia. She wouldn't even know I'm dating you... and... and now she might be involved in all this too and I..." At this, the watershed collapsed. In a gesture of pure affection, I cradled him in my arms.

"Watson," I mumbled into his hair, "It's alright darling, fall apart if you need too. I'm here."

"Julia?" he questioned again when he had recovered slightly. "Do you think... do you think sometimes that it's.... that it's not that people are bad... it's just that they.... make bad choices?"

"I don't think it, Jonathan," I whispered. "I *know* it. I know it *all* too well. We're humans and so we're flawed. All flawed children of Eve."

He nodded, oddly contented by my assertion. And then, a minimal margin above a whisper, he said something I will never quite forget: "It's just, no matter how old they are, I suppose everyone still wants their mum."

An assault to the stillness I murmured: "Or their dad."

It was his turn to take my hand. "Or their dad."

I reclined in my seat so that the terrestrial tapestry could be appreciated fully. "As cliched as it is," I said, allowing myself to be held in Jonathan's arms, "I like to think he's the brightest one up there. Looking down."

"He is, Julia." Gently, he cupped my chin in his hand, insisting I meet his eyes. "And he is *so* proud of you. Just the same way I am."

I nodded contemplatively. "But it's just hit me," I cast around wildly for the words. "He'll never see me graduate or... or publish my next book...and that *hurts* Jonathan. It hurts like *nothing* ever has."

I came undone then in his embrace. But as much as the emotion overwhelmed me, I trusted to something I never had before. That I probably should have learned long ago: sometimes, the strongest thing to do is to allow yourself to be vulnerable.

"But, Julia," he murmured. "You'll *always* have me. I promise."

Peculiarly giddy, an explosion burst from my lips. "We'll have each other."

He reached out to fondle my hair, running it between his finger and thumb in that way I knew contented him. A little like a child with his favourite toy. "Till death do us part," he murmured.

"No," I shook my head vigorously. "No. No, because if you love someone enough, not even death can break you apart."

I know this to be true. You see, the journey of life is long. It is arduous. Occasionally, it will take more than it gives and maybe, just maybe, give more than it takes. We mourn the past as we anticipate the future and attempt to enjoy what lies between. And in travelling this journey, we seek many things.

If we are fortunate, we will come to a place. We will not know what we are searching for but we will know it as we attain it. Its windows emanate warmth like the hope that sustains us. Its roof is the shelter of love. Its walls are the caress that eases our pain, like a gentle balm in all weathers.

It is known as home. The home within our heart.

CHAPTER 51

Julia

Despite its far from auspicious beginning, the remainder of our business trip to Spain was relatively uneventful. We spent two weeks scouring the selection of properties the area had to offer, meeting with potential clients and overseeing the decoration of the office in Marbella. Attempted murder, evil mothers and midnight visitors were mercifully absent.

As a result, a rather melancholic feeling infiltrated my heart the moment we landed back in Dublin. I had quite literally come back to earth. Ensconced in our bubble of the last few weeks, the reality of my recent tumultuous existence had become little more than a dream within a dream. Like it was someone else's dystopia and not mine.

About a week after our return, I found myself called upon to conduct a viewing on a townhouse in Ballsbridge and was preparing to leave work early.

"What are you up to this afternoon?" I questioned Jonathan, straightening the papers on my desk.

He gave a nonchalant shrug and executed a spin in his chair. "I have to head out as well. Need to value some place in Skerries. But I'd just rather be back in Spain." His expression turned wistful.

"We just got home, dopey-head," I rolled my eyes as I slung my bag across my shoulder.

"Love you too and all," he muttered as I made my exit.

Outside, the sun was shy and the clouds exuberant. A slight sprinkling of rain anointed the tip of my nose while I hurried down Dawson Street towards the car park. Slamming the door behind me, I deposited my bag on the passenger seat and began to negotiate my way through the heavy Dublin traffic. Typically,

I was early. I always felt more content to be excessively punctual for a viewing so that I could show myself around before the clients arrived and formulate the perfect pitch. Unlike Jonathan.

I was cautiously optimistic that I was in with a chance of securing a sale that day. This was a second viewing for the couple and I had managed to pique their interest the first time around, so the likelihood of an offer was tantalisingly close. When I had taken the job in Rockstar Real Estate, I had been unsure whether I would actually glean any pleasure from the work. Images of demanding clients and callous gazumping had haunted my mind. However, while such things were definitely prevalent, the thrill I experienced upon completion of a deal was something I had come to adore.

Optimistic and buoyant in my demeanour, the peal of the notification perturbed me. Sighing, my heart sank as a monotonous voice announed the message out of the car speakers.

My clients had cancelled. Great.

If I was Jonathan, I would have been delighted at the excuse to be relieved of my duties for the evening but the disappointment tugged at me unpleasantly.

With my tasks for the day already completed, I had nothing more constructive to do than return home. A smile dawned on my lips as I made the turn-off towards home and noticed a red Porsche, identical to Jonathan's, just outside our neighbour's gate.

When I swung into the driveway and sped around the side of the house, I initially noticed nothing out of the ordinary. My mum's Evoque was parked in its usual place on the concrete, Portofino blue lacquer gleaming in the diminishing sunlight. I pulled in beside it and sped hurriedly across the garden as the persistent rain shower scratched at my skin.

"Mammy? I'm home early!" I clamoured cheerily down the hall.

There was no reply. Brow wrinkling in confusion, I proceeded into the kitchen.

She was sitting at the island, gazing intently at her phone screen but with a slightly dazed look that evidenced the fact she was seeing little of what was before her.

"Oh, hi pet. Is everything alright? Are you finished the viewing already?" Her voice was dubious. I assessed her with a scintillating look.

She was hiding something.

"They cancelled," I said shortly. All joviality was depleted from my words.

"Right." She placed her phone face down on the countertop and stood up, brushing some imaginary speck of dust from her skirt.

"What's going on, mammy?"

At my question, a gnarled branch of fear coiled around her features, its dusky hued foliage the blush on her cheeks. "Nothing. Just surprised to see you. Anyway, would you like to..." she seemed to search for the words, "do something together? Get out for the afternoon saying as we're both off. It's been a while." Whether to seek reassurance that her speech had been effective or simply to find some occupation for them, she reached her hands out for me to grasp them.

I did not.

"*Tell me* what's going on."

Her laugh was hoarse. "I told you Julia, there's nothing-"

Impatient, I stalked from the room. There was only one way to find out and that was to do it for myself. Footsteps reminiscent of clattering cutlery, I strode upstairs. All was still. A tap was dripping. A pipe was creaking. A whisp of wind worried at a window.

I stalled in my tracks. Was I being paranoid again? After all, I had a tendency to be after recent events.

But no. Something was amiss. I knew it.

Ricocheting like a bullet, the sound rang out sharply into the landing. A sneeze.

From the first door on the right.

Horror and a sudden remembrance of that night in El Paraiso assaulted me.

There was someone in my bedroom.

CHAPTER 52

Julia

Inertia infiltrated my being. My every pore emitted a plea to cower in the corner and not face this situation. This was too much. Internally, my soul screamed. A scream that evaporated into the air and seeped beneath the paint of the walls encroaching around me. Stumbling blindly, I barged through the bedroom door and assessed the space. Empty. Then I saw it. The shadow lengthening across the ground, spilling from the walk-in wardrobe and confirming my suspicion. Had my mum allowed this person into my room? *Why*? Could I even trust her? What if she was involved in all this too? Thoughts were a million per millisecond but I could not focus on anything beyond the shifting shape before me.

Forcefully, I ran into the darkened closet and pounced on the figure, tackling them to the ground.

"Ow, ow, Julia get off me!"

I would recognise that voice anywhere. It was Jonathan.

My initial reaction was relief. Ultimately, at least it wasn't some random intruder all over again. But *why* was my boyfriend sneaking around my house whenever I wasn't there? Seriously, *what*?

"Jonathan?" I exclaimed incredulously. "What the hell are you doing here?" Scrambling to my feet, I turned on the overhead lights and illuminated the scene before me. He was still spreadeagled on the floor from where I had knocked him down but in his arms he clutched two objects: a notebook and a tape measure.

"Oh, hello, my darling! Sorry to frighten you, Angel. I was just... you know... waiting to surprise you." There was a triumphant note in his nervous squawk as he succeeded in imparting this last piece of knowledge.

I didn't buy it for a second.

Raising an eyebrow, I asked: "Really? By sneaking into my bedroom when you knew I was on a viewing?"

"Yeah, I wanted to be here when you came back to...." He trailed off pathetically.

"To what?"

"Do... stuff..."

"Jonathan, are you high? Because I swear to God if you are I'll-" I demanded.

"No! Of course I'm not *high*, Julia. You know I don't do gear like that."

Defensively, I folded my arms across my chest. "Well, you're doing a fine job of acting like you are. How did you get in anyway? Does my mum know you're up here?" My expression was far from congenial by this point.

Solace seemed to douse him at the offering of a straw he could grab. "Yes! She let me in. Eve's like... chill. She doesn't mind me calling round to see you." He was beginning to sound extremely childish in his desperate denials.

"Please stop talking crap!" My words severed his toxically. "What are you really doing up here, Jonathan? If you don't tell me the truth, I'll... I'll... well, let's just say you better have a good reason here!"

All of a sudden, he fell deathly silent. My brain turned through possibilities. At first, it alighted on nothing but then, slowly, realisation came under the spotlight.

"A valuation... in Skerries..." I began; each word deliberate. "My mum let you in... with a notebook and a tape measure... OH MY GOD, ARE YOU VALUING *MY* HOUSE?"

His chastened look was the only reply I required.

It was at this extremely opportune time that my mum decided to enter the room behind us. With one look at her, I could see she knew exactly what had happened. All colour had drained from her cheeks. She was ashen. She knew her secret was out.

Fury coursing through me, I rounded on her. "Mammy, are you *joking* me?"

"I'm so sorry Julia pet, I knew you would be annoyed so I thought it was better-"

"You thought it better to hide the fact you were planning to sell our *home*? And you asked *my boyfriend* to do it?" I spat the words with repulsion and venom in copious amounts. "I can't believe you wouldn't tell me something like that! What's happened to you, mammy? You've been so... strange lately. I used to think you were my best friend! Where did that go? Where?" Dissolving into sobs, my voice perished.

"My husband died Julia! In *this* house. How can you expect me to continue living here?" she said, exasperated.

"Well, my dad died but it doesn't mean I've started to tell you lies!"

"Please try to understand, Julia-"

Impatient, I cut her off: "Just stop, mammy."

With plenty of irate sentiments still to be expended, I turned my attention to Jonathan.

"And as for you, you deceitful git," I said hotly. "*How* could you do this to me? I really did think I could trust you but obviously not."

"Julia, I was only doing my job, I didn't-"

"How long have you known?"

"Only since this morning."

I shook my head. "I can't believe this, Jonathan; I really can't. I thought we were supposed to be a team!"

"Julia, after everything we've... please don't let this come between us. I thought you said nothing could break us apart!" he exclaimed his words with that same child-like quality that was characterising his demeanour. What I would once have found bashfully charming was now angering me further than anything ever had.

I laughed a short, sharp, mirthless rasp. "There is no 'us', Jonathan. Not anymore. So don't kid yourself."

With that, I turned on my heels and left two incredulous figures gaping in my wake.

CHAPTER 53

Julia

Hours later, my rage had subsided a little but was still far from exhausted.

Following my fit of anger with my mum and boyfriend, I had been unsure of what exactly to do with myself. Other than weep incessantly at the wheel of my car as I drove in a directionless manner to no specific destination. Obviously though, my tears were for the house and not Jonathan. Men are not worth tears. No matter how handsome, charming, kind or romantic they are. They're just not worth it. Like, at all.

All I really wanted was to get as far away from my house as possible.

Not that it was going to be my house for much longer.

Look, I don't want to seem selfish. I understood that one of the most horrific things that could possibly happen to a family had occurred within its walls. My mum's reasons for wanting to sell were more than understandable. After a few months of work in an estate agent's, I had become all too familiar with the three ds of property sales: death, divorce and debt.

We slotted all to comfortably into the first category. All I could hope was that we weren't secretly careening towards the last as well. I only prayed my mum wasn't concealing anything else that might regard the state of our financial affairs. I didn't really think so but my mind voyaged to some rather dark places in that unfortunate period after the altercation.

Unsure of how to occupy my restless brain, I found myself inexplicably heading in the direction of the train station. I paid for parking and bought a ticket on the next train into town. For the duration of the journey, I amused myself by observing my fellow passengers. It's a habit of mine, observing people. Their quirks, their mannerisms, the way they carry themselves. How they would take form as a character within the pages of a book. I've learnt some very interesting things about human nature in my relatively short existence and the surprises just keep coming. Namely, that those whom you wholeheartedly trust can betray you in an instant. I've often wondered what motivates us to behave in the ways that we do. A definitive answer has equally often eluded me. Humans really are the most vulnerable of creatures. Vulnerable to some intangible hand that manipulates their movements. Like actors on a stage. Actors who only realise the true dispositions of those with whom they tread the boards after the final curtain has fallen.

We are all vulnerable to sin.

My mood decidedly contemplative, I experienced the need to indulge myself in the simmering of quiet thought. When the train terminated at Pearse Station, I alighted and traversed my way to Merrion Square and the National Gallery. The space was familiar to me, somewhere I had visited many times in the past. Resplendent in its overt opulence, the intricately crafted patterns of the ceiling, Grecian pillars and elegantly sweeping staircases formed the oasis of serenity and culture I sought in that moment.

Mercifully, quietude reigned at this hour with the approach of eventide impinging. An area capacious in size, it somehow managed to feel desolate yet brimming with some abstract quality simultaneously. Much like the disturbance within me.

There were a multitude of artworks I could have selected to admire but there was no decision to make. I headed straight for Caravaggio's "The Taking of Christ."

I walked towards the painting. Each step I took echoed purposefully into the atmosphere. Deliberate. Assured. I allowed the pigments encased in the frame to flow away from their confines and swarm around me. The light. The shadows. Of one singular scene. They encapsulated human nature. How vulnerable we are when betrayed by a kiss. Just as I had been. So fearful yet so faithful. Trusting to everything that was to come. To tragedy for the sake of the future. To the altering of a life. Resigned sorrow. Powerless. Darkness brightened only by emotion. A passive figure with invisible forces overtaking them. Good and evil. The capacity for both in one who I loved. The capacity for both in me. Human. *Always* human.

"They thought it was lost, you know."

Gasping, I jolted myself back into reality to face the owner of the voice. Jonathan. Should I have been surprised? Maybe. But somehow I wasn't.

My eyes returned to the painting. "How did you find me?"

"Come on, Julia. You think I don't know you by now?" I was affected by the gravity of his words. The words of one who always struggled to be serious, even in the direst of circumstances. He sidled towards me, settling at my side. With affection in his tone, he said: "I knew I'd find you here."

"Leave me alone, Jonathan. I have nothing to say to you," I muttered bitterly.

"They thought it was lost," he repeated.

"What do you mean?"

"'The Taking of Christ.'" He intoned his words quietly. "They thought it was lost. But they found it again. In the nineties, hanging in a dining room on Lesson Street." He slid his hands into his pockets before continuing. "It really is so beautiful, you know."

"Yes."

"Imagine losing something so beautiful. You should never allow that to happen, Julia."

Suddenly, I looked him straight in the eyes. "Really? Well maybe you should have thought of that before you... before you snuck into my house and tried to stick a sign in it!"

"Julia, I didn't *sneak* in."

I shook my head, words deserting me. "I *trusted* you, Jonathan."

"You still can, my darling."

"Don't call me that. It's pathetic."

Ignoring my comment, he reached his hand out and stroked the back of mine. I tried to flinch away but was prevented from doing so by the inexplicable heat rushing through me. Blood pulsated in my veins a little faster. Pleasantly so.

"I'm sorry, Julia. I... I was wrong. I was just doing my job. Your mum... she shouldn't have made a decision like that without talking to you first. But I was wrong too. Honestly, I don't deny that." He took a deep breath and glanced at the painting. "But you have the power to forgive me. Anything can be forgiven, if you want to."

"I don't like you," I mumbled sulkily. However, it was devoid of vehemence.

A smirk stole onto his lips. "That's a shame. Because I love you."

Before I could protest, he grabbed me in his arms. Possessively. Passionately. Pleadingly.

"Please, *please*, forgive me Julia. I'll do anything. Anything at all. But I can't lose you... I... I just can't."

It pained me to admit it; I didn't want to lose him. I *could* lose him. I had a perfectly good life before he came into it and I was capable of having a perfectly good life after him.

But I didn't *want* to live without him.

Because I was, hopelessly and insensibly, in love with my Watson.

And I still intend to love him every moment breath remains in my lungs. After that, too. Wherever my home may be.

So, I allowed him to hold me still. "You're going to have to make this up to me. Big time." I said, giving him a wide eyed, reproachful look.

He winked and smiled. “Would a night in The Shelbourne help?”

Toying with the top button of his shirt, I feigned consideration of the idea. “It *might* improve things.”

“Good, because I booked us in. I know how high maintenance my little princess is.”

That earned him a playful punch. “Watch it, you’re on thin ice as it is, Johnny.”

It was frustratingly challenging to remain enraged with a boyfriend who booked you into The Shelbourne to make up after a row. I must concede he knows me too well. I couldn’t help but feel that I had just been rather effectively disarmed.

I sighed then as I remembered. “I’m going to have to go and pack. And face mammy.” My heart sank at this prospect. While I had been angry at Jonathan, I was simply infuriated with my mum. At least he was just following instructions. She was the one who had decided to put the house on the market without even telling me first.

“I packed for you. And,” he held his hand up, “before you ask, yes I brought you a book.” He winked again. “Anyway, your mum isn’t expecting you back. I told her I was taking you away for the night to apologise. She really is sorry too, Julia, she feels terrible actually.”

Unwilling to address the elephant in the room, I ignored the last part of his admission but landed on the first. “So not only were you wandering around my house uninvited, you were rifling through my knickers as well? You really *are* in serious trouble, Watson.”

But honestly? I forgave him easily enough. My mum however... well, that was only the beginning.

CHAPTER 54

Julia

Later that evening, we were settling down for the night in our expansive hotel room at The Shelbourne.

Following a lavish candlelit dinner, Jonathan and I arrived back at our quarters with our hunger pleasantly satiated and bond securely repaired.

"I'm sorry too, Watson," I admitted, sinking down into the deep-seated blue velvet sofa. "I flew off the handle a bit and my temper got the better of me. But you were always going to witness that at some point," I finished with a smirk.

He sat down beside me and wrapped his arms around my shoulders. "It's alright, you had every right to be angry."

There was silence for a moment where all that could be heard was the raucous chorus of a crowd traipsing through St. Stephen's Green below. "But let's not think about that anymore. How about I go down to the bar and get us a drink?"

I placed my hands on my knees and coaxed myself to stand. "I think that's a plan."

He departed the room and I crossed to the window. The last lingering embers of twilight were perishing from the sky, giving way to a sapphire night speckled with stars etched over the clouds by an invisible giant's paintbrush. Like great lumbering leafy monsters, laden trees bearing the emerald fruits of their branches undulated in the soft stirring of a wind. A wind of change. A wind that was preparing itself to distort life as I had known it. Suddenly, a ruby red flush prowled over my body. Despite the slight chill of the room, the heat was for some reason unbearable. For once in my life, I found myself unsure of how to proceed. Was I ready to leave behind the place I had called home for so long? I didn't know. I had experienced firsthand the myriad of emotions a property sale could invoke. Especially when the sale wasn't really by your own free will. I also knew that it was worth questioning whether my mum really wanted to sell or if she was in fact disposing of the house as some twisted coping mechanism. My head lolled involuntarily into my hands. I felt increasingly like I didn't know anything anymore.

Fishing "*The Dubliners*" from my bag, I began to read, seeking refuge within the pages of lyrical prose. The book became a shield that protected me from the cares of life, admitting me to worlds that were similar to my own in so many ways yet a rejuvenating flight from reality. Reading really is a lifeline.

I lost myself in the book for a while and when Jonathan came back carrying two cocktails I sipped one contemplatively. I had a foreboding feeling I was in for a restless night. However hard I tried; I simply couldn't shake the hovering disquiet.

Jonathan was being his usual charming self, regaling me with tales of difficult clients and property related disasters but for some reason, I really couldn't enjoy myself at all.

In bed, the Egyptian cotton sheets were soothing against me. I was lying flat on my back, gaze trained on the ceiling, fingers clutching the duvet. Jonathan was on his side, turned towards me, and I could feel the palpability of his eviscerating eyes.

"Julia? Are you alright?" He crept a little closer to me.

When I attempted to reply, I found an unexpected sob catching in my throat. "I... I... Watson, it's just so hard," I whispered haltingly. "It's... I'm not ready to lose the house and... I..."

"I know, darling, I know," he soothed, rubbing the familiar circular motions on my palm.

I sighed deeply. "Watson, do you think I'm being unreasonable?"

"You're not being unreasonable, Julia."

I moved onto my side so that I was looking directly into his eyes.

He reached up and tucked a stray strand of hair back behind my ear in that way I loved so much.

"I do see why she wants to sell," I mumbled, "but it's not *fair*, Jonathan. I should have had a say."

He shook his head sadly. "She was bang out of order. I didn't want to value your house, Julia, but at the end of the day she approached me professionally and I'm not allowed to refuse that. Plus, I didn't really fancy falling out with Eve." He grabbed another piece of my hair and began to twirl it around his finger. "Because, you know, that would have been a bit... awkward."

Rolling my eyes, I replied with a wink: "It's alright, you're back in the good books now."

"I'm glad," he smiled then and kissed my forehead.

I shifted uncomfortably against the mattress. "We used to be so close. We'd tell each other everything. She wasn't like my mum but... more like a sister or... a best friend. Something's *changed* her Jonathan. And I don't know what it is."

"She does want to make it up to you though. She was distraught about the whole thing after you left. Really she was, Julia."

"She hasn't taken it off the market but, has she?"

"Well, it isn't technically on the market yet but yeah she's... she's going ahead with it. I'm sorry, Julia." His words were contrite.

Unable to prevent them any longer, the tears began to flow unabashedly. After the multitude of unfortunate events Jonathan and I had experienced in the relatively short time we had known each other, I had become completely at ease being vulnerable to him. We had been through it all together. Life could throw nothing more strenuous at two people. Could it?

"Jonathan, where am I going to live now? What am I going to *do*?" I ejaculated suddenly.

"Julia, please don't worry. Everything is going to be fine," he began, caressing my cheek. "Your mum and I talked about it after you left and she said that, when you'd... settled down, the three of us would meet up and have a chat about things. See what you want to do moving forward."

I nodded contemplatively. "Maybe it's time... maybe it's time for me to get my own place. I've been saving up... from the books and obviously I have another one coming out..." As I said it, a flame of hope was ignited in my heart. I had always longed to own my own property, independent of anyone else, and maybe I was finally being handed the opportunity for that dream to come true.

"Only problem is," I started, "I'd have to put up with a complete plonker of an agent."

"Would you now?"

"Yeah, I happen to know this one. He drives a Porsche," I muttered sleepily.

"God, *definitely* a knob."

"He is. Gets away with it though because he's alright looking."

"Julia..." a shadow fell suddenly over his face, "I promise I'll find you somewhere perfect."

"That's not really that important," I said seriously.

"But it is-"

"As long as I can live in here," I tapped his chest, in the space where his heart resided. "I think I'll survive."

But as my words perished with the day, I knew deep in my soul I still had everything to fear.

CHAPTER 55

Julia

The melodic sound of our fingers dancing lightly over the keys in perfect unison had produced a peculiarly tranquilising effect on me and it was only as the sudden silence of the office crept in that I realised Jonathan and I were alone. Anto and Eamon had finished for the day and, as per usual, our boss was nowhere to be seen.

This was our chance.

After further extensive late-night discussion in The Shelbourne (at some ungodly hour) we had come to a decision: we would search the office of Frederick Featherington-Smythe.

With the whole melodrama of my house going up for sale, the mystery had taken an unusual position away from the forefront of my mind but, with our relationship repaired, our attention had turned to investigating our boss and any potential connection to the institution or, following recent developments, Jonathan's mother.

Freddie's personal office was strictly off limits. It was the golden rule of the agency that no one except for our glorious leader was permitted to enter. Under any circumstances.

Well, sorry Freddie, but sometimes I love to break the rules.

As expected, the door was securely locked.

"Feck!" Jonathan cried. "We can't get in!"

I rolled my eyes. "Stop being an imbecile. Of course we can, Watson."

"How? It's locked!" he moaned despairingly, looking imploringly at the door as if the heat of his gaze would magically break the lock.

"We pick it!" I declared as if it were obvious. "With a hair pin."

A puzzled expression lined his face. "That doesn't *actually* work, does it? They just do that in books."

"Trust me: it works."

"How do you know? Do you do this often or something?"

"Are you doubting your girlfriend, Johnny boy?" I said, cocking my head to the side.

"Of course not, darling," he mumbled apologetically.

"Good." With that, I removed a hairpin from the elegant chignon at the nape of my neck and stuck it in the keyhole. A few calculated movements later, the door swung open.

"How do you *do* that?" Jonathan spoke mostly to himself but with evident awe in his words.

"That's for me to know and you to find out, Watson," I declared dramatically, sweeping into the room and casting my eyes around it.

The place resembled a rubbish disposal facility. But that actually might be offensive to rubbish disposal facilities.

An antique writing bureau dominated the space. Its surface was littered with files and documents that were spilling over into residual piles on the grey carpeted floor. What seemed like multiple year's accumulation of empty takeaway coffee cups were dotted around the ground, the prehistoric sceptres of their contents still making their presence felt as dried dull brown stains. In each corner, a pair of filing cabinets stood sentry, drawers open and loads in no apparent order.

The focal point of the room however, took the form of a piece of art dominating the wall directly above the wing-backed desk chair: a portrait of Freddie. It was painted oil on canvas in the style reminiscent of a listed National Trust mansion somewhere in the Cotswold countryside and not a pretentious estate agency in

Dublin 2. Egotism at its finest.

"Why does the fecking twat need that on his wall?" Jonathan voiced my thoughts.

"Lord knows," I shook my head. "He certainly manages to make a lot of mess for somebody who's never here. Anyway, you take the left-hand cabinet and I'll take the right."

Many minutes passed in companionable silence, the quietude only punctuated by the rustling of papers and squeaking of opening drawers.

"Anything?" I questioned hopefully after ten minutes had elapsed.

"I don't think so," responded Jonathan despondently. "I haven't a clue what I'm after though."

"You'll know when you find it."

"Will I?"

Then, a second later: "Oh my God Julia, you have to look at this."

"See, I told you so," I smiled smugly, walking behind the desk to examine the red folder clutched in Jonathan's hands.

"The bloody paedophile! I knew he was obsessed with you!" he exclaimed angrily.

"What's the matter Jonathan? What is it? You need to show me," I said, suddenly alarmed by the puce colouring seeping through his features as he hurriedly examined its contents.

Silent and stony faced, he placed the folder into my outstretched palms and turned away, burying his head in his hands.

Embossed on the front, in chauvinistic calligraphy, was a solitary word: Julia.

An impenetrable boulder took up residence in the pit of my stomach while a gossamer veil of foreboding enshrouded my being. In that one moment, the mist of uncertainty alleviated to prepare for the arrival of the ominous clouds of confirmation.

Julia. There was no question that it referred to me.

My actions possessed a note of caution as, with a barely perceptible quake vibrating through my fingers, I opened the plastic and removed the documents contained within it.

Photographs. Of me.

I rifled through the pictures, only to discover documentation of myself at all stages of my life: baby photos, school prize giving, family events. Everything. On record in my boss' office.

I turned around to face Jonathan who seemed in genuine danger of projectile vomiting.

"What the hell, Julia? *Christ*, I always knew he was a sicko but this is too much!"

That was when I noticed it.

Framed in a simple cream casing and set in pride of place on the lacquered wood desk. Another photograph. One that I would recognise anywhere, even as my world began to crumble like a house erected by an incompetent builder.

Two people. A girl in her early teens and a man, his arm entwined protectively around her shoulder. Behind them lay the tapestry of nocturnal New York City, threaded by technicoloured ribbons of garishly lit motorways and punctuated by exclamation mark skyscrapers. On the highest floor of the Empire State Building, overlooking it all, were my uncle Nick and I.

"Jonathan," I began, nausea almost overwhelming me, "Freddie isn't connected to uncle Nick."

"What do you mean, Julia, I thought we established- "

"Freddie *is* uncle Nick."

CHAPTER 56

Julia

"I always thought I recognised him but I just couldn't place him, Jonathan!"

I had collapsed on to the Winchester sofa, kneading my fingers into my temples. For almost six months, I had been working for my uncle. The same uncle who, having once been amongst my closest relatives, had fled the country to Spain. After he murdered multiple people.

When I thought of it now, it just made such glaringly obvious sense. The institution's stronghold in Spain and his sudden decision to sell property there. Emily's disappearance. The sunglasses worn in all weathers. The avoidance of being in the office for an extended period of time. Lest I were to recognise him.

But why employ me? Why employ Emily in the first place? Surely that was an injudicious risk. That said, his disguise was extremely effective. The uncle Nick that I remembered possessed hair in a neat, dark coiffe. Frederick Featherington-Smythe had greasy waves that reached almost to his shoulders. There was definitely some fake tan involved in the whole process too. Plus, Nick was always a marvellous actor. He was well capable of carrying a character.

I was suddenly consumed by an inexplicable memory of the two of us together, shortly before it all happened, watching a property programme. The joke we'd always had; that Nick would have made the perfect estate agent.

And that is exactly what he had done.

I presumed he had needed a fresh start after the Emily and Maria debacle. His days in the medical profession were numbered. He required a clean slate. In real estate. What he'd always secretly wanted to do.

I had so many unanswered questions. He was still obviously involved with the institution. That was proved by the fact he had sent Jonathan to that development; where Emily had been taken after she confessed her suspicions to me. Where other girls were still being held. Just like back in Serenity Springs. She had likely been close to uncovering the whole truth and so, he got rid of her.

However, there was one fact that hurt me more than anything. Hurt doesn't even come close.

He had killed my dad. Why? For fear that the investigation into Lorraine's death would incriminate him all over again. That, second time around, his brother wouldn't protect him. He hadn't wanted to back then. It had been my mum who had encouraged us to keep the whole thing quiet. My dad would have revealed all to the world in an instant. There had always been tension between the two of them, not just fraternal rivalry, although I had never truly comprehended why.

"Right, that's it, I'm going to knock him into the middle of next week!" exulted Jonathan passionately.

"Ehh... no offence, Watson, I know he's twice your age but you've seen him. He works out."

"So do I! I'm a member of Malahide Tennis Club *and* Howth Sailing Club actually!" This was said rather smugly.

"Be honest, that's just for the status symbol and the free champers," I reprimanded.

His brow furrowed. "But you always say I've got lovely muscles!"

"Of course you do, darling but that's really not relevant at this precise moment." I rose to my feet and began to pace up and down. "Right, what are we going to do?"

"Go to the Gardai!"

Suddenly, I halted. My features darkened. "We can't do that and you know it!" I said sharply.

"Julia, our boss is a murderer!"

"He's also my uncle. And you know what that means," I began to pace again. "We withheld evidence back then. That's a crime! And if we go to the Gardai, my mum and I are going to have a hard time wrangling out of some very awkward questions!"

His tone was exasperated as he spoke again: "But what's our alternative, Julia? Keep working for the maniac?"

"I'll tell you exactly what our alternative is Watson," I intoned purposefully as I walked towards him. "We confront him ourselves."

Frederick Featherington-Smythe resided in the green leafy suburb of Drumcondra. A stereotypical Georgian façade, the red brick terraced house was accentuated by ornate plasterwork and cast-iron railings leading up to its red front door. Through the rounded glass panel at its top, an amber light emanated. He was home.

Jonathan parked the Porsche on the kerb and together we traversed the garden path until we stood facing the entryway. Fortunately, Jonathan knew his address but it had taken all my powers of persuasion to get him to take me there. Eventually though, he had relented when I threatened to go alone. I suppose sometimes the protective boyfriend who actually has a pair comes out.

With a firm hand, I knocked thrice.

I glanced sideways at Jonathan, who was still exuding the general impression of one facing internment in Auschwitz. "Buck up, Watson!" I chastised. If I was honest though, it was to encourage myself as much as him. I was existing on pure adrenaline in that moment. Had I stopped to consider what we were about to do, I would most likely have talked myself out of it.

It was too late for that now.

The door was opened by the man himself. Looking up into that tanned face while standing there on that doorstep, it struck me. Hard. It really was him; my uncle. How had I not seen it before? The uncle whom I had loved. Who had loved me. And, despite everything, who loved me yet. After all, why else would you keep someone's photo on your desk?

"How yis, Lads," he greeted us, brow furrowed in a mix of surprise and confusion, "to what do I owe the pleasure?"

Plastering on a pseudo smile, I greeted him warmly: "Oh, hello Uncle Nick, may I come in?"

The reaction that this produced was one exceptionally difficult to describe. He attempted to open his mouth but his jaw slackened and drooped, preventing coherent sound from escaping. No longer steady on his feet, I momentarily believed he was going to fall backwards.

"H... how did you know?" When he spoke, his voice was barely above a whisper. He gripped the doorframe in a desperate effort to support himself.

I did not reply.

"You'd better come in," he murmured faintly.

"Why, thank you, Uncle Nick," I effused, bounding over the threshold and into the hallway. "I must say, it really is *wonderful* to see you again. It's been far too long, don't you think?"

"Julia, how did you..."

"May we sit down? It's been a most eventful morning. Hasn't it Johnny, darling?"

"Yeah..." choked Jonathan, who was now looking decidedly jaundiced.

Eyes darting suspiciously between the two of us, he lead us off to the left, into an elaborate living room. Characterised by damask patterned sofas, gilded mirrors, curlicued cornicing and bold blue walls, it *screamed* the Nick I had once known.

I settled elegantly on the sofa nearest the door. Jonathan remained standing, shifting uncomfortably from foot to foot.

Suddenly, my demeanour did a full one-eighty.

"Now tell us what the hell is going on, Nick!" I demanded. "Or should I say, *Frederick Featherington- Smythe*? Which actually is it? Because I'm not sure at this stage!"

"Julia, I-"

"No, you hold on here", I said, jumping to my feet again. "What is the *meaning* of this?"

"Julia, honestly, whatever you're thinking, you've got it all wrong. I swear-"

"Nick," I interrupted, incensed. "You really don't have a leg to stand on. Forgive me, but I've lost count of the number of people you've... you've..." I couldn't bring myself to say it.

"Please, please, just listen Julia. I can explain everything-"

I laughed. Humourlessly. "Nick, I think I've given you enough chances before. Realistically here, give me one good reason why I shouldn't go straight to the Gardai!"

Those were the last words that made it past my mouth before my world imploded. For what felt admittedly like the millionth time.

Upon Nick's face, numerous emotions appeared to be waging war.

And it was telling the truth that won out.

"Because I'm your father."

CHAPTER 57

22 Years Previously

She stands. Rooted to the spot and gripped by a sudden lethargy. It feels... rejuvenating to be here. Her Garden of Eden. A place of paradise nestled amongst the cobbled streets of Mijas. With a tentative complexion, it embraces the rugged shores of Andalusia where the ravenous waves in their salivating hunger caress the golden sultry sands; their lover. Ecstasy tingles, a palpable entity, mingling with the hallowing humidity to lend this night an air of anticipation. On this evening, Eve Barnacle's life will be altered forever. As she awaits eventides approach, her slender pale hands rest lightly on the glass surround of the first-floor balcony. She presides over this property; her asset. It is the envy of all her friends. Being able to invite them here for the summer after their graduation provided Eve a sentiment of power, control. And if there is anything Eve Barnacle thrives on it is power and control. Her house, her rules. They owe this summer of gaiety to her and her alone. Eve smiles to herself. The wavering waters of the generously proportioned private pool glimmer in the perishing rays of sunlight. The glowing ruby from which they emanate dips below the horizon.

"Eve, come on! You're going to make us late!"

The voice that hails her is that of Alice, her closest friend. She is summoned. Very well.

Pushing open the sliding doors and re-entering the bedroom, Eve is taunted by pandemonium. A litany of makeup products is scattered miscellaneously across the marble tiles. Alice, as is customary, has secreted her features beneath innumerable layers of foundation, highlighter, bronzer and eyeshadow. The overall effect is rather pitiful; she is rendered a tangerine tint. She appears to have forgotten the other half of her dress at home; her entirely exposed legs are painted varying shades of white, orange and brown. That said, Alice is a good friend. Loyal. Eve values loyalty.

It is important.

Alice grabs a cocktail glass from the dressing table and downs the contents. "Where's yours?" she questions Eve, her words slightly slurred. Great. They haven't even hit the bar yet and Alice is already tipsy. There's only one way this night is ending and that is with a pool of puke on the bathroom floor.

"Finished long ago." Eve's reply is casual. A casual lie. She poured the concoction that was the nefarious negroni into the potted fern outside on the balcony half an hour ago. Alice doesn't need to know that though.

"Good because you know there's going to be loads of hot guys there, right? So, we need to lower our inhibitions. Just think, Eve, a sexy Spaniard..."

Eve giggles indulgently.

Catching sight of herself in the floor to ceiling mirrors built into the wardrobes, she is forced to concede that she *does* make a highly desirable impression tonight. Her naturally fair tresses cascade modestly, a spirited waterfall ending in a light curl. A lucid layer of makeup is tastefully applied and her scarlet gown cinches her waist while emphasising her curves in all the right places. It is a modest garment, leaving plenty to the imagination. The dress was costly but it shows in the elegant cut. Usually, Eve's skin is an almost transparent white; now, following a fortnight of Andalusian charms, it possesses a decidedly healthy glow. Briefly, she had considered a white dress, something though, told her that scarlet was more fitting for tonight.

Eve retrieves her Michael Kors handbag from the bottom of the wardrobe and descends the staircase in Alice's wake. The others are awaiting them in the open-plan kitchen and living area, resplendent in dresses professing their cleavage and skimping on skirt.

Surveying the group before her, Eve reflects on how similar yet opposing they are. She is blonde, Alice brunette, Kate a fiery red-head and Anna crowned by hair of a midnight black. At twenty-seven, they are young, liberated, single. They all, sans Alice, are recently qualified as medical doctors and after enduring the hard years of study and general training in hospital they are prepared to throw caution to the wind. All except Eve. Eve is perpetually cautious. No matter the circumstances.

Alice, in contrast to the others, is in the property business. Although her appearance tonight may be deceiving, she is highly competent in her field and has recently relocated to Spain permanently to master what she maintains is a highly competitive market. A market so competitive that it warranted a divorce from her husband and virtual abandonment of her four-year-old son.

"I was immature and I made a poor decision, Eve," she had admitted dolefully one night, shortly after she, Kate and Anna had arrived. "Michael was a good man but the marriage was impulsive, we were twenty-one and lost in lust, not even true love. I'm no mother, Jay is better off without me. His dad will look after him." She had shrugged dismissively then and sipped her martini. "This is a second chance for me, fresh as a property development straight off the plans." She smiled.

Anyone else may have found Alice rather neglectful but Eve had known her too intimately and for too long. Since their very first day of primary school, she had been erratic. She had brains and could put them to use when the notion took her. Which it often didn't. It felt like an eternity since they had spent this much time together and it was exciting to be reunited in this way. Alice was living in her own apartment just along the boardwalk but had been frequenting El Paraiso like it was her own since Eve's coming. Eve could not help but experience mild concern for her ambitious venture; there was every possibility Alice had bitten off more than she could chew. Although she seemed resolute.

Now, Anna is frantically ushering them all out the door to the waiting mustang taxi. "Dolls, tonight is going to be *cracker*!" she exults. Anna hails from Derry and can steadfastly be relied upon to "have the craic." Whatever way you wish to interpret the statement.

It is decidedly claustrophobic in the back of the car but even as perspiration wets their foreheads, nothing can dampen their spirits. The night is fraught with freedom; they are oblivious to the foreboding. Beyond the vehicle's windows, the motorway from La Cala to Marbella unfolds, an eternal carpet bordered on both sides by the twinkling lights of villas and apartment complexes. They zip by, held in their gaze for fractions of a second. They are illusions. Just as the illusion of youth, temporarily owned by us all but a home from which we will all come to be evicted, when it is repossessed by time.

"Vive Espana!" Anna's cry is almost feral. She extends her torso out of the window and sprinkles her shouts into the starlit night, sacrificed to a higher deity. Hormones and adrenalin are their lifeblood. No inhibitions. No fear. The story of tonight prepares to reveal itself.

CHAPTER 58

It is a practically incomprehensible phenomenon, at least to Eve, how anyone in full possession of their senses can find a nightclub such as this one pleasurable. The insistent thump of a bass penetrates her brain as pleasantly as a drill. She cannot feel herself formulate a thought. Neon lights assault her vision, beams like molten strands of fire dancing before her eyes in rhythm with the bodies on the dancefloor. Bodies. Male and female. Little to distinguish between them at this distance. Silhouettes gyrating aimlessly against a streaky luminous background. A supernatural quality about them...removed from mere mortals. The dark liquid in the glass she is clutching like a life buoy swims from side to side. Wine. Red wine. Another few hours and she will be able to abscond from this nightmare. Once back at the apartment, she will remove her dress and slip beneath the cool fabric of her bedsheets, their smooth texture lulling her towards slumber. She will be alone at last.

"Look who it is Eve! Can you believe it?"

Eve groans internally and prepares to face Alice, Kate and Anna and whoever they have in their company. This is the second time in as many hours that her tranquil reverie has been interrupted by her friends. She swivels on the bar stool, prepared to perform perfunctory pleasantries and orchestrate a subtle escape. And is momentarily astounded by the beauty of the man before her.

His demeanour exudes a lord of the manor, egotistical confidence. This is a man who is in no doubt of his purpose; he is gorgeous and he knows it. Slicked waves of hair, a sable mane, frame his handsome face. Expressive eyes, a strong jaw, full lips. Unbidden, her eyes travel away from his face and across his generous chest. The fabric of his linen shirt strains against pure muscle. Oh dear. Some primal instinct inside her is awakened from hibernation.

"Eve, can you actually believe it? It's Nick and Paul!"

The last occasion on which Eve laid eyes upon the twins Nicholas and Paul Joyce was on her final day of secondary school. They had seemed little more than children. Utterly uninteresting. Nick had gone on to do medicine too, Eve seemed to remember vaguely. Only, where she had gone to Trinity, he had gone to the Royal College of Surgeons and their paths had not crossed. Years had intervened and now Nicholas...

"Eve Barnacle." His voice is husky, low. "Well, well, is it really you?"

"What does it look like?"

It is a peculiar thing that when two people have known each other and formed an opinion of each other, no matter how much time has elapsed, the remnants of ancient emotions linger.

"As arrogant as ever, I see."

"I could say the same to you."

"Hi, Eve. It's nice to see you," interjects Paul tentatively.

"Hi, Paul."

"You look...different but...really...lovely." Of the two brothers, Paul was always the nicest.

Nick on the other hand, was the liability. She can't prevent herself from noticing his eyes all over her like some cheap imitation perfume.

For a few moments, there is an awkward silence. No party quite trusts themselves to speak.

"Well guys," announces Alice jubilantly. "I suppose you lot don't fancy getting out of here and heading someplace else? I'm so done with this stupid club."

Typical Alice, thinks Eve. Greatest advocate one moment, greatest critic the next. She won't be protesting though. This is her golden opportunity to leave this hellhole.

"How would you feel about coming back to my place? There's plenty of space... we can... party all night there if you like." The words have left Eve's mouth before her brain fully vetted them. Still, anywhere would be better than here.

"Sounds cool," concedes Kate's mild midlands accent

"Great craic altogether," approves Anna.

"Alright then," rumbles Nick like thunder.

CHAPTER 59

The cool concrete of the wall is soothing, calming her clammy skin. Inviting them back here was a mistake, of that at least, she is now certain. It is not the last mistake she will make tonight. Somewhere in her gut, she is instinctively aware of that, too. She had foolishly supposed that it would just be the six of them but alas that number appears to have almost squared; the population of the villa is encroaching perilous figures. With a little effort in extricating herself from the ongoing escapades, Eve has successfully moored on the upstairs landing. The hollering of revellers wafts maliciously to her ears. There have been drinking games, slanderous attempts at karaoke and now a diving competition is ongoing in the pool.

She is at peace once again. Until she isn't.

"You never were a party animal."

Nick. *How* did he get here?

"What do you want, Nick?"

"God, Eve, can't you ever play nice? You've always had such a thing about me."

"The last time I saw you was when I was eighteen."

"And?"

"You don't know me."

"Oh, but I do, Eve. I know you better than you could ever imagine. And I know you want to know me better too."

Eve laughs. It comes out as a rasp.

"What is that supposed to mean?"

"Merely an observation."

"Why would you be observing me? You detest me."

"I'm always observing you and for your information, I don't detest you." His voice drops further.

"Is that a threat?"

"I would consider it a promise."

For the first time since this conversation began, Eve looks Nick in the face. Hunger alights his eyes. Desire thrums in her veins. A magnetic field encloses around them.

"Let me prove how much I don't hate you." With that, his lips slam against her mouth. She doesn't resist. She cannot resist. For Eve is destined to succumb to the serpent.

CHAPTER 60

A Few Weeks Later

Something is amiss. Eve is forced to acknowledge the fact. This morning, following a restless night of tossing and turning punctuated by multiple trips to the bathroom, she had woken and promptly deposited the contents of her stomach in the toilet bowl. Retrieving her diary from her bedside locker, she gazes at the circled date. Three days ago. That is irrelevant, she assures herself. A cycle can be irregular. Can't it? She must ascertain things once and for all though.

In a similar fashion to every morning since their arrival in La Cala, the four girls are luxuriating on loungers beneath the sky of unblemished blue. Alice is at Eve's right hand. As always. This is her opportunity to say something and get it off her chest. Alice has faced this predicament. In her case, any suspicions were warranted. She was pregnant.

"Alice, can we...eh... go inside for a minute. I want to talk to you. Alone," Eve whispers barely perceptibly.

"Yeah, sure. What is it?"

Eve casts a glance across at Kate and Anna. They can't know. Not yet. However, their expressions are of complete bliss. Their only concern achieving a tan of even coverage. An unattainable dream.

"Just come inside, please."

"Ok, you're scaring the crap out of me now, what is it, Eve?" Alice's tone possesses a genuine note of concern. They are leaning against the island; Eve's knuckles have turned pearlescent white from gripping the surface so tightly. She inhales a gasp of air deeply into her lungs.

"I think... I think...well there's a possibility that... a chance...that..."

"For God's sake spit it out Eve!"

"I think I might be pregnant."

The silence roars. Then, it goes quiet.

"You...what?"

"You heard me, Alice."

"How... *who* the hell?" Alice is in danger of landing in a heap on the kitchen tiles.

"Nick."

"No! That... that couldn't be."

"Yes, Alice. The night of the party back here."

"And there's no other...possibility?"

"No, what do you think this is? Mamma Mia?"

"Okay...okay. I'm sorry, Eve. It's just I'm a little...surprised."

"Yeah well, join the club."

"There's probably nothing to worry about. You're on the Pill aren't you?"

"Yes, but I've been thinking and I took an antibiotic a few days before... it could have... interfered." Eve's words hang heavy, the implications laden in the air.

"You need to take a test."

"I know."

"Right, well. I tell you what. I'll run down to the chemist and you stay here. Don't say anything to the others yet. Keep it between us."

Eve does not protest. She is completely listless. As soon as Alice retreats from the villa, she sinks down on to the sofa and lies there, perfectly still, for a few moments. A freight train is tumbling through her brain. She cannot even begin to comprehend what this could mean. How could she have allowed herself to show such submission? To Nick. If this test is positive, she will possess no option but to inform him. It is impossible to imagine what he will think, say, do.

When Alice returns, she beckons Eve upstairs. Wordlessly. Standing here on the hostile linoleum floor of her en suite with Alice by her side she knows the result displayed on the small blue stick in front of her will alter the course of her life.

"You look, Alice... I... I can't."

There are some occasions in life when words are not required. The expression on Alice's face says everything that Eve needs to know. As the life she has led dissipates before her eyes, Alice runs to her and embraces her. Tightly.

"I'll always be here for you Eve. Everything is going to be okay."

Eve does not reply but slides slowly down the wall until she is nothing but a pool on the bathroom floor.

CHAPTER 61

She is merely delaying the inevitable. Eve knows this. She has to tell him. Tonight is as good as any; it has already been a week since she found out.

Nick and Paul are renting an apartment nearby for the summer. They have been in Eve's company multiple times since that fateful night but Nick has stealthily avoided being alone with her. Until now.

El Bombo is relatively crowded. It is a restaurant Eve is familiar with; she has frequented it on every occasion she has been in La Cala throughout her life. Something needs to be comforting tonight. Faintly in the distance, cutlery clatters and voices chatter. The sounds brush Eve's ears lightly but do not remain. She does not absorb them. Nick has agreed to meet her here for dinner "to talk." He is not yet aware of the news he is going to receive though. She casts a cursory glance at her wristwatch. Nick should have been here quarter of an hour ago. What if he plays truant? That would be an omen alright. An ominous omen.

He has probably just been held back by something or someone. That is what she tells herself. Although that little voice in her head that whispers, "Another woman?" cannot be ignored either. Nick is trouble. That is a cold, hard fact. If only she hadn't been quite so foolish. For the second time, the kindly waiter appears and asks her if she wishes to order. She repeats her excuse; she is waiting on someone. The realisation is beginning to dawn though that Nick is not coming. She should get out of here.

Seizing her handbag from the back of the chair, she slings it over her shoulder and exits the restaurant. What should she do? The others are most likely in Biddy Mulligan's, the Irish pub. It is only a few streets away. That is where she will go. She proceeds away from the beach and makes her way inland. The cobbles so quintessentially Spanish are uneven underfoot. Her tread on them uncertain. Just as the rest of her life ahead.

Panting and slightly lacking in breath, she eventually arrives outside Biddy Mulligan's. Eve scans the open-air tables, sheltered under umbrellas, which all appear occupied. The time of a sheltered existence has been covered by a curtain. None of her friends. No Nick. She sighs. This night cannot possibly get any worse. Except it can.

She enters the bar, barely hopeful now of meeting with any of her acquaintance. Inertia grips her. She must sit and rest her legs, so weary from the trek. Someone is positioned on a platform, strumming a guitar and singing "The Fields of Athenry." In spite of everything, a small smile tugs her lips. She has always loved this song. The soft musicality of the lyrics lulls her. Then, she sees them. At first, her emotions are of relief. Nick. Alice. They are here after all. Her journey was not in vain. She rises from her seat and prepares to greet them. The room alternates upside down. Her life does too. For here are Nick and Alice, their lips and arms locked together. Inseparable. A kiss that is not a first kiss but a kiss of two people who have kissed many times before. Eve's mind recedes to intangibility but her body gains control. It will not permit her to remain here in this bar, surrounded by betrayal and adultery. At the hands of her very best friend. Just as her feet cross the threshold, that one heart-shattering lyric assaults her: "You must raise our child with dignity."

CHAPTER 62

Her life is over. Finished. Doctor Eve Barnacle has no prospects. It is that singularly curious point of evening where the sun has fled but night has not yet fallen. The lights of the Costa del Sol are still to illuminate. Eve stares absentmindedly to her left, the settlements of Benalmadena, Torremolinos and Malaga an inky ribbon of black. To her right, Marbella, Estepona, a similar image. Above her, the sky is magenta, the purgatory between day and night. Waves lap insistently at the shore, their gentle crash still another element of this place that is familiar to Eve. The sand is grey in this light, its golden cast diminished. Then, gentle unobtrusive footsteps.

"Eve?"

"Oh, Paul. It's you." She is momentarily startled. Without invitation, he sits down beside her.

"What are you doing here? Kate said you were meeting Nick for dinner."

"I was... supposed to but he didn't show." There is an edge to her words and Paul notices.

"Why not?" he has the decency to seem surprised.

"He was too busy snogging Alice."

"They're an item?"

"Seemingly."

Silence reigns for a moment until Eve simply cannot bear it anymore. She starts to sob uncontrollably.

"Hey...hey, Eve, what's wrong? Is this about Nick and Alice?"

"I wouldn't care if I wasn't pregnant with his child."

Paul's jaw physically drops.

"You're not serious Eve?"

"Why would I joke about something like that?"

He is temporarily unsure of what to say and she can't blame him.

"I... I just didn't know that you two..."

"Oh, it was brief. Very brief. One night in fact but not...not brief enough." Her bitterness is only too obvious.

"Does he know?"

"I was planning on telling him tonight. That's why I asked him to meet me for dinner."

"But he didn't show." It is not a question. Paul knows his brother as well as anyone.

"No."

"I'm sorry, Eve."

"So am I, Paul. So am I."

"Nick is... well, he's a prat. I don't know how anyone in their right mind could choose Alice over you."

Something in his statement makes Eve sit up straighter. Paul thinks she is better than Alice?

"Eve, I ... I've been wanting to say this since...well, since that night we met up but I... I like you. I like you a lot and ... I think we could be good together." He stops short, breathless. Eve cannot help noticing how he cracks his knuckles, preparing to continue. "I've enjoyed spending time with you this summer so much. You are a good person, Eve. I've always known it, even back when we were in school. And... I want you to know that...whatever you choose to do about the baby, I will support you. This could...bring us together. So...what do you say?"

Along the coast of the Costa del Sol, miniscule pinpricks of light slowly begin to bloom into life. Reassuring, constant, steadfast.

They light the way ahead. Overhead, two timid stars have abandoned their shyness and there amongst the darkness, they glimmer. Together.

Eve looks Paul in the eye. With a steady voice she whispers, "I say we should give it a try."

CHAPTER 63

Julia

The silence stank. My hands were trembling. My head was pirouetting. My eyes were at capacity with tears.

My life was a lie.

Unable to contend with the enormity of the situation, Jonathan crossed to a mahogany drinks cabinet pushed against the far wall and uncorked a bottle of Middleton Very Rare whiskey. Without ceremony, he took a single long drag from the bottle and smacked his lips in satisfaction.

"Oi, Jono, leave the Middleton alone!" hollered Nick.

Looking mildly dazed, Jonathan replied: "Think this has gone way beyond that, pal. This is like... the time when you need a dram of that stuff that costs four grand in Adare Manor."

"That's actually the same bottle-"

"For God's *sake* would you two shut the hell up about fecking whiskey!" I demanded impatiently. "That is not the pressing concern here!"

"Okay, sorry," Nick mumbled contritely, turning back towards me. "So, yeah. Basically, I made you. So please don't call the Shades."

Jonathan emitted a slight whimper. "I think I'm going to call them just for the use of that sentence. Or else somebody get me a bucket so that I can boke!"

"Right, so hold on, this Alice person," I said, ignoring my boyfriend. "Where is *she* now?"

"Well, you met her." To his credit, he did have the decency to look mildly embarrassed then. "I haven't seen her since... that summer...

but she reached out to me a while back. Said she'd heard through the grapevine that I was extending the business to Spain and she would be willing to help us out. I didn't think about it really. Didn't even know where she worked exactly. But I thought it would do no harm for you to meet with her. All that was a long time ago and it wasn't like she would have known who you were. But then... Jono told me what happened. So... I take it she must have found out." He paused for breath. "I swear to you though, Julia. I was not involved in that in any way."

"Alice is Celia?" I screeched hysterically.

At this, Jonathan spoke again: "Scratch the bucket, make it a wheelie bin..." All of a sudden, he trailed off. "Wait... but... Celia's my mum!"

"Wha?" interjected Nick, features marred by complete incomprehension. "Who the feck is Celia? Lads, no offence but I'm lost here."

"Celia is Alice. Alice is Celia. Those two names are an anagram of each other," I said slowly in dawning realisation. "She's obviously using a different name now that she's big in the property world, not that you'd know anything about that," I shot daggers at him. "And she's also Jonathan's mum."

"Jaysus... wha?" It was Nick's turn to rub his temples. "So... hang on... you're Jay, the son she left behind in Ireland?"

Jonathan had turned the same colour as Nick's teeth.

"It... seems so." He put his head in his hands. "This is hurting my brain."

Nick sank down into an armchair. "Same, Jono."

"Okay, so... given all of that," I said, beginning my usual pacing. "Why would she want to kill me? I don't even know her!"

"Well," Nick became fixated on the ground. "It was never a real serious thing we had going on like. You know how it is... I was young, sleeping around-" Jonathan made some form of animalistic retching noise, "but like, she had a bit of an obsession with me. She was proper pissed that I broke up with her when I... when I found out about... you. I didn't think she'd still care after twenty years but... plenty of psychos out there."

"Pot kettle and all that!" exclaimed Jonathan with feeling.

It was a reflection of the severity of what was occurring that Nick ignored him.

"Great! I almost died for the sake of something that happened when I was a clump of cells!" My pacing intensified as I shook my head in an attempt to clear it. "Right, we've wiped that up but what about the institution? And, Nick," I fixed him with an aggressive stare. "You start at the very beginning and leave nothing out. And whatever you do, tell the truth."

I resumed my seat on the sofa, breathless now.

"Okay. So, about eight years ago, I was working as a psychiatrist and I got headhunted for a job in Serenity Springs, this private rehabilitation centre in Howth for mental illness and addiction. I thought it would basically just be a load of south siders who were a bit fond of doing lines." He cackled at this. Neither Jonathan or I joined in.

"I was earning loads of bugs bunny and it seemed like an offer I couldn't refuse," he continued. "I started working there and for a while, it was great. Everything that I'd imagined really. But then they started doing some weird crap. Like, it was only young females they'd take as patients. And, well... there was nothing wrong with them. It turned out the head honcho, Dr. Winchester, was into experimenting with obedience drugs and he used these girls to test them out. He'd always manage to spin some yarn to their family and have them 'admitted' to the institution. The whole thing made me uncomfortable so I handed in my notice." He paused then and sucked in a long breath. "But I wasn't allowed to leave. I knew too much about what was really going on. Dr. Winchester told me that if I left, they'd report me for...assaulting the patients. The girls would have testified to anything they were told to and so there was nothing I could do: I couldn't risk something like that."

Briefly, he became contemplative, hanging his head remorsefully.

"I had to go along with it, doing their bidding. Often, it was my job to lure the girls in. Through fake dates, usually. Then I'd take them back to the institution, make sure they got their first dose of the drugs and break the news to the family that they had been suffering from some kind of mental ailment. The plan was fairly simple and for a long while, it worked. Dr. Winchester continued to develop this drug and it got more effective as he made observations on the effects it produced. Over time, it grew into a cult. There was a whole religious side of it too; they were manipulated, told they'd go to hell if they didn't follow the rules." Again, he broke off, wetting his lips with his tongue. "That made me *sick*, Julia. It really did. Some of them were barely older than you at the time."

"Anyway, the next part you know: Maria. She was resistant to the drugs for some reason. Knew what was going on and started asking to be taken home when the family came to visit. They didn't believe anything she said but I knew they'd get suspicious eventually." By now, Nick appeared in genuine danger of bawling. "I panicked. And... and I overdosed her on the drugs and killed her."

Jonathan had slid down the wall and was now sitting back against it, cheeks flushed. The likelihood of him vomiting appeared to be increasing with every sentence.

"That was a mistake. Because then the family really did get suspicious. They were going to start legal proceedings against us. We might have got away with it but there were no guarantees that a bit of publicity wouldn't make some of the other families question us too."

He halted again, scratching his nose agitatedly.

"I'm not absolutely sure of what happened but Gerard panicked.

He knew we had to do damage control and so he... went to their house and cut the brakes on their car." He shrugged. "It worked."

"What a load of evil b-" began Jonathan.

"It was never my intention, Jono, you have to believe that," he pleaded, turning to look at the still crouched Jonathan.

"Anyway, after that we came to the decision that it wasn't safe to stay in Dublin. Gerard bought up a load of land outside Seville, in La Campina. And they began building this massive compound where they'd transfer all the girls. There'd be fake passports... the works. The families were told it was a temporary arrangement, that there were specialist facilities in Spain to avail of. And they believed it! If any of them did ask questions, it was too late by the time they got around to it. We were gone. And... Julia... it was the hardest thing I ever did. Because it meant I had to leave you."

Something happened then that I had long believed impossible. He began to cry. Genuine, heart wrenching tears of emotion. I experienced a tugging sensation in my gut and an inexplicable urge to comfort him. However, I restrained myself, taking care that my expression remained neutral.

When he had recovered somewhat, he continued: "So there I was; in Spain. Still forced to do their bidding for years. Then, about four years ago, I decided I wanted to move back to Ireland. They had grown so much in strength by then that I wasn't as vital anymore and thankfully, they allowed me to go. The thought of practising medicine again... I really didn't want to. I just felt so *done* with that part of my life. And I'd always had this unsatiated desire to sell property. I just... felt that I could do it. I took an online course and became an estate agent." A wistful cast came over him. "It was the best thing I ever did. It made me *happy* again." This was said almost in petulance.

"I built up the agency. Employed Lorraine, Anto, Eamon, Emily, you," he gestured at Jonathan "and then after Lorraine's death when the position came up and Julia applied... I knew there was a risk she'd recognise me and discover everything but I... it was a risk

I had to take," he smiled to himself and turned back to me. "I just wanted my little girl back," he began to sob heavily and to my utter surprise, I felt the wetness well in my own eyes.

"I've done a lot of terrible things in life, Julia. But there was one thing I did right and...that was you."

The sincerity of his words winded me like a physical punch. On reflection, I do think that the truth of the situation was yet to imbed itself in me at that point. Nick. My father.

It was Jonathan who broke the spell. "What's the craic now though? Are you still a part of that cult or...?"

"Yes and no."

"What do you mean yes and no?" I asked.

"Well, look, I don't have to pander to them anymore. I'm a free man now. But because of what I did, even though it wasn't of my own free will, I'm equally as bad as any of them. So, I have to protect myself the way they protect themselves, if you get what I mean."

"Ehh... not really if I'm honest," conceded Jonathan.

"Relax, Jono, I'm getting to it!"

Jonathan muttered wryly: "Well, I do apologise that I'm not relaxed when my boss, who turns out to be my girlfriend's uncle, who's really her father, is giving us a great story time about all the people he's murdered but, you know, maybe I'm just weird like that."

If Nick heard, he did not acknowledge the comment.

"It's why I had to fire Emily-"

"You fired her?" I interjected.

"Yes, I overheard her telling you the whole story about Maria that day, I had a hidden camera in the office, and so... I had to. If I didn't, I was risking two things; first of all, that she was going to make a fuss about it all and try to start an investigation again and secondly that it would make you realise the truth about who I really was. I had to let Gerard Winchester know about her. He... took care of it apparently."

"Yeah, well, he did that alright," piped up Jonathan. "That development you sent me to (it was a kip, by the way) is obviously under their control somehow. When I was there, I saw Emily. It was her; looking out of the upstairs window of one of the half-finished villas. I nearly had a heart attack! And that wasn't all, there were other girls there too. I caught that Luke dude knocking the crap out of one of them." He imparted this piece of information rather victoriously, as if glad to make some contribution.

"Luke... as in the developer?" questioned Nick thoughtfully.

"Yeah, him, seemed like a right- "Jonathan utilised some vibrant vocabulary.

"Again, look, I don't know him. We only spoke on the phone but there's every chance he is a part of it. They're still expanding as far as I know. Not that that I look into it much or anything but..."

Once again, silence descended as we digested the revelations. Surprisingly, it was Jonathan who tackled him next.

"Look, I think maybe it's time we addressed the more pressing concern," he started, an uncharacteristic assurance clinging to each syllable. "What about the more recent deaths? And by that I obviously mean Lorraine and Paul."

Nick was fidgeting absentmindedly with one of the tassels on a rug draped over the side of the armchair. His pupils irradiated.

"I killed Lorraine too," he said, his voice low, "but I didn't kill Paul."

The sound as gashing as a gunshot, he cleared his throat then revealed placidly: "Lorraine was the matron. You know that. She came back to Ireland at the same time as me and I employed her. But when Geard put the house up for sale with us after all this time... Lord knows why, it lay empty for so long..." he shook his head. "She balked. She couldn't deal with the guilt and she was threatening to go to the Gardai. Nothing I said could change her mind. I faked the appointment to view the house to get her alone. I planned to try and talk some sense into her. Remind her how we could all be ruined if she revealed everything. She wasn't having it and so I..."

The words were final.

"This is actually getting ridiculous," whispered Jonathan, half to himself. "You have some serious issues, lad."

Nick shook his head violently, as if attempting to expel some demon that lay within him. "No! Things got heated, it was spur of the moment, Jono."

"God, you always have an answer don't you?"

"It's not that-"

"Mate, cut it! You went there *with a gun*!"

The noise Nick expelled was an alliance of frustration and despair that was somehow deplorable and pitiful at once. " I didn't go there with a gun. It was her own. She pulled it on me and said she'd shoot if I didn't go to the Guards and confess. There was a struggle when I tried to get the gun from her and that's when it happened. I'm not trying to say I did nothing wrong but it was self- defence."

Jonathan nodded slowly. "Right. It happened, yeah, that's right Nick. Whatever."

Still burning, Nick's eyes alighted on me.

"Well..." I began, a slight tremor encroaching, "Wh.. what about my dad?"

At this, he flinched perceptibly but I did not retract my words. He may have been my father but he was not yet my dad. It was time that earned that title.

"I... I do know what happened to Paul, Julia."

The world halted.

"But... you're not going to like it."

Evading my notice until then, I realised Jonathan had filled the void beside me and wrapped his arms solicitously about my shoulders, skimming the exposed skin on my lower arms with his possessive hands.

"Julia... I did not kill Paul," Nick cantillated purposefully. "Your mother did."

CHAPTER 64

9 Months Earlier

Eve feels alive. Tonight is the night. She has been patient. She has been loyal. She has repressed her true urges for too long. Paul is working the nightshift. Julia is with a friend. Any questions they have as to her whereabouts will perish. Unlike her desire for Nicholas Joyce.

For almost twenty-two years, Eve Barnacle has spent every waking moment burning for that man. It is insensible. Pathetic. Feeble. After all, this is Nick. Nick who seduced her, got her pregnant and cheated on her. With Alice. Her best friend since childhood. What has sustained her all these years is that he did not know. About Julia. If he had, he would never have so much as looked at Alice. That, at least, is what Eve tells herself.

Paul was her saviour. There is no denying that. He guided her through when she thought there was no other way. He loves Julia so much. Like she is his own child. Not his brother's. He loves her too but that love is unrequited. It is such a desperate shame that she does not reciprocate his love. Yes, she cares for him deeply. So very deeply. But on every occasion Paul's lips touch hers, she dreams they belonged to Nick.

After that summer, when they returned home, she and Paul had presented a united front. Eve had feared her parents' reaction when she announced she was pregnant, but they had taken it well. They liked Paul. And Julia, their only granddaughter, meant all the world to them. Shortly after Julia was born, Eve and Paul married. No one ever knew the truth about Julia's real father.

Eve told Nick before they left Spain. She often wondered what he thought about her decision to build a life with Paul. He did not attempt to stop her. Request a second chance. Eve is certain and always has been, that if he had said the word her heart would have been his once more. But he had not. He remained a large part of their lives and had a relationship with Julia so wonderfully treasured by them both. Each day, it was displayed to Eve how very alike they were. Paul saw it as well. She presumes it crushed him a little inside. It crushed her, too. You see, Eve's life was perfect. A perfect daughter, a successful career, an attentive husband who would have done anything for her. Perfect in every way but one: Nick and Paul's roles were the wrong way round. It was Nick who should have been her partner and Paul the devoted brother-in-law.

She admits it: the desire has never cooled. Despite everything Nick did. For fifteen years, she had suffered, longing for him in the manner she had on that fateful night. Family holidays spent with the four of them together. Watching Nick on the beach, unapologetically flaunting his toned chest and tanned skin. Paul was handsome she supposed. Nice and sensible. Extremely tame like a cultivated flower. Not an agrestal weed like Nick. A weed she wanted with every fibre of her being.

Sometimes, she indulged herself in the fantasy that he felt the same way about her. That they were lovers divided by supernatural forces. Destined to become as one again. In another life. The altercations they had were quite an event to behold. Eve and Nick fought as only lovers could. There was such pent- up passion between them that it needed a vent of some description. Otherwise, they would have combusted. Overcome by the vehemence that should have released...in other ways.

Nick had demons. That much, Eve was apprised of. He was liable to make questionable decisions. That he had got into trouble with the wrong crowd barely came as a surprise to Eve. A restless spirit. A haunted man. She pondered then; if they had been together, would he have made better choices?

What he did admit though, beneath the front porch as he left for the final time, was that he loved her. That he would come back for her. Whenever he had sorted all this mess out. She simply had to be patient. He kissed her. Desperately. Before he slipped away with that parting phrase which has played perpetually on the gramophone of her mind ever since: "To be continued."

After Nick vanished, there was comfort in a form of...relief. She was no longer tortured by his beauty. She could commit herself to Paul. For the time being, until Nick came back for her. What they say, though, is true. Absence makes the heart grow fonder. It fans the flame of desire already so gargantuan it could light Dublin Bay after dark and Eve knows she would not have survived the waters of the last seven years without the raft that was his promise.

When the letter arrived, she was initially confused. After all, who even sent letters anymore? Turning the thick paper of the envelop over in her hands, she had recognised the handwriting immediately. Nick. He wanted to meet her, said he would explain everything, that it had been too long. As Eve's keen eyes scanned the curlicued words, she saw in print before her what she had interminably craved. Nick's second affirmation of love. He wanted her. Just as she wanted him. They could not withhold any longer.

She wrote back to the return address. Somewhere on Dawson Street. An office she presumed. If she found that peculiar, she did not dwell on it. Eve arranged a night she knew she would be alone in the house. When Paul and Julia were out. Soon, she would feel what she had not felt in well over two decades. The love of Nicholas Joyce.

Now, with his arrival imminent, she surveys her reflection in the mirror. Just as she did that night before they left for the club and her fate was sealed. Age has been kind to Eve Barnacle. She is an attractive woman still. Of this she is aware and in acknowledgement of it, she allows herself a minute nod of satisfaction. Her honey blonde hair is arranged in waves, her face beguilingly made up, her generous figure encased in the same scarlet hue it was then. Between then and now, there really isn't a marked difference and although she has not seen him in seven years, she is somehow assured that she will want Nick every bit as much. In the form of a finishing touch, she spritzes herself in perfume. She has done some research on seductive scents and has found that sandalwood is supposed to do the trick. It bloody well better, she thinks. The way Nick looked at her that night is something she needs to see again. Paul did so much for her, but he was never really romantic. Not once in their years together did he make a grand gesture, not once did she even receive a Valentine's present. In fact, the most amorous thing Paul would do in their relationship was pay the mortgage. He didn't even do that. Eve *always* paid the mortgage.

Every year though, Nick had gotten her and Julia a Valentine's gift. The two most important women in his life deserved it, he said. Nick had plenty of girlfriends over the years. A multitude in fact but none of them lasted. Eve likes to think that was because his heart lay with her.

The doorbell rings. Usually, Eve finds the sound shrill. Bleating. Now though, it is like the gentle strum of a violin. Calling her softly to love. The door is opened. He is there. Twice as gorgeous than the image that has been emblazoned across her mind since the last time those piercing pools of glacial fire swam before her. Those lips. That coiffed dark hair.

"Eve," he growls the word huskily. Growls it like it is precious.

"Nick. Oh my God, Nick." Eve's words are reverential.

He does not reply but winds his arms around her and embraces her, her face pressed against that chest of pure muscle.

Reluctantly, she retracts. "Where have you *been*?"

"I promise I'll explain everything Eve but just... just let me kiss you first."

She begins to protest but her words are as negligible as sunlight in winter.

"Eve," Nick starts again, placing one finger beneath her chin and tilting her face towards his own. "Look me in the eyes and tell me you don't want this."

"I...I..." stammers Eve, words deserting her.

"I thought so," says Nick with evident satisfaction.

Advancing hungrily, their mouths meet. It does not stop there. Nicholas Joyce has red flags emanating from every pore of his edifice but when Eve is in his company, well, she acts like she is colourblind. Twenty-two years ago, Eve did not see that a night with Nick would end in a broken heart. In this moment, once more, Eve does not see that a night with Nick will seismically alter the course of her life. Forever.

CHAPTER 65

Something about Nick has been altered. Eve is sure of that as she gazes at him lying beside her. He is still very much...Nick... yet somehow more...affectionate. Like he wants *her.* Not just physically but emotionally, romantically, in every possible way.

"I can't believe it's really you," he grins, flaunting the pearlescent teeth that catch the dim bedroom light and scatter it across the two of them.

Absentmindedly, Eve twists the wedding band around her ring finger. It is loose. She has never noticed that before.

"I probably should have taken this off."

Nick chortles. "You don't love him, Eve."

Some miniscule part of Eve finds itself compelled to defend the partnership she knows is little more to her than two close friends living together. "You don't know that."

"I do."

I do. Those two little words that say so much. They mean so little though. Eve said them to Paul, believing at the time that she meant them and yet she has now betrayed them. In the most extreme sense.

"Nick," she sighs. "You still have a lot of explaining to do."

The clock placed on the bedside table emits five rhythmic ticks. Each is the obtrusive blare of a horn.

"It was just my job."

"Your job? Really, Nick?"

"Yes! I didn't have a choice." His voice is hopeful. It seems he is begging her to believe him.

Eve turns onto her side and fixes his visage firmly in her line of sight.

"Nick. Cut the crap."

"Look, Eve. I didn't realise when I started working there that it was being run by... a cult."

"So that makes it OK?"

"No, of course it doesn't but I... never intended to kill anyone."

"But you did."

"I had to." He is becoming increasingly defensive. "To protect myself."

"To keep you on the right side of the bars," Eve offers sarcastically.

"Exactly!"

"Are you still involved with them?"

"Well..." That response is the shiest Eve has seen Nick.

"You are, aren't you?"

"I own an estate agency now. Rockstar Real Estate."

"That place that makes those idiotic property tour videos and plasters them all over Facebook?"

He throws back his head and guffaws at that. "You haven't changed a bit Eve, you know that?"

"Let's keep on topic here."

"Right. Yes, that's me. Frederick Featherington-Smythe, the proprietor of Rockstar Real Estate."

It is now Eve's turn to laugh. "An alter-ego?"

"It's who I am."

"I thought you had to leave the country?"

"I did...for a while but I came back a few years ago to set up the agency."

"But let me guess, you still have to be loyal to them. Or else they'll rat you out."

He sighs. "Yes."

"I thought so."

"You should see it though, Eve. I've got a great thing going. We're at the forefront of the property market actually! Eventually, I'll be able to break away from them totally. Leave it all behind me and turn over a new leaf. With you. We could run the place together. You could be my partner and not just in business." There is something almost childishly optimistic in the phrase.

"What about my job and... Paul? It's not that simple, Nick. I wish it were but it's not. I know he isn't romantic or... well...like you-" Nick smiles at that, "but he loves me in his own way. I'm sure of that."

He tilts his head closer to her and gives her that indescribable look. "Domesticated love, Eve. Be honest: that's not for you."

Eve toys with the lace at her neckline. "You *are* the type to be an estate agent. I shouldn't be surprised."

"The type? What do you mean?" He appears genuinely curious, joviality again infiltrating his tone.

"Incredibly persuasive, frustratingly charming."

"I'll take that as a compliment."

"You're assuming that *I* find you charming," she raises one eyebrow, an old habit and one Julia has inherited.

"Come on, Eve. I think we've established that," Nick says surprisingly tenderly, reaching for her hand.

"I don't blame you, Nick," she ignores the shiver coursing through her at his touch. "Everybody makes mistakes and... I want you to know that I love you. No matter what."

"I do know that, Eve." He pauses and becomes fixated on the ceiling. "Back then, with Celia. I only started things with her because I thought you weren't interested. It didn't last anyway. If we had talked..."

"She knew. She was with me when I found out and she knew it was your baby."

"What?" he is indignant. "That's terrible... that's..."

"Yeah, it is."

There is quiet then but it is far from uncomfortable. Nick speaks first.

"There wasn't a day that I didn't think about you. And Julia."

"She's studying medicine, you know."

"Oh, trust me, I kept tabs. Our Julia," he shakes his head. "I would apologise for... that night. We were foolish but...she was worth it."

That is when he is interrupted by the slamming of a door.

CHAPTER 66

"Eve? Eve, where are you?" her husband hollers.

It is Paul. Why is he back? Isn't he supposed to be working?

Nick and Eve simultaneously swear. They scramble up.

"Hide!" Eve hysterically hisses. Nick makes a beeline for the bathroom across the hall.

Flustered, she emerges from the bedroom and onto the landing. Paul is just ascending the stairs. He halts abruptly when he sees her.

"Eve...why are you...wearing so little?"

Feasible excuses as to why she is hovering guiltily on the landing adorned in a lacy nightdress unlike any other garment she possesses are scarce but she is going to have to play this off somehow. Despite the urgency of the situation, a poisoned dart pierces her heart at the fact that her attire does not affect him in any way. There is nothing in his words except confusion. Maybe if there was even one trace of lust, she wouldn't have spent almost half her life pining for his brother. In the earlier days she had almost convinced herself that she loved Paul. How deeply she regretted that it had been an illusion.

"Oh, hi, Paul. I was just... clearing out my wardrobe and I found this. Been a while since I wore it," she laughs in what is intended as a tinkling sound. In reality, It's reminiscent of nails on a blackboard. Change the subject. That is what she should do. "Why are you home? Aren't you on the nightshift?"

"One of the lads rang and asked me to swap with him. I'm on tomorrow instead."

The loudest silence Eve has ever encountered ensues. Paul is staring at her intently. Suspiciously. She can almost penetrate his forehead and see the cogs turning in his mind. The pieces slotting into place.

"Who is it?" he demands suddenly and sharply.

"Wh... what do you mean?" she queries.

Paul is no fool. Why is she surprised? It hardly takes a genius. Without another word, he barges past her and into their bedroom. He assesses the space with a cursory glance and then strides back out and over to the bathroom. Unceremoniously, he throws open the door. To reveal his brother. The same brother who, seven years ago, committed a heinous crime and was discovered by Julia. The same brother who went AWOL. The same brother who is now hiding in a bathroom in a half-buttoned shirt.

Eve's heart plummets to her toes. Paul swivels on the spot, looking between his wife and his brother. Syllables elude him. Until they don't.

"Is this some kind of joke?" he bellows. She did not think Paul was capable of bellowing.

"Afraid not, bro," Nick says casually, really not helping.

"HOW COULD YOU, EVE?" He is reaching unchartered decibels and, in that moment, Eve feels nothing but culpable. "After everything I did for you?" This is said close to a whisper that is somehow worse than the shouting.

"Paul, darling, I'm so, so sorry. I promise it's not what it looks like. I-"

"I don't want to hear it, Eve." His words are a knife that slices between them.

"But you," he points an accusatory finger at Nick. "After you betrayed her before, what you did in that...institution. You come back here after *seven years* and *sleep with my wife*?"

"Wouldn't *exactly* describe it as sleeping now Paul but you know-"

"God but you always were one sick-" With this, Paul lunges

forward and seizes Nick by the scruff of the neck. As their tousling intensifies, they spill out of the bathroom and onto the landing in harmony with the mutual fury that courses through their veins.

"Stop, please!" begs Eve, stepping between them.

Paul throws a punch at Nick which misses its mark by a margin, resulting in a clip around the ear.

"Don't do that, Paul!" cries Eve, rounding on him. Nick discreetly backs away.

"He deserves much worse and if it's the last thing I do I'll see that he gets it." With that, he springs towards his brother but before his fist can make contact with Nick's face, Eve shoves Paul sideways. It happens in slow motion. The fall down the stairs. Nick and Eve both hear the crack.

Their footsteps are thunder, pounding the steps. Eve's scream is lightning, illuminating the reality of the scene before them. Paul is lying, prone, on the cream tiles of the hallway. Motionless. She shouts his name. She shakes his shoulder. She knows that he is dead.

CHAPTER 67

In slow motion, Eve pulls back on her knees and coaxes herself into a standing position.

"Oh. My. God," she begins to tremble uncontrollably, every inch of her vibrating. "Sweet Jesus, Nick. What have I done?" He does not reply but gently moves her aside and crouches down beside his brother's body. "Cervical fracture... subarachnoid haemorrhage," he muses quietly. "Instantaneous."

"It's not your medical finals, Nick!"

He scratches his head. "Sorry, old habits die hard and..." Nick halts, the irony of his words hitting home.

"A broken neck." Eve is the one speaking pragmatically now. "We have to make it look like an accident. A fall down the stairs; it's common. Isn't it? Isn't it, Nick? Come on, Nick, speak to me!"

"It *was* an accident, Eve. You didn't murder him!"

"You need to go." Eve forces herself to say it before she can change her mind.

"No way, Eve. I got you into this mess and I'm going to get you out of it."

"Nick, my husband is dead. Your brother is dead. This is much more than a 'mess!'" she cannot conceal the exasperation.

"Right, I know, sorry. So... what? You call the police and tell them you...found him like this?" he asks.

"Do you have a better idea?"

"No."

Eve places her hands on Nick's shoulders and looks him straight in the eyes. "You need to go."

"I can't-"

"You have to," she says with steely finality. "This is my battle, not yours."

"Let it be our battle! Please, Eve, I love you!" he pleads.

Her lips find his and linger. "You kept me out of your trouble and now it's my turn to keep you out of mine."

He protests. She knew he would. "That's idiotic. You think I'm going to let you go again after all this time?"

She runs her finger along his jaw. That strong jaw that is now clenched in emotions she does not quite comprehend. "I promise you this is not the end. You just need to go. For now. Until this passes. And then... and then I promise we'll find a way. To be continued, Nick."

CHAPTER 68

Julia

"I'm so sorry, Julia."

My head shot upwards at my mum's voice.

She was standing there, framed in the doorway, face pitifully penitent. Limbs vibrating violently, she crossed the room and placed her hands on Nick's shoulders. He had kicked back further in the armchair, exhausted from the effort of telling the tale.

"Eve?" said Jonathan incredulously. "What are you doing here?"

I could not speak.

"I've been here all along."

"Why?" I managed; my voice strangled.

"Nick and I... we've started seeing each other again. In secret."

Nick chimed in then: "For the last few months now. We thought it was... best this way."

"Best this way?" I challenged accusatorily. "Best to keep secret the fact that I was working for my uncle... actually, never mind, my *father*?"

"Look, Julia-"

"And I suppose this is why the house is going up for sale. Because you're shacking up with him. Hmm?"

"Julia-"

"Mammy, is it true?"

"Yes, Julia, it is."

Her head hung low, her fingers kneading through the fabric of her dress like it was some sacred text that would provide the solution to an invisible equation. But it wouldn't.

The equation of my life was so far off balance it could not be solved.

"It's why I encouraged you to take the job. I knew it would be good for you to take a year out, with the grief and all that. Experience something other than medicine. Work for Nick. It's brought him so much *joy*, Julia. Believe me when I say that."

In one sudden movement, Nick stood up from the armchair, pulled me to my feet and enveloped me in an embrace. "Julia," he said tenderly, brushing my cheek with his thumb. "My beautiful daughter."

At first, I was stoic. Then though, slowly but surely, I reciprocated his action.

What I said next shocked me more than anyone.

"Daddy..." I mumbled as I buried my head in his chest.

I was falling. Back in time. A young child in the arms of her father. A young woman by a graveside, a single rose in her hand. Thinking that paternal love was gone forever. And then, somehow, I was both. A child. An adult. Merged as one. In the arms of her father.

Home at last.

Blinded by emotion, he clung to me still. Not willing to relinquish his hold. "I've... I've been waiting twenty-one years for you to call me that, Julia."

It felt right. It really did. A thing lost and found again.

Quietly, my mum burst the bubble. "Nick? Remember we have something else to tell Julia."

"Oh no, please, I can't take anymore," moaned Jonathan. "I feel like going on the lash just to clear my noggin."

"I promise this is the last thing, Johnny," mammy reassured him.

"Why do I struggle to believe that?" he muttered wryly.

Nick steeled himself. "We're moving out to Spain. Together."

"You're joining up with *them* again?" yelped Jonathan.

"No! Jono, don't be a spanner. Not everybody in Spain is in it you know!" said Nick.

"Really? Because I was kinda thinking they were at this rate," he whispered weakly.

"Well, where to? I questioned. "La Cala?"

"No. Frigiliana. Nick has a villa from when he was... out there before." My mum finished her sentence self- consciously. "It's why I'm selling up. We'll still be in Dublin some of the time so we're keeping this place." She gestured around her. "I'm sorry you had to find out everything like this Julia. We had been planning to break it to you gently. Nick was going to tell you who he really was at some point soon. But we didn't want to be too sudden," she reached out for Nick's hand. "Make sure things were going to work out this time."

"And... when are you... leaving?" I asked hesitantly.

"In a few weeks."

For a long while, there was quiet. Nick drummed his fingers along the upholstery. My mum continued to fidget with her skirt. Jonathan was breathing heavily.

"I'm happy for you."

The words sprang from me unbidden. As the pure and honest truth.

"I really am," I reiterated. "You... you deserve to be in love. It didn't work out ... back then." I swallowed. "But I... I hope it will now."

And, before I was quite conscious of what was happening, my

mum leapt on me. Throwing her arms around my neck, she held me. Tightly. “Thank you, Julia,” she said gently. “It means all the world to me, you know. To us both,” she added quickly. “Truly it does.”

I’ll speak plainly now.

Nick had sinned. My mum had sinned. I had sinned in protecting them.

But if there is one thing you would do well to learn about me, it is that I will go to great lengths for the ones that I love. No matter what.

Whatever life brings, I will stand by them. When rain cascades and the wind gusts high, I will be there. Sheltering them.

When the world is calm, I will be at rest. Beside them. And when the sun shines brightly, I will bask in its glow. Together with them.

Dysfunctional we may be. But we are a family. My mum, Nick, Jonathan and I.

In that moment, despite the utter absurdity of the past hours, I knew that the next chapter in my life was beginning. After all, each one of us deserves love. No matter the circumstances, nothing in this life should prevent you from being with the person whose heart calls to yours. To love is a right held by us all. For love is *never* a sin.

CHAPTER 69

Julia- 3 Months Later

It was Jonathan who persuaded me to accept the invitation.

The envelope was of parchment, tied with a neat bow. Formal but not exactly official. It had been delivered to my house. Yes, still the same house. Following the revelations of that day in Drumcondra, my mum had agreed to postpone the sale for a while. Until I had saved up a little more to allow me to afford my own property. The book would assist with that, I hoped. It was now completed and submitted to my publisher, within its pages the promise of my future.

Soon though, Jonathan would be primed to place a sign in the garden and it would be time to bid farewell. Over the past few months, I had reflected on this circumstance greatly. Finally, though, I had arrived at the conclusion that it was the right thing to do. We can at times be restrained by what is familiar to us and, if I were to remain in my childhood home, I would be forsaking the opportunity of fulfilling my own aspirations of ownership.

Now, companionably devouring our lunch in Bewley's, I presented Jonathan with the letter. Wiping his hands on a napkin, he scanned the writing hurriedly.

"Nick's 50th," he said, swallowing a bite of his sandwich. "At the villa in Frigiliana."

"Yes, Watson. I can read. What do you think?"

Shrugging as if the answer were obvious, he replied: "We go."

Rather disconcerted by his response, I shifted restlessly in my seat. "I... I thought we should maybe give it a miss."

His brow furrowed. "Why? My darling, it's an excuse to get away! Plus, there'll be a free bar."

Jonathan didn't exactly require an excuse; we'd been travelling together a lot lately. With Nick working in Spain (still under his pseudonym, likely to avoid any confusion amongst clients who knew him as Freddie), Jonathan was now practically in charge of the Dubin branch of Rockstar Real Estate and together, we had plans to expand the company even further. We had spent some time in Cyprus where we were keen to make an impression in the property market and I had a positive feeling our chances of success were high. Come September, I would be returning to university to complete my medical degree. But we all know Jonathan couldn't run the place without me, so, I'd continue to assist during my holidays and spare time. Despite my fears that all efforts would fail, I had even managed to secure the interest of several international buyers in Maycroft Demesne.

I don't mean to sound egotistical or anything but it turns out I make a fabulous rockstar.

Anyway, back to the invitation.

"But Johnny," I said with a sigh, "they want us to go out for a full two weeks!"

"So? Come on Julia, you've been on much longer holidays than that!"

"I know but... do you really want to spend that much time with them?"

At that, he fell silent.

I love my mum and Nick. After all, they're my *parents* but there's... a lot of history there. With all the lies they'd both been telling me for so long, I'll admit I'd been finding it rather difficult to be in their company for extended periods of time. Like I previously said, I would do anything to protect them. However, it's simply been... difficult lately.

When Jonathan spoke again, it was with understated purpose and intention. "Julia, look. You know I have no relationship with my mother. And... that's okay. I learnt to live with that a long time ago.

I had to." The downward cast of his eyes and rippling of his throat as he swallowed did not go unnoticed to me. Without a syllable, I reached out for his hand and grasped it protectively.

"It's okay, Watson. I'm here," I whispered.

He nodded before continuing: "And after what the jealous cow tried to do to you, I wouldn't want to have a relationship with her. Not for anything in the world." He paused uncertainly. "What you had with Eve though... that was special, Julia. I saw you together, you were like sisters! I know it's usually you giving me the advice," a smile waltzed on his lips, "but I really don't think you should give that up."

I knew he was right. Jonathan being right? Miracles never cease as they say.

Seriously, though, he was.

"That's... that's a fair point, Jonathan," I admitted.

Then, gripping my knife firmly in my hand, I said with conviction: "We'll go to the 50th."

CHAPTER 70

Julia

As a direct consequence of that conversation, we found ourselves arriving in Frigiliana a mere week later. Located east of Malaga, it is designated as one of the most picturesque areas in Spain and one where property is highly desirable. Characterised by Moorish architecture, an Arabian enchantment echoes evocatively from its position upon the slopes of the Sierra Almijara. Sprawling like some jagged multiplication square, the village's houses lie in respectful repose, their whitewashed stucco walls and red roofs an ink blot against the electric blue sky. Set slightly apart from the main town, there resides Nick's villa. It resembles an oversized traditional Spanish finca, the site occupying the majority of a hillside. With a low-pitched clay roof, a significant square footage spread over multiple levels, a veritable jungle of technicoloured vegetation, wide courtyards patterned in mosaic tiles and a swimming pool of Olympic proportions, it exemplifies the Spanish Colonial style to perfection. In defiance of its blatant antiquitarian ambience, the property exudes a cheerful demeanour, effortlessly transporting a ribbon of modernity through its soft arches and intricately carved wooden doorways.

My mum and Nick crossed the foreground to greet us, faces illuminated in welcome.

"Hey, hey, Rockstars!" Nick proclaimed at such a volume that I was confident all of Andalusia were now apprised of our arrival. He afforded Jonathan some masculine expression of affection in the form of a half hug- half handshake gesture that succeeded in almost knocking Jonathan off his feet. When he turned to me, it was with an exuberant kiss on the cheek and loving hug.

My mum embraced us both then too, with her usual warmth. I almost managed to relax. Almost.

Jonathan had been equally as concerned about the whole trip as I was, mainly due to the fact he remains slightly terrified of Nick, or as he thinks of him even now, Freddie. He had encouraged me to accept the invitation though and I was glad of it because I really did not want to risk damaging my relationship with either of my parents further. God, it still seems strange saying that. Nick being my father remains rather a foreign concept to this day. I suspect it always will to an extent. But it's a good foreign; if that makes sense.

"Like the statue," I remarked, assessing with a raised eyebrow the unclothed male figure rising from the middle of the decorative fountain that formed the focal point of the driveway. "Very... unique."

"I know, it's a self- portrait," Nick declared with a proud guffaw.

Jonathan looked as if he was going to turn on his heels and run all the way back to Dublin.

"You better behave yourself Watson," I whispered into his ear as we were lead into the house, "if you give me any grief, I'll take him down and put you up there instead."

Once Jonathan and I had unpacked, we reemerged downstairs where Nick suggested that he and Jonathan 'go for scoops' at an Irish pub in the nearby village of Nerja. Likely less than enthusiastic about this prospect, he none the less agreed and the two headed out together, leaving my mum and I alone.

Throughout my whole life, my mum was my closest confidante. I was comfortable telling her anything and I had believed there was nothing that could alter the dynamics between us. I was wrong. Anger was not my primary emotion towards her; although it was present. What greatly affected me however, was disappointment. Disappointment that she had failed to be honest with me. For my entire life.

"How are you Julia?"

Nestled in a sun saturated corner of the garden beside a fruitful grove of apple trees, we were reclining on their suite of outdoor furniture, sipping cocktails. Something in the mundanity of the question affected me and I bit my lip in discomfort.

"Really well mammy," I replied. "The agency's... flourishing and it's all about to get going with the book and..." I shrugged. "Things are wonderful actually."

She did not immediately reply but rather seemed to cast around for some elusive intangible.

"I'm so proud of you, Julia," she said finally. Enshrouding the words was a veil of sincerity. She meant it.

Running my forefinger along the surface of my glass, I watched the miniscule bubbles of condensation dissipate at my touch, each becoming a negligible entity as they merged into each other.

"Thank you," I replied simply. I allowed the words to linger, hovering to keep vigil in memory of an earlier time. A time when I had doubted myself, too. A time that seemed a forgotten century but was little more than a recent second that had just past in a fleeting breeze.

There was something I had to ask her. It was necessary. Although a large part of me feared her answer.

"Mammy, are you happy with Nick?"

Her forehead crinkled contemplatively. "What do you mean, Julia? Of course I am! Why would you ask that?"

Her words were edged with panic.

"Do you love him, mammy?"

She moved her lips as if to reply but nothing made it through them.

"I mean really love him," I persisted.

"I... I do. Why else would I have moved out here with him?"

What I was to say next was imperative. So, to compose myself properly, I tapped my nail three times against the glass. Insistently.

"I... I just want to make sure that you're not getting confused between love and lust." I spoke carefully but with faith in my sentiments. "Because there's a big difference."

I had almost expected her to become incensed by this. However, she nodded in a symbol of understanding. "It should really be me telling you that, shouldn't it?" she said slowly with a miscarried laugh. Abruptly, she stopped and then went on: "You're very lucky, Julia."

"In what way?"

She gulped a mouthful of her cocktail. "To have someone like Jonathan. He's... he's a lovely boy. And gorgeous." Her wink was devilish and, in that measure of it, it seemed as if no time had passed. That I was back in my childhood, cuddled close to the woman I believed could do no wrong. Momentarily, I salivated for innocence.

Then though, the moment passed and I came to the present again.

As it always did when someone mentioned his name, a blush infiltrated my cheeks. "He's... he's wonderful," I murmured quietly. "A plonker like but... my plonker."

We both laughed heartily at that.

"I knew from the very first time I saw you with him, Julia. You try to hide it but you're head over heels for him. As much as I know that's against your feminist morals."

Unable to cease smiling, I replied with meaning: "I am, mammy, I am."

There was silence as I broke off but I soon continued again.

"But that's the thing. I *love* Jonathan. Truly love him. For *everything* about him. The flaws, the vulnerabilities, the quirks," I swallowed. "Not just the polished exterior. The tarnished things too." My short outburst had left me moderately breathless. "And I want to make sure that's how you feel about Nick. Because anything less... that's not love. It's just... a crush, really. Or an infatuation."

Again, she made no direct response.

Instead, she turned her face upwards towards the sun. Glowing amber like a fortune teller's orb.

"You know," she began weakly. "They say it takes eight minutes for the sun's light to reach us."

Where exactly was the physics lesson going?

"I... I've read that."

"And you know what that means Julia?" she demanded firmly, fixing me with an expression rendered unreadable by her oversized sunglasses.

"What, mammy?"

"Everything we're looking at is the past."

With an unobtrusive clink, I placed my glass on the table before me, preparing for her to continue.

"And that means," she straightened up a little, "that there is no present. For we see the present only in hindsight. And, by then, it's too late."

Her voice cracked, hairline fractures fissuring through precious porcelain.

"If we could only *see* the present, then nobody would ever make mistakes. But we can't!" This was announced with an almost manic giggle. "So, we do! We make mistakes, we all-"she paused, "we all make mistakes. We *sin*, Julia."

The disturbance within my soul writhed. A palpable thing, it coursed through every cell, every pore, every inch of my body.

She became like a boat then. Like a boat when the wind dies down. Like a boat when it is deprived of its sails with the looming shadow of darkness encompassing it, returning to shore to escape the things it cannot control. Tenderly taking my fingers in her own, she intoned tearfully: "But Julia, if life has taught me one thing, it is that there is beauty in imperfection. There is beauty in sin."

My breath was stolen.

"And Nick... he is a sinful man. But it's like you say, Julia... I take him as he is. For better or worse, I take him. Because there's nothing else I can do!" She dissolved into irreconcilable sobs. I allowed her to cry. There I sat, her hand in mine, like a child's in her mother's. Roles reversed.

I will never fully comprehend the question that I asked then. But I asked it anyway.

"Mammy, did you love daddy?"

She emitted a strangled sound and I thought the tears were going to relapse.

They didn't.

Her words were wilting flowers, drenched by a summer rain: "Paul was... he was a good man. A good father to you, Julia. A better man than Nick." This obviously pained her. "I cared for him," she finished.

"But you didn't love him?"

She stood and crossed to the nearest tree. Hand trembling, she reached up and took an apple from a low hanging bow. Into its skin, she sank her teeth.

She ate the fruit.

"I remember, Julia," she began with a latent quality, "the day that he asked me to marry him."

I did not speak.

"You were a week old."

She resumed her seat on the sofa.

"I wanted you to have a father, Julia. I didn't want the shame of my sin."

A solitary tear absconded. A serpent from her eye.

"So, you know what I said?"

I did know.

"Yes, I said. Yes, I will. Yes."

CHAPTER 71

Jonathan

'Splitting the G' with my boss (who happens to be my girlfriend's father who happens to be the perpetrator of multiple homicides who also just happens to be a massive *twat*) was not *that* far up the list of things I was desperate to do today but anyway. There you are. The things I do for love.

Would you believe that Frigiliana, despite featuring in a Christy Moore song, does not have an Irish bar? I know, mad craic. As a result, we had to make the short trip to Nerja to get some black stuff and that is why we found ourselves in The Irish Harp, sipping creamy pints at a bar of polished oak.

"So, Jono," began Nick (it's still strange not calling him Freddie) while giving me a violent thump on the back. "It's great to get some man time. Those dolls can be hard work."

"Yeah..." I replied rather uncertainly.

"Right, tell us then, what's it like going out with Julia?"

Ehh... was it normal to be seeking particulars from someone who's dating your *daughter*? Did the weirdo wish *he* was dating her? Honestly, nothing would have surprised me with that dude by then. Even at that though, I don't require much encouragement to talk about my Julia.

"It's... amazing. She's my whole world, Nick." I shook my head. "I don't know how I lasted twenty-five years without her."

When I looked up at him, the emotions written on his face surprised me. He seemed... pensive. I was suddenly reminded of the phone call I'd had with him the night after Julia had the allergic reaction. He'd *cared*. A father worried about his daughter. A simple and natural thing.

"Jono, you're the luckiest man in the world, you know that don't you?"

"I...I do," I said slowly. "I don't deserve her."

Nick sat further back on the bar stool and assessed me critically. "Look, Jono. I know it's still sinking in but... I'm her dad. And because of that, I don't think anyone is worthy of her," he appeared to become fixated on something behind my head. "But you come as close as it's possible to get. There's no one else I'd rather her be with. Know that. Please."

That Guiness couldn't have gone to his head already, could it?

In all seriousness though, his words touched me.

"I appreciate that, Nick," I replied firmly. "She'd hate me saying it but... I'll take good care of her."

He threw his head back and chortled openly. "You're right she would. Bit of a bra burner is our Julia."

At my rather offended expression, he hastened to add: "Not that I think it's great. I mean... I'm incredibly proud of the woman she's become."

I couldn't prevent the grin of affection that leapt to my lips. "She's... just not like any other girl I've ever met. I love her for it." I probably sounded hopelessly lovesick but who cares. I am, at the end of the day.

"I can see how much you love her, Jono."

Quiet enveloped us then. It was companionable, possessing a silent camaraderie.

"Jono?"

He startled me out of my thoughts. "Yeah?"

"There's a few things I wanted to say to you. As her dad." There was a certain light that was born on his face as he said this. It was like he had longed to be able to say it for a very long time.

"I'm all ears."

"Julia... Julia's a complicated girl. And again, I mean that in the best way possible. She's been through quite a lot and she doesn't really publicise it to people because she's very resilient and... she believes in getting on with things. In her own way," he started. "She's not one to follow the crowd; never has been. That's because she's always been quite mature for her age, looking at the world differently from people around her. Do you understand me, Jono?"

"Yes," I wasn't exactly sure how best to respond. He summed her up well. All the things I loved most.

"You can be sure of one thing; there'll never be two days the same," he said with a laugh. "But you understand her, Jono and she's grateful for that. I can promise you."

"She's my everything," I repeated unambiguously. Because it was the truth; plain and simple.

"But please just remember that... the beautiful woman you love was, not so long ago, my little child. I couldn't openly acknowledge it and that hurt me every day but I knew in my heart that she was. And I clung to that, Jono. For dear life. I still remember the first time I held her, kissed her little head, saw her little smile." He glanced up and I could see that his eyes were moist. "I loved her then and I love her more with every day that passes."

Inexplicably, I welled up too.

"So be gentle with my little girl. Because no matter how old she grows, I still think of that little child. And I know that she's lurking in there even now. The same spirit, the same capacity to love more than anyone I know. Never take her for granted. Love her, Jonathan, with all that you are. She'll love you back; just the way she is."

His monologue was so moving that I was barely able to speak a response. Eventually, I managed a quiet: "I will, Nick. I promise you."

"You're a good lad, Jono, and you're damn good at what you do as well. Even better since Julia started doing half your job for you." He supplied his characteristic wink.

I made to defend myself but he cut across me.

"All jokes aside though; it's been an honour to have you work for me and it's an honour to have you as part of the family. You're a fine young man, believe me, Jono."

It struck me then that, really, he wasn't so awful. In fact, he was grand to have a few pints with.

After all, we were united now. United in our love for Julia Joyce.

CHAPTER 72

Julia

Nick's fiftieth Birthday bash was scheduled for the following evening and it was no understatement to say that it was to be quite the occasion.

The guest list was extensive, the villa's nightclub area and bar fully stocked and the array of culinary delights plentiful. He had hired a team of staff from a catering firm in Malaga who arrived early in the afternoon to conduct preparations, proceeding to whisk over the house like a colony of aggravating ants, getting under everyone's feet and causing a copious amount of general frustration.

However, as I stood bedecked in my carefully selecting evening finery, the sounds of the arriving partygoers wafting upwards towards me, I experienced a divergent feeling: serenity. Of the kind that occurs when you trust to the future despite the stirring within you that something is changing. That something beneath the ground is moving. A corpse called evil, rearing its head, flexing its limbs, longing to walk amongst the living again.

Voluminous in quality, my dress rippled around me in cobalt waves. The sleeves were puffed and the bodice expertly tailored to emphasise my waist; the garment oozed elegance, class and beauty. I had permitted half of my hair to fall with its natural blonde kink, the rest swept up in a halo braid that circumnavigated my head, threaded through by miniscule petals that matched the hues of my outfit. Stacks of alternating gold and silver bracelets secreted my forearms while earrings and a necklace set with sapphire stones accompanied them. As always, I wore several rings, the power of their diamonds catching the light. Distorting the light.

I had never looked better.

I had never felt such power.

Beyond the confines of the bedroom, the Sierra Almijara soared. Curving exponentially upwards, they undulated in noiseless rhythm, the haunting choir of their voices deafening the silent landscape. Clouds were scudding like passing friends, casting an insipid eye on all below. Their shapes in constant transposition, singing a melody of changing tune. The form you thought you knew borne away. To be replaced by something you would love still. Albeit differently.

Within the bedroom, light had depleted and shadows grew over the surfaces. Warping and twisting and contorting and morphing they were. Living. Breathing. Drowning. Dying.

A meek tap on the door that led into the main room from our dressing area was heard. Jonathan.

I crossed and opened it.

There he stood. In a tux.

Don't swoon, Julia, that would be *highly* idiotic, I reprimanded myself internally. It took effort though.

In the strips of depleting daylight, the waves of his boyishly fair hair glimmered. The precisely tailored tux encased him perfectly, the damask pattern of the waistcoat pulling out the flecks of colour in his eyes. He was so *very* handsome.

My Jonathan.

My Jonathan who would do anything, and I mean anything, for me.

"My darling... he trailed off as he took me in. "You... you look..." Unable to form coherent words, he instead placed his lips gently on mine. "Ethereal," he breathed finally as he moved reluctantly away. The look on his face said it all.

"You're aggravatingly handsome yourself, Watson," I said, wrapping my arms around his neck. "I must admit."

"Julia," he began with a smirk, "I don't know if I like you looking this gorgeous."

"Why, Watson?"

"Because other dudes are going to want to steal my princess," He rubbed my cheek with his thumb.

"Are said dudes annoying little plonkers called Jonathan Crookshank?"

"I hope not."

"Well then," I said, leaning confidentially towards him. "I don't give a *damn* about them."

It came as no surprise that the party was also doubling as a networking event for property professionals. Winding amongst the charcuterie style starter buffet were some of the most eminent figures in luxury real estate. I wondered passively to myself whether this evening would transform from black tie to black eye whenever, sufficiently lubricated by alcohol, the simmering rivalries bubbled to the surface. Droves of drunk and doggedly competitive estate agents? A recipe for disaster.

The villa boasted an impressive area designated for hosting parties such as this. It was located on the lowest level and kitted out with a gigantic dance floor, surround sound system and, most importantly, the bar. Nick had arranged a band who were scheduled to play for a few hours before a DJ would take over. Although I had been rather dubious about the whole occasion, I surprised myself by enjoying the night immensely. There were certainty plenty of interesting characters present and I found it a most comical biopsy of high society. At one point, there appeared to be a high-stakes dance off to ascertain which agency was most competent in the Macarena before everyone got on the ground and began doing Rock the Boat. Anto and Eamon had also flown over and Eamon, excessively inebriated, stood up on a table, removed his tie and began singing 'Lisdoonvarna' in a thick Tyrone accent.

It was a truly wonderful night.

At least it was before... well, before it wasn't.

She appeared like a mirage. A lone figure amidst the sea of bodies thronging the dancefloor. At first, I thought I had imagined her. Admittedly, I had consumed quite a few cocktails and I was fairly certain there had been at least a bottle of champagne present earlier in the evening. But I have a strong constitution. I had not drunk nearly enough to hallucinate. Not nearly enough to hallucinate that I had seen Celia.

Or Alice. Whatever the hell her name actually was.

'Maniac 2000' was pounding through the speakers but as she appeared once again from behind a cluster of Cypriot agents doing shots of ouzo, I saw that it was her. Unmistakeably.

Oh God.

Suddenly, I felt myself detach from the room, the music, the gaiety and the craic. I was floating above it all. I was back in the café in Marbella, the poison coursing through my veins, my airways closing. Then, I was in the garden at El Paraiso, realising she was my boyfriend's mother. Next, I was in the living room of the terraced Drumcondra house, discovering that this woman, this woman who had made an attempt on my life, had once been my mother's best friend. A best friend who had been by her side when she was found out that she was pregnant. With me. Such a friend that she began a relationship; with the man she knew was my father.

Feck her.

I had to think logically. She must have gate crashed. There was no way she had been invited. My mum hadn't spoken to her since that fateful summer and I was confident she wasn't exactly flavour of the month with Nick either due to the fact she tried to kill me for the grave offence of being born. The woman was obviously ill in the head. Was she *still* obsessed with Nick?

There was another possibility though: that she was back to complete the task she had failed in accomplishing. Getting rid of me.

Barging through the crowd, I emerged out of the nightclub area into the night. The temperature was now decidedly boreal, the mountain air possessing a frigidity that eluded the rest of the country. Where was Jonathan? Nick, my mum? So thick was the mass of people that I had somehow lost them all.

My dress benefitted from deep pockets, in one of which I had secreted my phone. I removed it and called Jonathan. No answer. My mum and Nick yielded voicemail too.

Unsure of what else to do, I made my way back to the main house and ascended the stairs to my bedroom. Adrenaline rushed through me but it was laced with that all too familiar undercurrent I had believed was dead and gone: pure terror.

CHAPTER 73

Jonathan

It was her; my mother.

What was she doing here?

Originally, I foolishly supposed that I had seen her but she had not seen me. That was wrong. The moment her eyes alighted on mine from halfway across the room, she made a beeline for me. Coming quickly. I had to run. I couldn't face her. Not after everything that she had done. After trying to take my girlfriend's life.

My eyes darted around the cavernous room, searching desperately for any route of escape. The main entrance was up a flight of steps, too far away for me to reach before she would be upon me. Anything would do. Anything at all. Relief doused me like a lighthouse's spotlight on a struggling sailor: a small wooden door in the far corner. I wasn't certain where it led but if I could only slip out unnoticed everything would be alright. I could find Julia and we'd have her removed. We'd call the police; have her arrested for trespassing.

Get her behind bars, where she belonged.

As it transpired, the door led out on to the pool terrace. Julia. I needed to find Julia. If I could only find Julia, this nightmare would end.

Julia. I saw her then, in my mind. Backlit in the low light of the bedroom as her image swam meanderingly before my vision. Golden locks lapping about her shoulders like the wavering waters of the pool. Personage cast in panels of shadow; she was as the unpigmented moon above. A light only made possible because of the darkness.

I wanted her. I *needed* her to sustain me. To breath her scent that was the scent of lilies. To hear her voice that was the voice of an angel. To do what she wished because what she wished was right. Always right. No matter what.

"Johnny?"

My blood froze in my veins. My mother had found me.

"Johnny, oh my darling boy!"

Unwillingly, I turned to face her. That woman. I abhorred her.

I *adored* my Julia. My Julia. Anything for Julia.

She was stumbling along the ceramic tiles unsteadily, as if at any moment, she would lose her footing and slip. I could see it now; she was absolutely wasted.

How dare she? How dare she sneak in here, an uninvited guest, and get *drunk*? Where was the class? She had no class. But Julia did. My Julia was elegant, so demure, so pure. All for me. For no one else. What she hid from the rest of the world, she did not hide from me. All mine. Forever.

"My Johnny, come to mother!" she slurred revoltingly.

Don't go to her, Watson.

"What do you want from me?" I snarled, lips curling in rage.

"I'm here for you, Johnny! I'm here to take you home!" Her words were childish. She had no claim to me. Only Julia had a claim to me.

Are you being a wimp, Watson?

"It was you." I began to advance towards her. "It was all you. Celia, Mrs. J. You did it all."

That's right. She did.

"To save you, Johnny. Save you from *her*."

No one can save you from me.

"Why would you want to be with her, Johnny?" This was pleaded. Desperately. "With *Julia Joyce*." She spat her name like it were poison. "That girl ruined my life!"

She almost ended mine.

I laughed pityingly then. "Ruined your life? Enlighten me mother, how did Julia ruin your life?"

In the short time that had elapsed since the conversation began, she had begun to sway violently. The slightest breath of wind would have knocked her over. Feather light. Like my Julia's touch.

"Eve Barnacle," she began. "That *woman!* She took my Nick. Took him from me! I loved him, Johnny. Loved him so much. But one night with her and it was gone. All of it gone!" She gasped for air but seemed to be denied it. Like she was drowning already.

Because of me.

When she continued, she did so breathlessly. "It was one night. It meant nothing. He came back to me. Just like he was supposed to! But then he found out about that stupid, stupid baby." She stopped. "And he ended it! Ended us. He felt he had to but he didn't. It was Eve's fault; she should have been more careful." She cackled grotesquely.

It was then that the incandescence began. It flowed through my veins not as a red-hot heat but as a cool fire. Cool as my Julia's skin as I enfolded her in my arms.

What if she'd taken me away from you?

"It was Julia's fault, Johnny. If it wasn't for her, I could have been happy!" She was blubbering pathetically now, droplets sliding down her cheeks.

I scoffed. "She wasn't even born, mother! How can anything have been her fault when she wasn't even born?"

Suddenly, the swaying ceased. She stood stock still. "Because Johnny," she swallowed with purpose, "of Original Sin. That girl was sinful. Sinful right from conception!"

What if I had died?

Those words had an effect on me. I hate to admit it but they did. "Don't... don't be silly, mother. This is nothing to do with Julia."

You'd never have felt my breath again.

"Have you any idea, Johnny, what it was like to find out that my son was dating that-"she swore vulgarly, "that she got her claws into you? Just like her mother got her claws into my Nick! I couldn't have that. I couldn't! I had to save you, Johnny. So when I heard the two of you were coming out to Spain, I agreed to meet with her. I thought it would have to be poison but then I heard her tell the waiter she had a nut allergy." She shrugged. "It was so simple; a switch of the plates."

You'd never have heard my voice again.

Bile rose in my throat.

"But why send the hit man, why call yourself Mrs. J? That still doesn't make any sense!"

She began to sway again. Gently. "The hit man was just a little show of theatrics. To shake you up a bit. But calling myself Mrs J," she shook her head. "That was intentional. Mrs. J, Mrs. Joyce, who I always should have been. If I could only have had my Nick."

I'd never have touched you again.

My laugh this time was a bark. "You should actually hear yourself. That's the most pathetic thing I've ever heard! You're nothing but a sad woman, mother. Not that you've any right to be called my mother. What have you ever done for me? What *one thing* have you done?"

Good boy, Watson. What a man you are.

"I'm saving you Johnny! Getting you away from her before it's too late."

It's already too late, darling. You're mine now.

"I don't need saving, mother. If anybody needs saving it's you. But I think... I think it's gone beyond that."

Her lurching increased. Grew frenzied. And before I quite knew what had happened, she was in the water.

That's where she belongs. You know it, Jonathan.

The lapping waters overtook her immediately. She could not make a sound. The alcohol pressed down on her, rendering her body unable to combat the waves as she sank, sank, sank...

You're so wonderful Watson. I love you so much, darling.

"Help me Johnny! Help me, *please*!" She somehow managed to coax out the words. But they were feeble. Just like her.

Say it, Johnny. You know you want to.

"I'm afraid mother, that we've had this date with each other from the beginning."

My words were impassive.

Just as the syllables settled like stars at the coming of night, the last shuddering breath left her lungs.

Well done, Watson.

I did it. I watched my mother die. I avenged my love.

I'm so proud of you.

What was I supposed to do then? To where did I turn?

You're coming home.

Home? What was that? What did *I* know about home?

I'm your home, Watson. You come to me.

That is exactly what I did.

CHAPTER 74

Julia

She was coming to get me.

And why was Jonathan not answering his phone?

The room was close, laden down with some incorporeal quality. Air. I needed air. With a turn of the handle, I opened the doors leading out on to the balcony and allowed the night to take me. An electricity stabbed at every inch of my exposed skin. Providing a nervous enchantment. Underscoring that certainty that something, that everything, was about to change.

A selenian mirror of the soul, the moon presided overhead. I was not aware of the exact time but I knew we were safe within the confines of an hour meant only for repose. Cloaked by invisibility, the mountains were singing again, stretching on and on. En perpetuum. Onwards through Granada, through Murcia, through Almeria and beyond. To Catalonia and to the region of the Basques. Across the Iberian Peninsula, an area renowned for its mountains; for its peaks and its troughs. A reflection of life.

Like life, it was a changing landscape. Infringing on the inky carpet above, the first tentative footsteps of dawn rang out.

I looked down.

Bathed by the moonlight were two people: Jonathan and Celia. Jonathan and his mother.

Something drained from my heart. In that moment, I knew what was about to happen. She was embarrassingly intoxicated, that much was her own fault. The slip into the pool was an accident. But the fact that my boyfriend watched her drown, ignoring her pleas for assistance, was anything but.

My heart contracted.

Ferally, he tilted his head backwards and began to laugh. A low, rumbling sound that germinated into a high-pitched scream. Thunder into lighting. The noise was not loud. It was unassuming, appearing weak.

But beneath its exterior, it possessed an unrivalled strength. Matched only by that conviction which lay within me.

My Watson and I. Two flawed people who had come, despite the odds, to do the most human thing; to love and be loved in return.

Two negative products, branded by sin, as one becoming the light of a positive promise.

Together. Human. *Always* human. Sinners.

I retreated back inside the bedroom, pulling the door behind me with a quiet thud.

Facing the dressing table mirror with a defiant expression, I settled on the stool in front of it and succumbed to the silence. There was not a sound to be heard from any pore of the night.

Jonathan was a murderer. My boyfriend who was afraid of spiders, hotels less than five stars and confrontation, had killed his mother.

He had killed her for me.

Dear reader, I promise you something; I know right from wrong. Truly I do. Or at least I know that sometimes, to do the right thing, you have to do what is wrong.

You see, I warned you earlier that you should feel sorry for Jonathan. If we are to pinpoint the victim in this situation then really, it is him. Not Celia. Excuse my crudeness but she deserved to die.

Honestly, she did.

So did Lorraine.

My dad did not deserve to die. But that, as it transpires, was really as simple as it looked. A tragic accident and nothing else.

Jonathan was the victim. Before he met me, he was an innocent boy. The most heinous crime he had committed was listing a property as a four-bedroom when it was really only a three. That was as bad as it got.

Then, he met me.

He learnt how to be deceitful. I taught him to lie. Under my tuition, he became a morally flawed man.

A man who was capable of murder. Not just any murder but matricide.

I was so *very* proud of my Johnny.

Just then, the door to our bedroom was opened. Framed in the residual light of the hallway was my boyfriend. He did not say a word as he crossed the room, my eyes tracking his progress in the mirror. Reaching my side, he knelt beside me. He lowered his lips to the nape of my neck, some uncontrollable instinct staining his pupils.

"I was hoping I'd find you here," he mumbled. His words sank into my skin. Just the same way his mother sank beneath the water.

I made no reply.

"Did you have a good night, princess?"

Still, I said nothing.

"Julia?" His question was insistent as he reached up to tuck a wisp of hair behind my ear.

So, this was the way it was going to be.

"It was... perfect," I smiled as genuinely as I could muster. "Wonderful, actually."

Insistently, his fingers crept gently down my arms. "Do you have any idea how beautiful you look?"

"You flatter me."

"Of course I do," he stroked my cheek. "You're my little angel."

I tried to resist the heat in my veins, the desire in his features. Alighting on the looking glass, my eyes took him in. Painfully attractive as he had always been. The truth? No matter if he murdered a million people, I would want him regardless. As twisted, as flawed, as antithetical as that was. The key to my heart was within his grasp. And the key to his was in mine.

Purposefully, I turned to face him. Our foreheads collided. Our lips followed suit.

The love that was the root of all evil.

Later that night, I lay in a now familiar position with my head on Jonathan's chest. He was stroking my hair, letting it slip through his fingers. Confident in the knowledge that I was safe in slumber.

I was not.

"I love you, Julia," he whispered. He paused then and even though the next words were intended only for himself to hear, he deliberated them with caution. "She can't hurt you again. *No one* can hurt you. Because I'm not going to let them. Everything I do, Julia, it's all for you."

I did not blame him. I did not.

After all, just as sin entered the world through one man and death through sin, in this way death came to all people.

Because all sinned.

CHAPTER 75

Epilogue

Julia Joyce can barely believe this day has come. The day that she will leave her home.

But when the creak of a floorboard is the ache of your heart, the sign in the lawn shooting its scintillating stare cannot be ignored any longer.

Home.

It is a strange thing. Intangible; a concept really, more so than a thing. Yet it speaks to us, travels with us, resides perpetually within the four walls that are our minds.

Home is a silent witness, a keen observer who is impassive despite seeing everything. The hopes, the fears, the dreams and the tears. They are entrusted to it. Secreted there under lock and key.

Home will give you its heart, without reluctance and possessing generosity. It takes nothing in return.

Home embraces you deeply, enfolding you in its arms. Radiating warmth, it keeps you safe.

Home is freedom like the jovial mirth of laughter. It is untamed. Wild. Incapable of being manipulated or controlled. It will be as it will be for as long as it exists.

Home is the favourite hello and the hardest goodbye.

Yet, home shelters you with compassionate restraint. A restraint you will resist. You will leave its confines. But it will not desert you. Like all-encompassing vines of germinating ivy, it remains. Growing within your heart, its boughs linger as they stretch into your mind.

Calling you home.

Now, Julia's footsteps ring out. Each one is purposeful and measured, tempered with a decided intent.

She stands in the hallway of her childhood and she surveys around her. Her ears are ringing with the laughter of three people; a girl and her parents. She yearns to hear the sound she is not really hearing. It creeps into every crevice, every nook, every cranny. And echoes.

The images are flashing before her eyes. All emotions that have been. The firsts, the lasts, the nothings and the everything.

A home. Nothing before it is everything. Everything before it is nothing again.

Before its inhabitants move on, obedient to the passage of time.

"Julia?"

Jonathan's voice startles her. Not unpleasantly though. In a solicitous gesture, he winds his arms about her shoulders. "Are you okay, darling?"

Wiping the moisture from her cheek, she intones quietly: "Yes... I... I am but it's just... so hard, Jonathan. So bloody hard."

"I know," he says simply. "I know."

The sceptre of conclusion is hovering, waltzing elegantly, taunting. Some intangible disturbance of the atmosphere, it is jeering and caterwauling in plaintive protest. Crying with the ignorance of an infant, it perishes with the aspersions of the ancient.

"I'm not ready to say goodbye." She looks up at him and in her eyes there is fear.

"You are, Julia."

Resolutely, she shakes her head. "I'm not."

"You are," he repeats with intention, drawing her closer to him.

"I'm here, Julia. There's nothing to be afraid of."

For a moment, silence reigns.

She is barely aware of their command, but somehow her feet carry her to the front living room, Jonathan's tread unobtrusive in her wake. Night has fallen, the illumination of an outside light spilling through the windowpane in golden liquid as it drips from the sill and anoints the heads of Julia and Jonathan while they settle in their perch seated upon the ground. The space around is foreign to Julia. She does not know it but she has met it many times. Barren. Funereal. Comfortless. It is the soulful sobbing of isolation, the demonic shriek of anger, the warbling of fear. Home when it is home no longer. But then she is reminded. The memories greet her. They are thundering along the floorboards, footsteps on Christmas morning. They are liberated, a child soaring on a garden swing. They are the quiet whisper of secrets, confided to the two people who meant most to her in life. They are the murmur of turning pages, a girl enveloped in the protective shawl of a book.

They are what home has meant. What is no longer but what it will perpetually be in the utopia of memory that becomes almost imagination.

"And anyway," he begins again suddenly. "You of all people should know that it's not goodbye. You're simply opening the door to the next chapter." With love in his eyes, he looks at her. Long and hard. "Or the next book."

Julia cannot help herself. Despite everything, she smiles. "Yes," she swallows the lump in her throat. "The next book." She pauses. "Jonathan?"

"Yes, Julia?"

"I... think we need to go back to Spain."

His expression is unreadable. "Why?"

"For Emily. We owe it to her, Johnny. To bring her back. To bring her home because... because we all deserve to come home. No matter what."

He nods. Cautious but assured. "I know," his whisper becomes quiet. And there is so much within that silence. Everything that he has done. Everything that they will do.

He takes her hand as they rise to their feet. "You can do this, Julia."

"I can." Her voice is firm. Inwardly, she trembles. "I have to."

And with that, Julia Joyce turns her back and crosses the threshold.

With a click of finality, the door is shut.

Before her, the sweeping driveway unfolds, giving way to the path ahead. Flowers in technicolour line its periphery, each hue keeping vigil of a memory. A memory that belonged to a house that was home.

She makes her way along it; her hand held securely in Jonathan's. She has accepted the past. There is the future for which to proceed.

But before they exit through the gates, she turns to face the cream façade once more. Standing in front of the house, there is a girl. Her hair bounces about her shoulders in blonde ringlets, the smile cavorting on her lips marred only by the gap between her front teeth.

There is a man holding the girl's hand. That man is her daddy.

As Julia watches, the two figures raise a hand in farewell. She waves back. While she does, she looks the little girl keenly in the eyes.

Julia knows that life will throw many things at that little girl. And she knows that with conviction in her soul, hope in her heart and just a little faith, she will overcome them all.

Of that little girl, Julia is incredibly proud.

Growing fainter, the figures dissipate.

But Julia knows where they have gone.

In the end, they are home.

THE END.

Acknowledgements

Somehow, I can barely believe that I'm actually writing this: the acknowledgements to my first novel. It almost feels like I'm in a dream and that, in a few moments, I'll wake up and realise 'Original Sin' does not exist.

Except, this time, it does.

I've longed to be an author since... well, as long as I can remember. When, little older than a toddler, my fingers first caressed the covers of the Famous Five, Secret Seven and Malory Towers, I dared to hope that maybe, just maybe, there would one day be a book with my name on the cover.

That dream never died.

Instead, it became a reality.

Practically every person I've encountered in the course of the last nine or ten years has inevitably heard the phrase: "I'm going to write a book!" So, it's with great satisfaction (and just a little relief!) that today I tell you: "I finally did it; I wrote a book."

Now you see, I wasn't lying.

Anyway, enough of my rambling (I assume, as our friend Eamon would so tastefully describe it, that you're well and truly 'scundered' of it by now) so I'll move on to the thank yous and at least attempt to keep it brief (and yes, I know everyone who knows me is thinking, 'she *really* doesn't do brief.')

To my teachers, past and present, of St. Patrick's Primary School Castlederg and Loreto Grammar School Omagh. I truly wish that I could name each and every one of you (but Anto would likely tell me to 'Ger up outta dat' and remember my promise to be succinct) so please just know how grateful I am to you all. Thank you from the bottom of my heart.

I do want to mention in particular Mr. Adrian Doherty (my P.7

teacher) and Miss. Catherine Cumiskey (my English teacher.)

Adrian, the day I left your classroom was not the day your support ended. Thank you for appreciating my penchant for telling a story before I truly did myself and being among the very first to read 'Original Sin.' Now, not only are you my former teacher but a friend too.

Miss. Cumiskey, without your encouragement and unwavering support, this book would not exist. Thank you for reading excerpts as they were written (not in chronological order, thanks to my rather erratic writing style) and the pre and post class chats about the characters, plot and publishing. You made this possible.

To Michael Lunney, my amazing cousin. Since I first saw one of your theatre productions at the Gaiety in Dublin, aged just six, the flames of my love for literature were fanned. Your example proved to me that writing a literary piece was not an unattainable fantasy. Thank you as well for your continuing advice and guidance as I take my first steps into this whole new world. They are invaluable.

To Clodagh McHugh, my best friend of ten years. Everyone deserves a friend as true as you have been to me. Thank you for always being there.

To Fr. Paddy Doherty, for your support and belief in me and the constant prayers throughout my life.

To my Godfather/uncle Ed and my aunt Louise, for the memories made in their very special property in La Cala that inspired the Spanish sections of this book.

To Jonathan (not the fictional one!) and Andreas. Thank you Jonathan for being an early reader and Andreas, thank you in advance for the insider Cypriot knowledge that will doubtless come in useful for the sequel.

To Teresa Bradley and Kathleen Arkinson, for the early encouragement.

To my entire extended family and friends, the Tyronians, the Dubs and all in between. Again, I wish I could list you all.

To everyone reading this. Thank you for picking up this book, taking a chance on its narrative and allowing its characters into your life. I assure you they'll be back for more in the future. Remember not to be afraid to follow a path in life that is uniquely yours, regardless of what anyone might say. Be your own person and follow your dreams wherever they may lead you.

I promise you; it'll be a journey worth making.

And finally, last but most certainly not least, to Mammy, Daddy, GG and Granda. Thank you for believing in me before I could believe in myself, for putting up with my endless discourse on all aspects of 'Original Sin' and for accepting my demands for silence in the house while I was writing.

I know I was definitely hard work when I was a baby (some might argue I still am) and as a result, I owed you an easy teenage years. But I do hope that, in publishing this book at fourteen, I'm doing something to fulfil that promise. Everything I do is for you.

Oh, and I do apologise to Granda that this wasn't a biography of a Man United player but I think you still enjoyed it anyway!

Seriously, though, after all that has been said in this little volume, there is one thing that remains: you four are my forever home.

With a love that 84,101 words cannot describe,

Isabella.

Xxxooo.

About the Author

Isabella Coughlan is a fourteen-year-old student at Loreto Grammar School, Omagh. Following a lifelong passion for literature, she began writing 'Original Sin' while still just thirteen. This is her debut novel and, she hopes, the first of many.

Born in County Tyrone, she spends weekends and holidays with her parents in her dad's native Dublin and as a result considers herself very much half- Dub and half- Tyronian.

Her great loves include travelling, music, reading and writing and, of course, watching every property programme ever aired on television!

Printed in Dunstable, United Kingdom

74354572R00190